Sister Creatures

A NOVEL

Laura Venita Green

ᴜɴ
THE UNNAMED PRESS
LOS ANGELES, CA

AN UNNAMED PRESS BOOK

Copyright © 2025 by Laura Venita Green

All rights reserved, including the right to reproduce this book or portions thereof in any form whatsoever. Permissions inquiries may be directed to info@unnamedpress.com

Published in North America by the Unnamed Press.

www.unnamedpress.com

Unnamed Press, and the colophon, are registered trademarks of Unnamed Media LLC.

Hardcover ISBN: 9781961884-57-1
EBook ISBN: 9781961884-58-8
LCCN: 2025940202

"Chapter 1: Stuck" and "Chapter 7: Mama Prayed" first appeared in *Story Magazine*, as well as "Chapter 2: I Want More" which first appeared in *Fatal Flaw*, and "Chapter 10: Banned" excerpted in *The Missouri Review* & the anthology titled *Talent: Stories of Authors and Artists*.

This book is a work of fiction. Names, characters, places and incidents are wholly fictional or are used fictitiously. Any resemblance to actual events or persons, living or dead, is entirely coincidental.

Cover photograph: "Consolation Self Portrait" by Laura Makabresku
Cover design and typeset by Jaya Nicely

Manufactured in the United States of America by Sheridan

Distributed by Publishers Group West

First Edition

For Tom

Contents

Part I: Louisiana

Stuck / *Tess* 1
I Want More / *Thea* 23
Für Amelia / *Lainey* 32
Gold Star / *Olivia* 52

Part II: Beyond

One Trick / *Tess* 75
Palsgrave House / *Thea* 102
Mama Prayed / *Olivia* 113
Slovenly Tess / *Tess* 133

Part III: Homecoming

Hintergarmisch / *Thea* 155
Banned / *Lainey* 163
Jesus & Booze / *Olivia* 181
Sistercreature / *Gail* 191
The Strays / *Summer* 213

Acknowledgements 235

Sister Creatures

Part I
Louisiana

Stuck

Tess

Not too long ago, the Thompson kids' dad sold the black walnut trees behind their house for timber, and now clusters of big, sad stumps spoiled the backyard. Tess was living with and caring for the Thompson kids—ten-year-old Miles and eight-year-old Minnie—while the Thompson mom recovered in some facility for broken-down women and the Thompson dad drove a long-haul truck to try to pay for everything. During her first week on the job, Tess rummaged through the drawers in the master bedroom and came upon the receipt from the timber company: $787 for all of it. To Tess that sounded like both a fortune and not nearly worth it. Now there was nothing to shade them from the early May sun already beating down and promising a hellscape of a summer.

Miles acted as if the stumps were the best thing that had ever happened to him, and maybe they were. He was constantly inventing stump games that called for ever-increasing acts of physical prowess that Minnie couldn't match, which was absolutely his point. Minnie—too old to play with dolls but obsessed with an ugly plastic one dressed in hand-crocheted pastel pink plantation garb that some church lady gave her right after her mom got taken away—set her doll on the lawn chair by Tess so they could both watch as she attempted a wobbly little headstand on one stump while Miles pelted her with Ping-Pong balls from another.

"Be careful," Tess said because she was the grown-up. Twenty-one next month. If Miles and Minnie had taught her anything, it was that she'd never have kids of her own, but as far as jobs went, this wasn't bad. She could spend much of her time doing the two things she loved most: drinking and reading. On her last library visit she'd checked out a stack of horror books about malfunctioning women. There seemed to be no shortage of books featuring women who lose control or lose their minds, and the librarian was always good at helping her find things she liked. It was one of the good things about quitting the community college. She could read what she wanted now. As for the drinking, she was pretty good on weekdays because she had to drive the kids around, but Saturdays meant no rules. The sun shone directly overhead, and Tess was on her third vodka tonic. Lovebug season was the worst in years, thousands of copulating insects stuck end to end for life while they drifted in flight like snowflakes—if snowflakes were black and red and drifted both down and up. Louisiana snow. Tess fished a drowned pair from her drink, flung them on the grass, and sucked from her bendy straw.

After Minnie toppled out of another headstand and Miles yelled, "You *suck* at this!" Minnie crawled over to the lawn chair and apologized to the goddamn doll. "I'm so sorry, Thea." That was its name, Minnie had announced one night last week after she'd pretended that it had whispered its name into her ear, and ever since then, that name, *Thea*, had wormed its way into Tess's brain. "Thea, you're so smart and pretty, if you were playing you wouldn't fall over like I did. I'll do better, I promise."

The phone rang inside the house. They'd left just the screen door shut in the back so that they could hear in case their mom called from the facility, which had not happened even one time in the five weeks since she'd left, but the kids were ever hopeful. At the first sound, Miles shot off his stump and darted toward the house. Minnie whined after him: "It's my turn to answer the phone."

"Come here," Tess said. She put her arm around Minnie's bony shoulders while the little girl sat in the crabgrass next to the lawn chair and picked lovebugs from the doll's frizzy brown plastic hair, squishing them between her fingers and wiping their guts on her shorts.

Tess noticed something moving in her peripheral vision and looked up to the woods that bordered the property, pine woods whose timber the Thompson dad couldn't sell because he didn't own them. It was Sister Gail again, watching. Tess shouldn't have been surprised, but she was, which irritated her.

"Go away!" Tess yelled, and the girl shifted behind a tree but didn't leave.

Minnie clutched the doll to her chest and whispered, "Hi, Sister Gail."

"Just ignore her," Tess said, and took another sip of her drink. The girl, who was maybe fourteen or fifteen, wore a thick denim skirt with a hem that brushed the ground and a dingy blouse that covered her neck and wrists. She had scraggly white-blond hair down to her ass. Pentecostal. Everyone knew that Gail's family lived off-grid in the woods, with well water and no electricity, and were the most Jesus people in all of Pinecreek, a town full of Jesus people. This was the third day in a row that Gail had shown up to watch them but wouldn't come any closer than the trees and ran off if they tried to approach, only to come back later. Tess felt suffocated seeing her, covered in all those clothes. Perhaps as a rebuke to the girl, or maybe just a taunt,

Tess took off her T-shirt so that she was just wearing her bikini top and cutoffs. More sun on her burnt skin.

Miles ran back outside, saying to his sister, "That was Mom. I would've got you, but she told me not to. She didn't want to talk to you."

He was obviously lying, but of course Minnie's face crumpled. "It *was*? You knew I wanted to talk to her, Miles. You knew I did!"

"Shut up, Miles," Tess said. "We all know that wasn't your mom. Anyway, she'd want to talk to Minnie way before she'd want to talk to you."

The way Miles's shoulders hunched in on themselves at her words made it apparent that she'd gone too far. A low blow, but come on, Miles, don't dish it out if you can't take it. A few days before his mom was taken away, after things had gotten really scary (though Tess didn't know all the details), Miles had said that he couldn't live with her anymore. The Thompson dad had told Tess a little about it to explain that, although Miles acted like a bully, he was carrying a lot for a ten-year-old boy. Tess shouldn't have suggested his mom might not want to talk to him. But the kids grated on her, and that Gail girl was still over there, staring, creeping her out. All she wanted in life was to read her books and finish her drink so she could make another while the sun beat down on the unshaded yard and the bugs got all over everything.

"Hey," Tess said, reaching over and circling her hand around the boy's skinny ankle. "I'm messing with you so you can see how Minnie feels when you mess with her like that, okay? Of course your mom will want to talk equally to both of you when she calls, which I'm sure will be soon." Both of the kids still looked miserable, so she added, "Know what? I'm ordering pizza tonight."

Minnie jumped up, still embracing the doll, and Miles yanked his leg from her grasp. "Really?" they said in unison.

"Hell yes," Tess said. By which she meant... maybe. If Miles was still really upset, it was possible. But if he'd gotten over it by dinnertime, well then, she wasn't going to spend money on something like that when she could open a can of soup.

The kids ran off to play some more on the stumps, and Tess flipped over so she didn't have to look at Sister Gail, who was still standing there motionless, staring. Tess wasn't sure how Gail had gotten that nickname, but this town could be mean, and it thrived on gossip. Tess lay on her stomach with her head hanging off the edge of the lawn chair, her drink next to her notebook on the ground below. The notebook had been a birthday gift last year from her former best friend, Lainey. It was the five-subject spiral kind that they sold in the school section at Market Basket. Lainey had written *Tess Lavigne, writer* at the top of the front cover and then completely covered the rest with cutesy horse stickers. But on the back, she'd stuck on a single horse with its head ripped off, blood in red ink spurting from its neck. It made Tess grin every time she saw it. Anyone who knew Lainey knew how wholesome she was and how hard it would have been for her to decapitate even a horse made of paper. But the gruesome joke was a testament to her love for Tess, because she knew it would make her friend smile. Despite the fact that Lainey recently ended their lifelong friendship like it had been nothing, the notebook was Tess's most prized possession.

Tess caught her straw with her mouth and pulled from the notebook folder a booklet containing an old short story, "The Yellow Wallpaper," that the librarian had actually lent to Tess from her personal collection. It was only twenty-three pages. Tess had read it last night after finishing *Carrie*, but the ending was hazy because she'd started the weekend early, drinking-wise. She couldn't tell what was really happening, if the character actually went insane at the end, hunching low and creeping around her room in a perpetual circle, her shoulder just fitting "in that long smooch around the wall"—Tess flipped her notebook open to a fresh page and wrote *long smooch*—or if she'd really hanged herself with the rope mentioned a few pages back and this whole last part wasn't even real. *But it's scarier to imagine her crazy and hunching and CREEPING around the wall, circling with her shoulder in the LONG SMOOCH, than it is to think she killed herself,* Tess jotted down in her notebook. *What even is a smooch?* "*A very funny mark on this wall, low down, near the mopboard."* (*What's a mopboard? Can't picture it exactly.*) *And is she like bending and walking? Or belly to the floor, crawling? Slithering?!* Tess took a break. There was something on the previous page she'd scribbled so hard that she could see the ink through the paper and a few spots where the pen had poked through. She flipped back. **SMOOOOOOOOOCH!!!!!!** took up almost the entire page, the letters scrawled over many times, although she didn't remember even reading the part with the long smooch before now. Any white space around the word was filled in with the doll's name written over and over, *Thea Thea Thea*. All of it, needless to say, in Tess's own handwriting. She shut the notebook and felt lightheaded.

Both of the kids started yelling—those exhausting kids—and then Minnie ran to Tess's lawn chair and started shaking her. Tess sat up. "Tell him to stop, tell him to stop," Minnie said.

Miles came over to the closest stump and kicked up into a perfect handstand. "You're such a baby," he said. "And that doll is butt ugly."

Tess expected Minnie to start crying again, but instead she got really quiet for a second and then charged at her brother, tackling his upside-down body. His sister knocked him off the stump so violently that Tess rushed over, dizzy, terrified he'd broken his neck. Miles lay there groaning, his arm splayed out at an unnatural angle.

Then, from the edge of the woods, Sister Gail approached.

On New Year's Eve a few months back, Tess had left a party early after getting a beer poured over her head by the girlfriend of a guy she'd just hooked up with in the upstairs bathroom. She had been crashing on Lainey's couch, but Lainey had kicked her out the previous day. In hindsight she could see that she'd overstayed her welcome; Lainey had a lot going on, particularly with her little sister, who had some major issues, and Tess hadn't exactly been helpful. After the party she'd driven around for a while to avoid going to her parents' house, though she had nowhere else to go. She blew through Pinecreek's single stoplight, and even though there was no other traffic, a cop pulled her over. They'd known each other in high school; the cop had been a senior when she was a freshman. The surprise on his face sobered her up a little, and she could imagine the way she looked: beer-matted hair, beer paunch not at all hidden by her strapless dress, still wearing beer-logged glasses in the shape of *2000* and made of cardboard and glitter. The fact that she'd been well loved throughout high school—voted class favorite each year, always fun and easygoing in a way that people had appreciated back then but for some reason did not appreciate now—paid off, because he didn't arrest her but made it clear that he would if it happened again.

"Do you know how to drive?" Tess asked Gail, now standing with them in the backyard. The way everything had gone dark for a second at the edges of Tess's vision when she'd jumped up too fast hinted that maybe she shouldn't get behind the wheel. But looking at this odd girl up close with her dirt-smudged cheek and a big toe sticking out of a homemade leather shoe, maybe a more appropriate question would have been, Have you ever been in a car? Have you ever even *seen* a car?

Gail shook her head. She was kneeling over Miles and was, for some reason, holding Minnie's doll. Miles kicked his foot up and onto the ground, hard, groaning in pain, while Minnie hid behind Tess's leg and muttered "I didn't mean to" on repeat. Tess did not want to be doing this job anymore.

"Are you okay, Miles? Do you need to go to the hospital?" Tess asked. The Thompson dad was due to come home on Wednesday for a couple days off, and an injured kid was the last thing he needed. "It would cost a lot of money," she told Miles, "and your dad would probably have to work even more hours to pay for it. But tell me if you need to go."

Gail placed a steady hand on Miles's forehead and said, "Can you touch your shoulder? Like this?" She brought her left hand up to touch her right shoulder. "Try and do that now." Her voice was unexpected, strong, deeper than Tess would have guessed from looking at her. Miles stopped moaning and strained to raise his injured arm, which barely lifted from the ground before he gasped and shook his head.

Gail stood up and looked at Tess. "It's dislocated, I think. His shoulder. We have to get him up on something high, so his arm can hang and not touch ground."

Tess nodded. "Kitchen table. Minnie, go and clear it off, okay?"

The relief on Minnie's face to have something useful to do matched the relief Tess felt that this strange teenager was taking charge. Before she ran inside, Minnie reached out to Gail to take her doll back. Gail hesitated a moment before she handed it over.

Then they helped Miles off the ground, careful to avoid his injured arm, and the three of them walked into the house. Minnie moved the last of the breakfast dishes to the countertop, and they propped Miles on the table, face down, with his bad arm hanging off the side.

Gail lay down on the floor and grasped his arm above the elbow with both of her hands. "Deep breaths, Miles, relax if you can," she said. "I'll be gentle."

Minnie sat in a chair on the opposite side of the table and took Miles's good hand. Tess stroked his sweaty hair; sometimes she forgot what a little boy he was. And then Gail pulled, pulled and held on tight for several minutes, until finally they all heard a dull pop, the shoulder snapping back into place.

※

They stayed inside for the rest of the day. Tess gave Miles an Advil, and Gail made him a sling out of one of his mom's old scarves, on which he kept resting his cheek, breathing in deeply, eyes closed. Tess and the kids had gotten into the habit of sleeping in the living room for the week to ten-day stretches that they were alone. The kids' mattresses were shoved together in front of the TV, piled with pillows and blankets, tangled sheets, and many days' worth of dirty clothes that Tess would clean up and put away on Wednesday in time for the Thompson dad's evening return.

The kids, Gail, and the doll lounged on the mattresses in front of the TV. Tess turned the tower fans on high, both because the house was stuffy and because Gail stank of someone who'd gone through puberty but hadn't yet discovered hygiene products. Then she got the basket that held their collection of VHS tapes, old movies from Blockbuster sale bins. Miles's all-time favorite movie was *The Little Mermaid*, but he would rather die than admit it. If asked, he'd always choose either *Misery* or *Die Hard with a Vengeance*, both of which technically the kids weren't allowed to watch but had several times after promising that they wouldn't tell their dad.

Tess pretended to consider the options and then picked up *The Little Mermaid*. "Have you seen this before?" she asked Gail.

Gail shook her head.

"Let's watch this one," Tess said. "For our guest."

"Sweet!" Minnie said.

"Oh, man, no. Not that one," Miles protested. Very convincing.

"You're going to love it, Sister Gail!" Minnie said.

Tess turned it on for them and then went and got her drink from outside. The ice had melted, and there were several dead bugs floating on the top, which depressed her. The reality of her life was that she couldn't afford to waste the alcohol, so she drank it anyway (along with the bugs). Added protein.

Back in the living room, Gail sat at the edge of the mattress cross-legged, staring at the screen every bit as intensely as the little girl in *Poltergeist*. From how everyone talked about the way her family lived—the Liebrechts, that was the family name—it was likely she'd never watched television before. Gail clutched one arm of Minnie's doll while Minnie held the other. Miles sprawled across both mattresses. The kids whisper-sang along with Ariel about all the stuff she's collected and how neat it all is. Tess sat on the couch behind them and, instead of starting her next book, took some more notes on "The Yellow Wallpaper" and tried out a few lines of her own about a woman taken from her children and forced to rest for her own good. When the movie was over, Gail asked if they could watch it again, and they did.

※

At dinnertime, Tess made herself another vodka tonic, at first with only one shot but that was too disappointing, so she topped it off with another splash or two. She got a bag of baby carrots out of the fridge and a couple cans of Chef Boyardee from the pantry. When Tess closed the pantry door, Gail was behind her, crowding her. Tess flinched. She hadn't realized the Liebrecht girl was even in the room.

"What are you doing?" Gail asked.

"Making dinner," Tess said.

"Miles said we were to have pizza."

Tess shrugged off the query. "Do your parents know you're here? Shouldn't you be heading home?"

"Miles said that *you said* we were to have pizza."

This girl had no social skills: she made eye contact and held it fixed.

"Pizza's expensive," Tess said. "And you can't undertip the delivery guy because he knows where you live."

"The delivery guy doesn't know where I live."

"No, I didn't mean—"

"And you don't know where I live. Even if I told you where I live, you couldn't find it on your own. Too many winding paths. Too much forest."

"All I mean is we're not getting pizza."

Underneath the dirt, Gail had a perfect little heart-shaped face. When she smiled at Tess—a charming smile in spite of (or because of) her overcrowded teeth—Tess couldn't help but smile back.

"No, I can see," Gail said. "I know that you are a woman of your word."

Tess couldn't help but laugh at that. A woman. This kid telling her she was a woman of her word. Uh, nope. And what was everyone's obsession with one's word? Before she'd quit a few weeks ago, she'd been taking Miss Rachel's Louisiana Literature class; it had been one of Tess's favorite things, even though it had zero long-term practical value. Miss Rachel had been so disappointed when she found that Tess had snuck a flask of vodka into the first class and made her promise she wouldn't do it again. She *hadn't* done it again, not technically. But in a class in late March she had put the tiniest bit of Everclear into a water bottle. Miss Rachel had zeroed in on the bottle right away, didn't believe her when she'd said it was water, and, in front of everyone, had poured a little from the bottle into the palm of her hand and tasted it. From the expression on her face, you'd think Tess had physically slapped her. The class had gawked while Tess packed up her books and left for good.

Tess got the can opener out of the drawer and was just about to puncture one of the Chef Boyardee cans when Gail clapped and called out, "M and M, we are getting the pizza!"

The kids both cheered from the other room. The voices on the TV switched off, and they came shuffling in with little dance steps, whooping in excitement.

Putting down the can opener, Tess closed her eyes for a moment. When she'd brought in the Everclear, it was to help her face some people in her class she'd just been camping with over the weekend in Kisatchie National Forest. She'd been trying to make new friends since all her old ones had dropped her. But Tess had woken up the final morning sharing a sleeping bag with her patchy-bearded classmate whom she wasn't even into, her boobs on display for everyone in their six-person tent. So despite the obvious downsides, there was one benefit of this babysitting job, in this secluded house nearly a mile away from the closest neighbor: it was a great place to hide out.

"Okay," Tess said. "One pizza. One large pepperoni is all, and if you're hungry for more we'll have something here. And minimum five baby carrots per slice. With no whining."

The three of them nodded in unison.

"You," Tess said, pointing to Gail. "You need to get on home."

"I'm not going." Gail shook her head. "I've never had pizza."

"Let her stay," Minnie said, stroking Gail's arm with her doll's plastic hand.

"Yeah, let her stay," Miles said. "She's never had pizza." He winked at Tess when he said it, and they both pressed their lips together to keep from laughing.

※

After dinner, when Gail made it clear that she was spending the night, Tess suggested she take a bath. Gail asked Minnie if the doll could keep her company, and Minnie sulked but handed it over. Gail propped it on the tank of the toilet where it could watch over her.

"Why do you like that ugly doll so much?" Tess asked.

With a painful little hitch in her voice, Gail said, "I've never once in my life had anything of my own. Not once. I've never been permitted."

Tess didn't know what to say, so she just ran the tub. The faucet was finicky, the water either freezing or scalding, no in-between. Tess alternated between the two temperatures until she had filled the bath with lots of bubbles. Before she could leave, Gail stripped naked with no hesitation, surprising Tess with her lack of modesty. The girl was thin, undernourished, with pinkish nipples and pale blond pubic hair, unshaved legs and armpits. Tess tried not to stare, though she couldn't help but inspect Gail's body for marks. There were cuts and scrapes like any kid, but were those also fading bruises circling her ankle? Tess couldn't tell for sure.

Gail got right into the tub, held her nose, and dipped her head back underwater. "Are you going to wash my hair for me?" she asked when she came back up.

Tess moved the shampoo and conditioner to the edge of the tub where Gail could easily reach. "I think you can manage it yourself," she said. She looked at Gail's filthy clothes crumpled on the floor, her grayish underwear with a hole at the seam near the hip. She couldn't even imagine the type of life this girl lived. "I'm going to put your clothes in the wash, okay? You can borrow some pajamas."

Tess picked up the dirty clothes and opened the bathroom door, but the Liebrecht girl's voice chased after her before she could escape. "Your hair. It's like a boy's."

Tess put her hand up to her short hair.

"Why is it like that?"

"Well, it's easier. Better in the heat. And sometime during the last year or so, I started chewing on it, compulsively. I couldn't stop. Now I'm used to it. I like the way it looks."

Gail nodded. "I like it, too."

Clutching the dirty clothes, Tess gave a tight smile and tried to leave again, but Gail said, "Sounds to me as if you had a problem and you found a solution."

"Uh-huh," Tess said.

"M and M both really want their mother to call," Gail said.

"Uh-huh."

The phone had rung three times while they were inside that afternoon. Telemarketers twice, and once the crocheting church lady neighbor asking if she'd see them at service tomorrow. She wouldn't. The kids were hyperexcited and then disappointed each time. Watching them, Tess was almost grateful that her own parents were worthless. They treated her exactly the same when she'd aced the state assessment test in reading comprehension as they had the time she got caught shoplifting from McKee's. They thought as little of her when she'd been the town's golden child as they did now that her reputation was trashed. A stance that was oddly freeing. There was no scenario in the world that could make her care about her parents the way Miles and Minnie did about theirs.

"Do you think she'll call? Their mother?" Gail picked up the shampoo bottle and squeezed it directly onto her hair. It started to ooze down her forehead.

"Watch out, don't let that get in your eyes," Tess said, and tossed Gail a washcloth from underneath the sink. Maybe she should just help the girl, but it was too awkward, this naked stranger in the tub.

"I bet you could get her to call. You'd figure out a way." Gail rubbed the washcloth into one tiny spot on her scalp. Not very good technique.

"I don't think so," Tess said. "I even told Mr. Thompson that maybe she could just call and read to them. Something comforting, like *Anne of Green Gables*. I could put the phone on speaker, put us on mute, and there wouldn't be any pressure on her. But they'd at least be able to hear her voice. Anyway, he said she's not doing well right now." And Tess didn't even know where she was staying, though she'd looked, rummaged through all the drawers trying to find out where they'd taken her.

"But you'd figure it out if you were forced to. You could make it happen."

Tess didn't want to push it with the Thompson dad. Either he was too distracted to know how everyone in town had turned on her, or he was too desperate to care. For now, this job was the best thing. "Look, I'm going to put these in the wash, and I'll have some clean pajamas waiting right outside the door."

But before she could step out, Gail let some soap suds get in her eye, and Tess caved and helped the girl wash her damn hair.

※

The kids said they were going to pull an all-nighter and that was fine with Tess. She had an entire unopened bottle of vodka if she got through the current one, and she was starting *The Turn of the Screw*. Plus, Sunday sleep-in.

Tess was on the couch and the kids sat cross-legged around Gail, who looked almost like a normal teenager in Tess's Nirvana T-shirt and a pair of sleep shorts. Tess hadn't really been paying attention to them, but then Gail said:

"Thea told you to do it, didn't she? To hurt your brother. Thea is boo-sah."

Minnie started to whine—"*No*"—but Tess cut her off. "She's what?"

"Boo-sah," Gail said. "It's German for evil."

Tess opened her notebook and handed Gail a pen, tapped on the page, and Gail wrote *böse*.

"You speak German?" Tess said.

"Yes," Gail said. "My father is German, and my grandfather is staying with us right now. He only speaks German." She wrote again in Tess's notebook and then pronounced it. "*Meine Enkelin ist böse.* My granddaughter is evil. He says that all the time."

Well, that's messed up, Tess thought. Concerning even. Definitely something she should ask Gail more about, make sure everything was okay. But with Miles and Minnie looking at Tess to see how she'd react, for now she just said, "*Are* you evil, Sister Gail?" and they both giggled.

"Yeah, *are* you evil?" Miles echoed.

Gail paused, looked each of them in the eye one by one, and then said, "I'm not. But Thea is. She told you to hurt Miles."

Minnie protested. "No, she didn't!"

"Oh, great," Miles said. "You did it on your own?"

"No!" Minnie said.

"Thea told me she told you to hurt him. You're saying she lied? Or you can't hear her when she speaks?"

"No!" Minnie said. She clutched the doll tight as ever and whispered, "I hear her."

"Shush," Tess said. "Stop teasing Minnie."

They were quiet for a moment, but then Gail said, "I had a sister once. Her name was also Thea."

Minnie turned her doll around to look it in the face as if it could confirm. "Really?!"

"What happened to her?" Miles said.

"She was my twin sister. We were always together. The best of friends. But then she died."

"How?" Miles said. Minnie hid her face in the doll's hair and peeked one eye at Gail.

"You don't want to know," Gail said.

Tess dog-eared her book and put it down. "You're saying you coincidentally had a twin sister named Thea?"

All three of them nodded.

"And she died?"

All three of them nodded.

"How old were you?"

"Not even a month."

"And your parents told you this?"

"No. She did."

"Look, I don't think we want to hear the story of your dead twin sister, Thea, okay?"

"Yeah, we do!" Miles said, and looked to Minnie for backup, but she shook her head.

Gail propped herself up and knelt in front of Tess. "Then spend time with us," she said, and gestured for Tess's drink. Sure, okay. Tess herself had had her first drink when she was only eleven; a taste wasn't going to hurt. She handed her drink over, and Gail stood up and rushed to the kitchen. Tess went after her, but it was too late, it was already slipping away down the drain.

"What the hell?" Tess said. She felt an odd sense of panic, helpless. This girl in her house pouring her drink down the sink, and there was nothing she could do about it. "Go home," she said. "I'm sick of you."

She went to get her bottle from the freezer to make another drink, but Gail grabbed her wrist before she could open it. "You don't need that."

"Who said anything about need?" Tess said. "Of course I don't need it, but it's the weekend, so give me a break."

But Gail didn't let go. "I can see. I know you can do without."

Tess wrenched free from Gail's grasp. If this girl says "I can see" one more fucking time, she thought. But Miles and Minnie stood in the doorway giving her a look like, Yeah, maybe you shouldn't have another. Ridiculous, because truly she wasn't even drunk, she'd been pretty good with her pacing since they had a guest and last night she'd sort of blacked out. But hey, whatever. She'd wait until tomorrow morning after the Thompson dad's scheduled phone call.

"Fine, then," she said. "What do the three of you want to do at almost midnight on a Saturday night?"

"Dance party!" Minnie said.

Miles looked a little pitiful in his sling, his face pale and drawn. "Don't worry," he said. "I can watch. I like to judge."

So they danced. Minnie chose Metallica, probably to impress her brother, and they headbanged. Miles chose Pearl Jam, and they jumped and jumped. Tess chose Fiona Apple because Fiona Apple was the shit, and they mostly twirled. Gail didn't know any musicians, so she sang a somewhat concerning song about walking over burning hot coals for Christ, and they all swayed. When they finished, Tess and Gail were tied at four points each, Thea had three, and Miles must have been feeling generous, because even Minnie had a point.

※

Tess didn't remember falling asleep, but sometime during what felt like the middle of the night, she woke up on the couch to Gail shaking her. She almost cried out, but Gail put her hand over Tess's mouth. Outside the window, there was only the barest hint of dawn.

Gail put her finger to her lips—*shhh*—and pointed down to where the kids slept huddled together, Miles's bad arm tucked awkwardly to his chest, Minnie with her doll in a headlock. Tess got up and followed Gail through the kitchen and out into the backyard. It was nice out, this early time of day. Warm but comfortable, bugs not yet swarming.

"I watch the sunrise every morning," Gail said. "I thought you'd want to join me."

Gail was back in her own clothes and was carrying Tess's notebook. They sat on two wide stumps situated close together halfway between the house and the woods.

Before Tess could ask what she was doing with her personal notebook, Gail opened it: "I'm writing you a little letter. It's in German."

"What does it say?"

Gail smiled. "You can figure it out later."

Tess listened to the scribble of the pen and smoothed her hand over the surface of her stump. So many rings, from once grand trees that had been here long before Tess was born, before they'd been cashed in for a fraction of a hospital stay. There was a not-so-distant past when Tess's life had been good. Lots of friends, and they'd all laughed together, ran wild, queens of the open country, always a good time.

Something rustled through the grass, a small brown snake slithering toward them from the pine trees. Instinctively, Tess whipped her legs up to her chest, but Gail reached over and put a steady hand on her knee.

"She's okay," Gail said, nodding toward the snake. "Not going to hurt you."

Still, Tess's sudden movement had startled the snake, made it change course and rush back to the woods. Gail handed Tess's notebook to her, finished with her secret note.

"I have to get back in time for worship or they'll be out looking for me. Miles said if I stayed for breakfast, we could probably convince you to make pancakes. But I can't."

"How's everything at home?" Tess asked. The girl's clothes, her isolation, the shadow of a bruise that may or may not have circled her ankle. Tess was supposed to be the grown-up, but instead she was inadequate, unqualified for this job, for life in general. "I hate getting involved, and the last thing we need around here is any trouble. But, you know, tell me if you need help or anything."

Gail tilted her head, fixed on Tess's eyes for a moment, but then shook her head. "Don't worry. I'm going to live up north with my aunt at the end of the summer. My mother's sister. That's why my grandfather's here, to try and talk me out of leaving. But he can't."

Something in the girl's face seemed less certain than her words, but Tess left it there, hating how relieved she felt not to have to deal with anything.

They walked back toward the house so that Gail could say goodbye to the kids, but just before they opened the back door, Gail gave Tess a hug and whispered, "I'm sorry about this, but I know you'll figure it out. I know you will. I can see."

Before Tess could react, Gail went inside and was flipping on all the lights and clapping her hands, yelling for the kids to get up, get up! "M and M," she said. "Great news! Your mother is going to call today." And the kids were stirring, confused. Tess was confused. Miles winced, holding his shoulder, trying to adjust his sling back in place.

"Do you hear me? Your mother will call! Thea told me."

"She is?" Minnie said. "She did?"

Miles just seemed stunned, yanked from a dead sleep, looking from face to face, trying to get a handle.

"Stop," Tess said. "What are you doing?"

"But," Gail said, her voice so loud for the time of day, for the barely awake children, for Tess. "Thea will only allow that to happen if she comes with me."

"Really?" Minnie said, her eyes filling with tears.

"Gail, you go on home. Now," Tess ordered. Minnie had made herself into a tiny ball, wedging herself with her doll between the mattress and the foot of the couch.

"Mom's okay?" Miles said. "She's going to call?"

"Ignore her," Tess said. "We barely even know this girl."

"Thea's been preventing the call," Gail said. "Because she belongs with me. She's been calling to me."

Miles stood up over his sister and poked at her. "Give it to her."

"No!" Minnie said.

"You have to give her to me," Gail said, "or your mother won't be okay."

Miles started jabbing his sister hard with his foot. "Give her the ugly-ass doll, Minnie. Do you hate Mom or something?"

"Quit it," Tess said. "Please."

Miles kicked his sister, and Tess pushed him off, not very hard, but he tripped backward off the mattress and onto his bad arm. He shrieked in pain.

Minnie sat up and looked at her brother, then at Tess, total panic on her face. She loosened her hold on the doll. Minnie nearly hyperventilating, Miles writhing on the floor, a fire in Gail's eyes that could burn down the world. What might that girl be capable of if she didn't get what she came for? Tess took the doll from Minnie's little hands, which relinquished it without much of a fight, and handed it over. Gail Liebrecht took one deep breath, the most blissful smile lighting up her face, before she sprinted out of the house, dodging stumps across the bare yard, and disappeared into the tangle of trees.

I Want More
Thea

THEA CHECKED the box trap behind her cabin and found a massive timber rattlesnake coiled and ready to strike. Without hesitation, she grabbed the metal rod resting near the trap and flipped open the lid. She used the rod to disorient the snake, catching on to the length of its body and knocking it back and forth against the sides of the box. The moment its attention wavered, Thea darted her hand inside the trap and secured the animal, pinching tightly just below its diamond head, her thumb pressed into the vertebrae that connected to its skull. She pulled the snake from the box, held it out in front of her, looked it in the eyes. The snake hinged open its jaw and bared its fangs. It flickered its forked tongue, hissed. Thea hissed back, and then ran her own tongue over the flat, even row of her top teeth. It lashed its powerful body at her torso, thrashed up between her legs, wrapped around her arm. The snake's efforts were useless, of course; Thea had all the power. She caught hold of the snake's tail, let go of its head, and in one swift motion cracked it like a whip, snapping its neck. With a hook, she pierced the space just behind its head and hung it from the cord that draped between two longleaf pines behind the cabin near the woodpile.

The snake joined a dozen other recent kills that hung in a perfect row, where they'd stay for a couple of days while their skins loosened, making them easier to peel and flatten into pelts.

On her way to check another trap deeper in the woods, a pine cone struck the top of her head. Thea looked up. Through the tangle of branches and needles, she noticed beyond the treetops the sky shone blue, the day was brilliant and clear. Lately, her home, a cabin nestled in a dense pine forest—one of many in a land called Louisiana, according to her husband, Frederick—had become stifling to her, with its ever-present dampness, its bug-teeming undergrowth, and its vegetal stench of decaying leaves. The fact of the sky, the blue sky, made the air around her feel damper and more shadowed. She felt the disparity that existed between the narrow world she inhabited and the vast one above.

Instead of continuing on to the trap, Thea located the tallest pine and ran her fingers across the slippery lichen-covered bark at the base of its trunk. With her powerful legs and calloused hands, she climbed up to the lowest branches and then farther, not to the top, but as high as she could go without the tree snapping. And for one blissful moment, everything was perfect: the whoosh of air around her—free of sap scent and pollen dust—the unadulterated view of distant hills and billowing clouds. Perhaps, Thea thought, what she really wanted was to live in the trees.

Then she saw the hawk. He was perched one tree over on a slender, high branch too delicate to carry Thea's weight. The bird of prey, compact in body and regal in the tilt of his head, wore feathers in every shade of rich brown. He regarded Thea coolly as she stretched her arm toward him, overwhelmed by the need to touch, until she lost her balance, barely grasping the trunk in time to prevent her fall. He looked away, dropped from his perch, and darted toward the earth.

Thea's breath caught in her chest as she watched his plummet, broken only at the last instant when he swooped inches from the ground to sink his talons into the body of a rabbit, which he carried right back to the branch. When his sharp beak tore into the neck of the thrashing rabbit, that was it. Thea knew nothing else in the world would ever matter. She knew love.

※

From that moment, Thea spent much of her time in the pine. She caught squirrels and rats as offerings to the hawk. He spurned her efforts, cocking his head and narrowing his eye at whatever limp animal Thea held by the scruff of its neck. But she persevered. Every once in a while, if her offering was sufficiently plump, he would seize it from her hand without the slightest show of appreciation and fly in the direction of the morning sun, to a tree far off in the distance she assumed was his home.

She cultivated a taste for raw meat. She was tentative at first, but then ravenous, devouring the still-warm flesh from the snakes she trapped. She no longer made pelts from their skins, which she'd sold through Frederick to various leatherworkers, but instead left them in a heap around the woodpile. Though she still descended from her tree when the stars emerged and went inside the cabin to Frederick, she stopped sleeping in their bed. His featherless pink skin now revolted her, his awkward arms and long stick-legs pathetic. She stopped chopping the wood and tending the house and making their dinners. She stopped speaking to him almost entirely.

One night, Frederick coaxed her down from the tree and into their cabin, which sparkled with roaring fire and candlelight. He pulled from behind his back a bouquet of tiger lilies. Thea understood that these had been her favorite, but she felt so removed from the version of herself who cared about flowers. When she didn't take the bouquet, Frederick arranged it in a vase. On the table was a feast of roasted mushrooms and stewed rabbit made from what Frederick foraged and hunted for her pleasure. Not so very long ago, she would have cherished this gesture.

Frederick worked as a park ranger for Kisatchie National Forest. When they sat down to dinner, he performed their old routine, telling her about his day.

"There's a group staying at the lodge for some corporate team-building retreat," he said. "I took them on a hike down the main trail. There was this guy, and, I swear, Thea, he was wearing Italian leather shoes that cost more than my annual salary."

Here he chuckled and looked at her, expecting something. She picked at the long-dead meat but couldn't ignore the nausea she felt from the earthy reek of the fungi. She stood to scrape them from her bowl into the fireplace. When she sat back down, Frederick flicked his eyes between her and the fire, and then resumed his story.

"And this guy, once we get to that clearing by the lake where you and I first met, he goes, 'How do you tend this entire forest? The manpower it would take to landscape this much space, I can't imagine.' As if he'd never been in nature before. My god, some of these people!"

Still, Thea said nothing. Frederick hesitated a moment but then got up and came around the table, kneeling beside her to take her hand. His clammy touch was so repulsive that she jerked back, grating the legs of her chair against the wooden floor.

"Please," he said. "Sweetheart. What can I do? What can I possibly do? We have so much. Nature, trees, labor, love. Every single thing you've ever said you wanted."

She looked up at the wooden beams that supported the ceiling, the ceiling that hindered access to the sky, and said the last words she would ever speak: "I want more."

Thea left the house and entered the nighttime forest. Frederick tried to follow, but she stopped him, placed both of her palms flat on his chest, and shoved. He stumbled and fell, and Thea heard a crack, followed by silence. But there was no looking back. She trudged far into the woods, through the understory that grew beneath the pines, saplings and thorny shrubs tearing at her skin. She went in the direction that her beloved flew when he took her offerings. And though it took all night and she had to climb dozens of trees, just before dawn, she found what she was looking for.

※

Long ago, before Thea was Thea, her form had been that of a snake. Lowly slitherer. Full of nothing but venom. Burrowed with her then-mate in a woodpile behind a ranger's cabin. He found their den, showed kindness, left them in peace. From the time she first saw the man, first flickered her tongue and caught his scent, she knew love. Forest king, strong arms, legs that gave power to come and go as he wished.

She knew her fate, though not the *how*. No matter what it took to be with this man she was sure of success, as love left no doubt. Her mate she once prized for threat and cunning now was only beady eyes, scaled hide. Hideous. The long muscle of her body shuddered.

She stalked the ranger while he patrolled woods and visited camps. One day the man found a tent pitched in a clearing by a lake. Next to it stood a lone woman. Long black hair, powerful legs. She saw that the woman pleased the man. He smiled, spoke, listened, lingered. When at last he left, she stayed near the woman's tent, sensed what needed doing. She waited for night. Slithered into the tent. Coiled tight at the foot of the bag until the woman climbed in for sleep. Ever so slow, once sure of slumber, she slid up the body, explored. Up between strong legs, onto the torso, cold skin on warm. She lifted her head to look at the woman's strange, oval face reflecting moonlight. Her tongue flickered. She sensed that she had dwelt in other forms, lower forms, sub-awareness, since the beginning. She sensed her power, owned, innate, born into every being willing to use it. The power to create a supreme ideal, to become what she wanted. More. But not without loss, sacrifice. Not without cruelty. The eyes of the woman opened, snap, and she sank her fangs into the neck, on a fat vein locked her jaws. She held through struggle and thrashing. She felt life drain from the woman's body and into her own.

Once it was over, she slunk home and waited for what she knew was coming: the agony of the shift. The end of her long tail tore apart to form legs, flesh slashed from her sides for arms, her body expanding into the shape of the woman. Scales shedding in one horrible slough. By the time she reached the woodpile, she was no longer slithering but crawling, suddenly aware of cold, ecstatic. She heard her throat make a *ha* noise. A *haha*. Her jaw hinged open and air pushed out from her chest, making a *ha!* Her voice, first hoarse and then strong, a loud *HA!* Her hand on the step leading to the cabin—*HA!*—open palm slapping the wood of the step—*HAHA!*—and a light came on, and then there was the man.

He shone a flashlight on her naked form. "Thea?" he said, and scooped her up into strong, capable arms, carried her inside, and nursed her to health.

Beneath the hawk's nest, Thea hid in the tree under a branch thick with plump green needles. As the sun broke the horizon, her beloved flew off, leaving his family unprotected. Thea climbed, ever so slowly, up to the nest, careful not to wake his mate. She regarded the female, her feathers more black than brown, her razor-sharp beak, and her wings that gave her freedom to break free of the trees and roam the sky. She touched the warm body, so lightly, enjoying one last time the pleasurable sensation of soft texture on fingertips. When the hawk's deep brown eyes opened, Thea didn't hesitate. She grasped the bird's neck with one hand and squeezed with all her strength, enduring the talons that slashed her arms to shreds. She snatched the eggs one by one and flung them to the earth below, watching as they burst silently on the forest floor. The nest cleared of the unwanted offspring, at last she felt the departing life fill her up.

The transition was more painful than before; the horror of the last time had settled into her frame and magnified the effect. She wasn't securely in the nest when her arms failed her, and she could no longer hold on, snapping branches and bones on her way down to the earth, where she landed in the ooze of the underdeveloped embryos. Eggshell lodged into the tender skin of her neck. She tore at the ground, uprooted saplings, fighting the agony of bony wings sprouting from shoulder blades, of legs contracting, of talons pushing up underneath fingernails. What started as a scream turned to a harsh, high-pitched cry that came from her newly forming cartilaginous beak.

Yet she knew as she rested that she was everything. She was almighty.

As soon as she could bear it, she hopped and staggered on her new legs and stretched one wing, then both, then called out as strongly as she could, a sharp call that she repeated over and over until her beloved swooped down from the treetops and landed at her side.

※

In their nest, her one true love tended to her health. Though she felt no remorse—confident in the necessity of violence to secure her perfect life—she was honest in mourning with him the loss of their hatchlings. He brought her nourishment until she was back to full strength. She conveyed her taste for snake meat, and soon, the smooth, papery skins outfitted their nest.

It wasn't long before she was delighting in her sleek new wings that lifted her higher than she'd ever been, in her crisp eyesight that put the world into focus for the very first time, in her sharp beak and talons, in the overwhelming bloodlust for stalking prey. She lived enough seasons flying high above the treetops to learn that spring was her favorite. Spring, with the relentless rains that kept the lake water fresh. Spring, with the proliferation of new life to hunt.

Until one spring night, after another flawless day flying and hunting with her mate, soaring ever higher until she touched the clouds, she felt that familiar and oh-so-unwelcome sense of void when they settled down in their nest. All she'd done, truly done, was trade in her days walking inside the forest for days flying above it. But she was no closer to breaking free. Or maybe emptiness and disappointment were just part of being alive, the burden of possessing an imperfect soul.

Her mate assumed their usual sleep position, nestling his head into the feathers of her neck, making space for her to do the same. Before closing her eyes, Thea tilted her head and looked up into the heavens that surrounded them, to the glittering stars that pierced through the dark. Her focus turned to one star that shone brighter than all the rest, and even from this distance, she could feel its warmth, its all-encompassing light that radiated the promise of perfection, the promise of obliterating all sense of futility. How stupid she'd been, looking for heaven on earth—earth, a place defined by limitation and decay—when it could only exist *beyond* anything she had ever known.

When the coming dawn obscured the star from her sight, she knew she would think of nothing else all day until they were able to meet again in darkness. She turned her attention to her mate and found that his coat of feathers, full of dander and lice, disgusted her. She pulled away from him and burrowed into the pile of snake skins on the other side of the nest, ignoring his inquiring look. Because from the moment she'd seen that brightest star, that was it. She knew love.

Für Amelia

Lainey

LAINEY GOT OFF work early to drive her younger sister, Amelia, to the annual high school music competition. She could hardly believe they'd made it. Their dad had urged Amelia to compete, but Lainey felt that by doing so he was setting her up for failure. Amelia had a hard time with most things, even small, everyday things, and got through life only by making deals with herself. For this competition, for instance, she finally decided she could manage it, but only if she didn't watch TV for a month and if she made herself smash her favorite night-light with the stained-glass butterfly. And still, for the three days prior, Amelia had one of her episodes where she shut herself in her room and refused to leave even for school. Their dad always let her be, said they needed to wait it out, so that's what they did. Yesterday the vice principal left him a couple of messages warning of excessive absences. But eventually Amelia made some other deal with herself in order to leave her room, and now here they were.

Their dad was late, but he managed to sidle into the chair Lainey saved for him just in time, clapping enthusiastically for the Leesville High clarinetist whose performance he'd missed. But then Amelia was up. Lainey and her dad reached for each other's hand as she wandered onto the stage, staring down at the music she cradled in her arms, knocking her hip into one of the mic stands that then shrieked high-pitched feedback through the speakers. Up onstage Amelia looked so skinny. Her flowing peach-toned dress clashed with the Christmas decorations heaped throughout the auditorium, making her skin and long blond hair too pale. When Amelia made it to the piano, Lainey heard her dad exhale, and when he squeezed her hand, she squeezed back.

In order to avoid the awkwardness of her sister onstage, shuffling around the bench instead of just sitting, Lainey read through the competition program. According to its mission statement, the Rural Musicians Project was a nonprofit that focused on fostering talent in "underserved teens" in Vernon, Beauregard, and Calcasieu Parishes. That word—*underserved*—caught her up. It felt like one of those labels used behind people's backs for the sake of donations, not something to hand out to the people themselves.

Amelia finally sat but then took forever setting up her music. The audience fidgeted. The program coordinator peeked nervously from the curtains at the side of the stage. Maybe Lainey should just get up and take her underserved sister away from all these people staring, clearing their throats while she shifted her sheet music a millimeter left, then right, left-right, left-right, over and over again.

Amelia had played piano obsessively and incessantly ever since their dad bought an old one at a flea market several years ago. She could play a range of music, but she'd fixed her singular focus on Beethoven's "Für Elise," a song she'd quickly mastered. Eventually, the song had morphed into something all her own—still recognizable as the original but altered. They called it "Für Amelia." She'd vary the usual refrain, or convert the key signature, switch to a stiff staccato, or maybe add a series of grace notes and over-the-top embellishments. The way she played changed each time. None of that explained why the effect was... what? Weird and unnerving. Beautiful and energetic. An overplayed composition taught to every kid who'd studied piano became something more.

All at once Amelia began to play, and the bored parents and jittery kids stopped squirming in their seats. Lainey sat there and watched, one of many in an audience, while her sister set herself apart with her creation. Amelia came alive when she played. Lainey thought she'd heard every iteration of "Für Amelia," except now her sister was doing something completely different, where she converted the melody of her left hand from sixteenth notes to thirty-second notes, flying through octaves while her right hand kept a slow pace for the tail end of each measure. Lainey couldn't exactly analyze it, although she herself had tried piano for a year before she'd quit. There was an element to her sister's playing that defied explanation.

As Amelia finished, Lainey had to wipe away a tear that threatened to drop onto her shirt.

Lainey's dad elbowed her in the ribs. "Crybaby," he said.

Lainey got a tissue and blew her nose as applause erupted throughout the auditorium and Amelia slunk offstage. "Shut up," she said, and smiled. His eyes were wet, too.

※

At the reception, Amelia buried herself in the crook of their dad's arm while he accepted the congratulations meant for her. The nonprofit director came over to where the three of them stood by the snacks table.

"That was very impressive, young lady," he said.

Amelia leaned her head on their dad's chest, turning away.

Their dad shrugged and gave the director a good-natured eye roll and shake of the head.

Lainey smoothed her sister's hair. "She didn't even manage to sleep last night, she was so excited for the competition," she said. That wasn't true. What was true was that Amelia didn't want to stay for the reception, but their dad urged her to since she'd won, and she'd made a deal that she could stay if she didn't talk to anyone. These deals, sacrifices, trade-offs, or whatever were integral to Amelia's life but hard to describe to outsiders, so Lainey and her dad didn't try.

In any case, the sleep explanation seemed to work for the director. He asked Lainey if she played any instruments and what grade she was in.

"I tried piano for a while, but I wasn't very good at it," Lainey said. "I graduated a couple years back."

"Oh?" the director said. "Are you continuing your studies?"

"No, sir. I'm working full-time over at Clark Farm, midway between Pinecreek and Crider."

"Ah." The director gave her a sad little smile, perhaps contemplating the tragedy of this poor, underserved rural teen whose talent he'd failed to foster, and turned to address their dad. "Halfway through her freshman year, correct? She's our youngest-ever winner."

"Yeah, well, she's a total prodigy." Their dad reached into a bowl of tortilla chips, picked one out, and double-dipped it into the guacamole. Lainey grabbed a paper plate, heaped on a pile of chips and guac, and handed it to him, pulling Amelia close to her side so he could eat.

"Wonderful," the director said. "She's in the right place then. Our program's very rigorous. Her scholarship means that starting in the new year, she'll be studying here twice a week after school and all day Saturdays."

"If you could see how much she practices at home," their dad said. "Piece of cake."

Lainey doubted Amelia would even begin the program, let alone stick with it. And if she did, that meant they'd have to drive her over an hour to Lake Charles and back three days a week. Amelia was eligible for a driver's license on her birthday in a few months, but that was unlikely. Their dad just wanted Amelia to get out and take part in the world, and so did Lainey. It was the reason Lainey was still living at home. To help out.

The director shook hands with their dad and then with Lainey. When Amelia eyed the director's hand but didn't make a move to take it, he gave her a final odd look that suggested he was beginning to regret the judges' decision. "Why don't you call our office tomorrow so we can give you all the program details," he said to their dad.

Lainey felt her dad clap his hand on her back, and through his last mouthful of chips, he said, "Actually, Lainey here will be the one to handle it all. She'll call tomorrow afternoon."

*

The next day, when she pulled up at home after work, Lainey saw Tess's beat-up Honda and then Tess herself. She was waiting on the front porch, wearing a ratty pair of jeans and her Pinecreek High letter jacket, resting her head on her knees and clearly hungover, which had been her steady state for the past year or so. Lainey's stomach dropped, and she had an ungenerous thought: Tess was one of those people who peaked in high school.

If Lainey was being honest, their friendship had been faltering for a very long time, and in her heart it had officially ended back in July. They'd hung out after Lainey spent the morning helping a mare through a grueling labor that probably would have resulted in her and the foal's deaths if Lainey hadn't been there. It was profound, visceral, beautiful. And when she tried to talk to Tess about it, Tess's eyes had glazed over until Lainey shut up, at which point Tess confessed in a breathy, scandalized monologue that she'd been sleeping with their old high school English teacher, whose wife finally called Tess the night before to tell her she'd better stay the fuck away from her husband. Lainey tuned out after that. Immersing herself in that kind of exhausting drama had become Tess's entire life. Lainey just wanted to grow up, be a responsible adult.

Now, Tess stood from the porch step, put her arms around Lainey's neck, and said in her most pitiful voice, "I lost my job and my roommates kicked me out. Can I crash here for a few nights?"

"Seriously?"

"You know I can't go home."

Lainey relented, brought her old friend inside, and made them grilled cheeses before she had to turn around and pick Amelia up from school. They'd been inseparable their whole lives. Everyone had always thought of Tess and Lainey as a single unit. Childhood, the awkward years, puberty, heartaches and disappointments, successes and failures, challenging family dynamics, even death, they'd weathered together. So much history. Lainey knew that Tess, an only child, considered her a sister. But Lainey already had a sister who needed support.

They agreed on two nights on the pullout couch in the den. But two nights turned into two weeks where Tess stayed up drinking and reading horror novels all night and then rolling out of bed whenever Lainey got home from work. Not helping out at all, except to be the fun one on Christmas Day who surprised them all with gifts. She'd gotten Lainey a yellow toy duck for her dog, Red, who lived over at Clark Farm, which was actually really sweet. Her dad got a *Girl Dad* coffee mug. Amelia got a tape recorder for her piano practice.

The day before New Year's Eve, Lainey came home to Amelia playing the piano in the living room as usual. Their dad was still at work. She checked on Tess. The den reeked of vomit. Tess was passed out on the couch under a comforter covered in puke. Lainey ripped it off her and immediately threw it in the washing machine. She went back and shook Tess awake. Amelia was trying something with "Für Amelia" where she'd play a measure as softly as she could and then bang out the next one, a chaotic soft-loud, soft-loud, soft-loud that was admittedly hard on the ears. But this was Amelia's house, and this was how she lived her life.

Tess squinted up at Lainey. "Oh my god," she said, and then raised her voice. "How can you stand that fucking noise?!"

That was it. This grown-ass woman with self-imposed problems was being a jerk about her little sister? And Tess being one of the few people who really *knew* about Amelia's challenges? Lainey began picking up Tess's mess from the floor and threw everything into her duffel bag. She went and got her toothbrush and toiletries from the bathroom and threw them in, too. She cleared the dirty dishes and the empty vodka bottles from the floor by her bed and brought them to the kitchen.

Tess was slow to react, but then she understood. "Where do you expect me to go?"

"I don't know. Go to your parents'. They might suck, but they're not going to *not* let you stay there."

"You know I can't stand to do that."

"I really don't care anymore. Go anywhere but here."

Tess pleaded, tried to reason with her, reminded Lainey of all the prior for-better-or-worse promises they'd made, and finally cussed her out for her lack of loyalty.

Lainey grasped Tess by the shoulders and moved in close so there could be no mistaking her words. "Look, I'm at the point where I can either be a responsible, productive person who moves forward in life, or I can be friends with you, Tess. Do you hear me? I can't do both. Not anymore. I'm sorry." Then she carried Tess's bag to her car and waited until she drove off. When she went back inside, Amelia paused long enough to ask if Tess was gone. When Lainey confirmed that she was, Amelia said, "Oh," and resumed her playing.

※

Three months later, in March, Amelia was surprising Lainey by still attending her music lessons. However, in order to go she'd given something up each time. She gave up certain types of junk food, she gave up wearing socks, she gave up talking to people at school who weren't her teachers. A month ago, she gave up sleeping between the hours of two and three a.m., and Lainey often woke to Amelia's alarm clock blaring through the wall. She gave up a few items from her bedroom. Gone were her stereo, her new tape recorder, her beanbag chair, the Cat Stevens poster that had been their mother's. Gone were the curtains on her window, her quilt with the stars. She allowed herself only one pillow now.

"Another month or two of lessons and she's going to be living like a monk," Lainey said to her dad after he knocked and came into her room on a Thursday afternoon carrying the mail. He handed her the electricity bill, which was the "rent" she paid to still be living at home. Then he handed her another fat envelope.

"You know your sister's so dramatic sometimes. A true *artiste*. And don't worry, I'm storing everything in the basement for when she eventually deals it back to herself. Anyway, we could all do with less stuff in our lives."

Lainey wondered if part of becoming an adult was hearing her father call what Amelia was doing the work of a "true *artiste*" and thinking he was fucking nuts. She scrutinized him closely. He looked different, his version of suave: soft flannel under a worn gray hoodie, laces conspicuously missing from steel-toed boots, thick-framed glasses, carefully messy stubble. Lainey wondered if he was dating again. He used to have a serious girlfriend, Linda, but Amelia had been paranoid about her coming around, and eventually they broke up.

Lainey opened the big envelope, and when she saw the first words her heart boomed in her chest and she quickly stashed it in the top drawer of her desk. She'd applied for a twelve-month apprenticeship at a nonprofit called Wildlife Rescue & Rehabilitation, which provided on-site housing and a monthly stipend on its two-hundred-acre property just outside San Antonio, but she never expected to get in. It almost exclusively took college graduates, though every once in a while people went to college after and the apprenticeship counted for a ton of credits, but that made it a multiyear commitment. Its website featured one apprentice who stayed with the nonprofit all the way through a doctorate. The site also featured a detailed story about a litter of orphaned baby opossums that volunteers successfully raised and released into the wild, which Lainey had read easily a dozen times. She'd applied only because Tara had given her the materials and insisted. A dream job, but she wasn't going to leave her home. She was needed.

"What you got there?" Lainey's dad said.

Lainey didn't want him to know about the job. For some reason that she couldn't explain, even applying had felt like a betrayal. To change the subject, she said, "I see you need some shoelaces," and she went to her work jacket that hung from a hook on her door. From a waist pocket, she pulled some twine that she'd snapped from a hay bale that morning.

He laughed when she offered it, sat at her desk, and propped up his feet. "By all means."

She cut the twine in half and laced them in. They were only long enough to reach the ankle eyelets, but that was almost better, rough fibers splintering low down with the upper flaps of the boot falling open. Lainey knew he'd go ahead and wear them like that; that's the kind of guy he was. A semi-helpless, good-natured guy.

"Beautiful. Truly top-notch work." He got up and kissed her on the top of her head. "You and Tess make up yet?"

"We're not going to make up. I told you."

"I heard she quit her community college classes the other day."

Lainey was so far removed from the town's gossip mill that she hadn't heard that, but she wasn't surprised.

Halfway out the door, her dad turned back. "Oh, hey. Any chance you can take Amelia to practice tonight?"

Here was the real reason he'd come to her room, played as an afterthought. "Uh-uh. No way."

"You can't?" he said. "What you got going on?"

"You do weekdays, I do Saturdays. I get up in the morning at like four o'clock, Dad. We made a deal." Lainey didn't like the whine in her voice, but her dad was always pulling this kind of thing. And Lainey wanted to spend the evening poring over the packet from Wildlife Rescue, to discover as much as she could before she turned it down.

"Okay, no problem. I'll call the studio, tell them I need to come in late and leave early," he said, and closed the door.

Lainey's dad worked two jobs. Early morning to mid-afternoon at the RV rental down in Moss Bluff. Then he worked part-time—very part-time—as a sound engineer in a local sound studio that was just a buddy's converted garage. Maybe he really did have a date tonight and didn't want to tell her.

She stepped out into the hall where she knew he was waiting for her. "I'll take her."

He turned and walked away, giving her his signature rock-and-roll fist pump over his head.

※

The Monday of Amelia's spring break, when she was off from both school and her music lessons, she came into the kitchen hours before dawn while Lainey was making coffee to take to work. Amelia was dressed up in a white miniskirt and a light pink crocheted blouse, with matching pink tights and white boots.

"Is that Mom's?" Lainey asked. "Did you get into Mom's things?" All these years later, their dad still kept a couple of chests full of her old stuff in the basement. The sisters used to play dress-up with it when they were younger. Last time Amelia was in their mother's clothes they hung off her, dragging on the floor. Now they fit perfectly.

"Let's go visit her," Amelia said.

Lainey poured her sister a glass of orange juice. "I need to get to work, but we could go this afternoon."

Amelia shook her head. "No, I'm coming with you. We'll walk by Mom's spot. Bring her some things."

Lainey inspected her sister for signs that something was off, but she seemed normal enough: relaxed, making eye contact, completing sentences.

"Okay, let me call Tara. Tell her you're coming and that we'll be a little late."

Lainey wondered if hearing her mention her boss would change Amelia's mind. Tara used to come by a lot before Amelia banned her from the house. And though many of Amelia's deals and sacrifices were temporary, bans were conclusive. Last year, Amelia had gone through a particularly bad patch where she got really paranoid and ended up insisting that they couldn't keep their dog, Red, because Red was spying on her. Not a dog, according to Amelia, but a spy in a dog costume. Because things could get scary with Amelia if she got something in her head but didn't get her way, Red went to go live with Tara at Clark Farm, where, good for him, he was living his dream and Lainey still got to see him. Tara, who'd been friends with their parents since forever, began suggesting to Lainey's father that Amelia needed professional help—a suggestion that was overheard by Amelia one afternoon, leading to Tara's banning. It was the indiscretion, more than the suggestion itself, that also resulted in the rift between Tara and their dad.

But Amelia didn't flinch at Tara's name, so Lainey went and made the call and finished breakfast with her sister. Amelia wanted Lainey to wear something of their mom's, too. Together they went down to the basement to look through her stuff. Since Lainey needed to fix a broken stall door at work and walk the fields rounding up cattle, she chose a simple navy-blue shirt with a white lace collar that she wore under her work jacket. Amelia rummaged through their mom's rusted jewelry box and selected a hoop earring that didn't have a mate. She also brought the Cat Stevens poster that used to hang in her bedroom.

Lainey usually drove to work, but they could walk there in thirty minutes if they cut through their back pasture and took a path through the woods. The path led to the dirt road that the farm was on. If they went in the opposite direction for a quarter mile or so, they would come upon the spot where their mother died in an accident thirteen years ago when her car slammed headfirst into a tree.

Sunrise wasn't for a couple of hours, and the sisters both carried flashlights on the walk. Lainey knew the land so well—both of them did, really—but without the light it was easy to stumble on a root or step on a snake. It turned out they needed the light, because since the last time they'd made this trek, four pine trees had toppled onto one another like dominoes, blocking their path just as it bordered the spring. But they both managed to climb over the trunks with no problem.

There was a pre-summer chill to the air that Lainey savored. They made it to the spot and found the wooden cross, still standing, though it tilted to one side. Their dad had burned an epitaph into the wood: *She hath awakened from the dream of life*. It was barely legible, and Lainey wasn't sure if she could make out the words only because she already knew what they said.

Amelia bent down and placed the earring on the cross, then unrolled their mother's Cat Stevens poster that was older than either of them, its psychedelic colors promoting *Majikat, Earth Tour '76*. Lainey found four rocks and placed them on the corners so it wouldn't roll back up. Their parents had never officially married, and the family lore was that it was because in her heart, their mom was already married to Cat Stevens.

When the poster was positioned to Amelia's liking, she nodded at Lainey and they walked on to Clark Farm. When they got close enough to smell the cut hay and manure from the barn, Amelia slowed way down.

"I don't know, Lainey. Tara's banned."

"She's banned from our house, but you're not banned from seeing her at the farm."

"I could maybe go if I don't talk to her."

The two sisters stopped at the driveway. Lainey didn't mind that Amelia didn't want people around—Lainey herself was quiet and introverted—but Tara was a loss. She was like family.

"How about instead of not talking to Tara, you can go if I make sure Red stays in the barn out of sight and we don't step on the grass the whole way to the house?" Not often, but sometimes Lainey was able to help her sister negotiate better terms with herself.

"Okay, but also we don't let our arms touch our sides until we get there," Amelia said, so the sisters both walked together with their arms held stiffly away from their bodies, and when Tara greeted them at her front door, Amelia looked up and said, shyly, "Hi."

※

Lainey got her work done while her sister sat in the shade of the porch with Tara and worked on refinishing the leather horse tack, wearing a heavy canvas smock so she didn't ruin their mom's clothes with the stain. People acted like living in Pinecreek was the worst thing in the world, but to Lainey it was beautiful. Green and trees and open space. Fresh air, the smell of hay and pine. Horses with tails that swished as they grazed. The chickens always kept her company on her daily rounds, bopping and swaggering around her feet while she put out feed and filled water troughs. Many of these animals were being raised for slaughter, but Lainey tried to give them as happy a life as possible for as long as they had.

At lunchtime, when Lainey crested the hill in the pasture heading back to the house, she could see something was wrong. Amelia was standing up on the porch, her back to Tara and her arms wrapped around her head in that protective position she took on when she didn't want to deal with something. Lainey set down the barn cat she was carrying and picked up her pace. Tara was close—too close—to her sister, clearly trying to talk to her while Amelia made herself as small as possible. Lainey started jogging, calling out her sister's name.

When Amelia heard her, she turned and looked and then rushed off. Lainey tried to catch her, but she was too far away. Tara intercepted her at the gate.

"What's wrong? What happened?" Lainey said.

"She'll make it home okay without you."

Tara reached across the gate and touched Lainey's cheek. Tara wasn't exactly like a mother to her, but she looked up to the older woman. She was strong, confident, and capable, youthful even with her hair that had prematurely grayed.

"But what happened? You didn't tell Amelia about the job, did you? She didn't even know I applied."

"You know it's the perfect opportunity."

Lainey unlatched the gate and came through. "That's none of your business. She's going to feel like I betrayed her, Tara. She hardly trusts anyone."

"Your mother was my friend—"

"Leave my mom out of this."

"—and she wouldn't want you to throw your life away. I see you making your life smaller and smaller and using your sister as an excuse. That's not fair, Lainey, to either of you. The truth is that Amelia's life will always be limited, but yours doesn't have to be."

Lainey removed the leather rucksack with the tools that belonged in the barn and dropped it at Tara's feet.

"Your mother needed help, too, but she was a grown adult and refused it, and I felt at the time that I had to respect that. Amelia can't make that decision for herself, though, Lainey. You must know that."

Their dad had tried to take Amelia to a doctor when she was in eighth grade, but it only made things worse. They'd been saddled with a $200 bill, and Amelia had closed herself up in her room for so long that the school held her back a year. Lainey started to empty the pockets of her work coat, but realized that the coat itself was Tara's, so she took it off and handed it over.

"Your dad. He knows about your job offer, too, but I bet he didn't tell you that. I went by his work weeks ago to make sure he got the message. He'll take responsibility if you're not around to do everything for him, Lainey. Life will go on without you."

Lainey started walking home while Tara called after her.

※

The damage was done. Lainey was banned. No matter what she did, Amelia wouldn't talk to her, look at her, remain for long in the same room with her. It didn't matter when Lainey tried to explain that she wasn't actually going anywhere, that Tara was mistaken. It was as if anything that came out of Lainey's mouth didn't register. As if she were dead to her sister.

Amelia refused to go to school and to her music lessons if Lainey was the one taking her. Their dad had to adjust his schedule. He seemed defeated, stopped keeping up with himself. If he'd been seeing someone, he broke it off. He didn't seem to know what to do or say; he half-heartedly congratulated Lainey on her job offer but otherwise said very little. Lainey felt invisible. She felt as if she'd done something wrong. One week later and Amelia refused her lessons entirely. She told their dad that for every day Lainey stayed, something else had to go in her place. In addition to giving up lessons, she gave up playing their home piano. She got rid of item after item from her room. She buried in the backyard her half of the walkie-talkie set she and Lainey had used together for years. She took a pair of kitchen scissors and chopped off half of her hair. She stopped eating meat. When she brushed her teeth, she skipped her back molars. She stopped leaving the house in daylight. The school sent notice that it was holding her back another year.

Lainey had quit Clark Farm the day Tara had spoken to her sister, effective immediately. She felt unmoored, sleepless nights followed by groggy days. Nothing she did helped anyone. She felt so isolated that she'd considered calling Tess, but she asked around and found out that Tess had taken a live-in babysitting job, which sounded like a disaster waiting to happen that Lainey didn't have the energy to deal with.

Instead, she walked by the farm and watched from the edge of the woods. Part of her wanted to go make up with Tara, ask for her old job back, but she saw that everything functioned as always. A new guy whom Lainey didn't recognize groomed the horses with a sure hand, the chickens dancing at his feet. Lainey had overestimated her own importance. Nothing had collapsed in her absence. Tara had been correct: she wasn't needed.

※

The evening of the deadline to respond to her job offer, Lainey knocked at her sister's door. When Amelia didn't answer she went in anyway. The room was completely empty now. Just ratty old carpet, bare walls, and a fixtureless bulb blazing from the center of the ceiling. Amelia lay on her back on the carpet in the space where her bed used to be. Her legs were zipped together, her arms held in tight to her sides.

Lainey lay next to her sister, not too close. She was wrong, the room wasn't completely empty. A single star was stuck to the ceiling directly overhead, one of those stickers that glowed in the dark, but with the harsh light of the bulb, it hid like a ghost against the plaster.

"Mom put those stickers up, you know," Lainey said. "There used to be a bunch. I thought they were all gone."

If Amelia heard her, she didn't show it.

"You used to make Mom laugh so much. You were so funny. I remember, when you were maybe six months old, you used to sit in her lap when we were all eating at the table. And you wanted to be like everyone else but didn't eat food yet, so you'd wave your arms until she slid her plate or bowl to the edge of the table and you'd latch on. Just latch on and start gumming it. I was only, I guess, five or six, but I remember because once we were all laughing and you were going to town on that bowl, I started copying you, chewing on my bowl, and Dad did this Cookie Monster voice: 'Must eat bowl!' I remember us all doubled over in our chairs, laughing so hard, and you smiling all proud, like, See? I do the eating thing just like everyone else."

Still, Amelia didn't move a muscle. The air conditioner clicked on, and a soft mechanical hum filled the room. A slight vibration.

"I'm leaving," Lainey said. "I called the place I'm going to be working for and they're expecting me at the end of summer. I'll be living in this really rustic cabin out in the middle of the woods with two roommates. We'll have our own bedrooms but share the living space. I'm going to be learning about all kinds of native Texas animals, how to care for them and feed them, go out on rescue calls, all kinds of things. I'll be working up to seventy hours some weeks. I have to get a rabies pre-exposure vaccine before I go."

Though Amelia hadn't moved, Lainey could feel her sister's energy shift slightly in her direction.

"But all of this depends on you," Lainey said. "You have to agree to a major deal if I go. I mean I'm going to be asking a lot."

Now Amelia shifted onto her side, resting her head on her arm. Her skin was almost transparent; delicate blue veins ran like vines up her neck. "What kind of deal?"

"I'll go, but only if you don't keep depriving yourself of all your stuff. We're moving everything back into your room, and I mean tonight. All your recent restrictions are over."

Amelia thought about it for a second. "I don't want that old beanbag chair, though. It's all stained and it smells bad."

"Okay, not the beanbag, we'll throw that away. But everything else."

"Done," Amelia said.

"Yes, but I'm just getting started. I'll also only go if you don't quit playing the piano. You can never quit playing the piano. You're too good."

"I hate those lessons, Lainey. I just want to play our piano and work on 'Für Amelia.'"

"You need to be able to tell Dad that kind of thing, okay? I think he'd be fine with that if you just told him. We'll talk to him about it together tomorrow."

Amelia nodded. "Okay, deal."

"One more thing, and this is going to be the hardest. This is the one that you're going to want to say no to, but you can't. If you say no to this, I won't leave, do you hear me?"

"What is it?"

"Dad made an appointment for you with a specialist up in Alexandria. A really nice doctor, a woman. We looked into it and made sure it was someone you'd like before we made the appointment. But I'll only leave if you don't say no, okay?"

Amelia shut her eyes tight, curled her legs up to her chest, her cheek pressed against the coarse carpet. Lainey didn't want to consider what would happen if her sister didn't agree to this. Once a girl cleared out her bedroom and stopped going to school and stopped eating regularly, something had to happen, whether voluntarily or by force.

Lainey waited a long time until finally Amelia spoke. "You said you're leaving at the end of summer, but when exactly?"

"They want me on the Tuesday after Labor Day. It's about four months."

"Okay," Amelia said, and looked Lainey in the eyes for the first time in weeks. "I'll do everything you said, and you will leave on the Tuesday after Labor Day. That's our deal. Tara told me you deserve to have a good life."

"So do you, Amelia. You deserve that, too." She took hold of her sister's hand that was balled into a fist at her chest. When Amelia relaxed, she got up and pulled Amelia up, too. Their dad was making a real dinner—chicken and rolls and green beans—and she led her little sister out of the room and downstairs to have a meal together as a family. When they got to the kitchen doorway, their dad saw them and beamed as he poured out glasses of Coke. The relief on his face was plain. Lainey felt it, too. For the first time she let herself feel excited about her new life.

She squeezed her sister tight into a hug and said, "I'll be back to visit, okay? I'll be back all the time."

Amelia didn't pull away from the hug, but she didn't respond to it, either. After a moment, she whispered in Lainey's ear: "Once you leave you can never come back. You're banned. Forever. It's the only way."

Gold Star
Olivia

OLIVIA PULLS INTO LOT C and parks in her usual spot, excited as always about getting to work because it means she's minutes from seeing Nora's face. Today's a particularly good day, because she has a great piece of gossip, the kind that Nora lives for. Also, this morning the principal announced Olivia's full-ride acceptance to LSU—a first for their mediocre rural school—over the loudspeaker during homeroom. No one in her class seemed particularly happy for her, and Olivia had the pleasure of tolerating half-hearted applause and fake smiles.

In Olivia's final high school semester, she attends class only through the period right after lunch and then works three hours each afternoon at Boise Cascade, a wood-processing plant about a forty-minute drive from Pinecreek High. Once she parks, she speed-walks across the concrete, onto the sidewalk past the main warehouse and then to the long row of office trailers. The burnt tar smell of creosote makes her eyes water. Chemical vapors plume from the ventilation stacks on the factory roofs. Although the complex is surrounded by forest, the property itself is devoid of all plant life other than sickly, yellowed grass.

She works in the seventh trailer on the left. It's a cool April day and only the screen door is closed to keep out bugs. Olivia composes herself and then goes inside, forces herself to politely greet Miss Pam before she turns and walks down the length of the trailer to her desk, which is so close to Nora's.

Nora is on a phone call, but her eyes light up when Olivia passes by her desk, and she holds up a finger to signal *just a sec*. Every day, Nora wears jeans and an open flannel shirt over a tank top. Today it's a maroon tank top under a green-and-brown flannel with flecks of gold.

Olivia opens her day planner and pulls out the filing left over from yesterday, waiting for Nora to get off the phone. This has become their routine. Nora, who is a decade older than Olivia and never got to finish high school, loves to hear all gossip first thing. Olivia, laser-focused on her future, never before cared about gossip but is now a careful collector.

Nora ends her call and swivels her chair around, nudges Olivia's shin with her foot and then leans in. Olivia leans to meet her, intertwists her pinkie with Nora's, and then waits three beats—the optimum number to create the most anticipation, she has discovered through trial and error. She keeps her voice low.

"So, Jaden Nickel snuck into the girls' locker room right after gym class this morning and stole a random pair of underwear that I guess someone left lying around. It was this dirty gray cotton pair that had some sort of, I don't know, crotch smear—"

"Oh no," Nora says, eyes wide, already swaying a little into the drama.

"—and at lunch he turned them inside out and ran from table to table shoving them into people's faces and yelling 'Mustard!' Finally he got to Amelia Bordelon sitting in the corner where she always eats alone, and since she wouldn't give him any reaction, he kept yelling

'Mustard!' right in her ear and then started trying to shove the underwear in her mouth."

"Jesus, why would anyone want to mess with Amelia Bordelon? That poor girl has got to be twenty years old by now. Just let her graduate already."

"Right? But finally, Jenna Mullin rushed over, screaming at him to stop. Which he clearly thought was hilarious. He held the underwear up over his head, and she kept jumping and trying to snatch them away. Jaden's like six foot six, and no way was she getting them. But then Coach Kyle came in, so Jaden put the underwear on Jenna's head like a ball cap, yelled 'Mustard!' one last time, and sat back down."

"That motherfucker," Nora says, not whispering anymore, and immediately Miss Pam scowls at them from her desk at the other end of their office trailer.

"Shhhhh. Nora!" Olivia feels the keen sense of glee she always feels when Nora acts inappropriately at work, which is so much of the time.

Nora lets go of Olivia's hands, turns and pushes off her desk with her feet, rides her rolling office chair until it bumper-cars into Olivia's. And then she moves in close and whispers, "That inbred worthless redneck motherfucker." The dimples high up on Nora's cheeks dent just under the outside corners of her eyes like they do when she's excited. "I bet if we got hold of *his* dirty underwear they'd be loaded with shit stains." The office phone rings at Nora's desk, and she rides her chair back, picks it up: "Boise Cascade. This is Nora." Nora's voice can turn from vehement to neutral like *that*—she is endlessly fascinating. "He's away from his desk at the moment. May I help you with something? Or I can transfer you to his voicemail." Nora touches her pen to the corner of her mouth, and for a split second her tongue slips out to probe it before she says, "One moment." She presses some buttons, hangs up, and wheels back over. "He can drop dead. That shit stain."

Miss Pam calls from across the room. "Olivia, you finished the filing I gave you?"

"No, ma'am. I'm almost finished."

"If you need extra help, Nora can help you. She seems to have time on her hands."

Nora rolls her eyes and digs her heels into the carpet, inching her chair back to her desk.

"In fact, since you're heading off to college soon—congratulations, by the way," Miss Pam says, and Olivia feels her breath catch and her hand shoot out from her side as if she's trying to throw the words back across the room. Theirs is a small town and news travels fast, but she thought she'd get away with waiting to deliver her rehearsed speech to Nora about it over the weekend. She glances quickly at Nora, and the dead-eyed gaze she receives says it all. She's screwed. Why hadn't she told her before?

She definitely knew she'd be accepted—Olivia has always found a way to get what she wants—and for weeks now she's been contemplating a way to convince Nora to move with her to Baton Rouge. They could get an apartment together and even bring along Nora's tedious twelve-year-old daughter, Kasey. Of course. Obviously they wouldn't leave Kasey behind.

But Miss Pam keeps talking. "Since you're heading off to college soon, why don't you come up with a project or two to make our office run more efficiently. You can think of Nora as your employee for the next few months before you leave."

Olivia tries to give Nora a look to acknowledge Miss Pam is a nightmare while still appearing respectful to Miss Pam, who is their supervisor. She nods at Miss Pam and turns back to her desk. A yellow jacket hovers outside the tiny square window. She tracks its movement while she labels color-coded folders.

Eventually Miss Pam rises and goes to the restroom, and the instant the door closes, Olivia hops up and throws herself at Nora's feet, circling her arms around Nora's legs and looking up into her eyes. Nora can hold a grudge like no other, but a silly, dramatic gesture like this, Olivia has learned, is the best grudge prevention.

"I was going to tell you this weekend. There's a reason I didn't tell you yet."

For a second, Nora's dead look remains, but then—thank god—it clears. "Calm down, we both know Pam's a stupid cow."

"Jesus, you're my favorite human, I love you so much." Olivia places her head on Nora's lap, she's so grateful.

Nora nudges Olivia to sit up and pulls a flask of vodka from her purse, takes a swig, and hands it to Olivia. Olivia puts her tongue over the opening before she tilts her head back, then mimes a swallow and that *oh god, it burns!* expression that always makes Nora laugh. By the time Miss Pam returns, they are both back at their desks, toiling.

※

The next day, Nora has to sit in on the annual audit meeting and take minutes, so Olivia waits until they get to Nora's house to give up the gossip. They've had a routine for precisely the past six Fridays. After work, Olivia swings by and gets Kasey from basketball practice while Nora buys frozen daquiris from the drive-through Liquor Barn, and then they meet back at the house. Olivia's mother thinks that this is a babysitting job, and technically it is, even if she doesn't get paid and Kasey won't speak to her.

At home, Nora and Olivia lie on the couch while Kasey plops herself on the beanbag chair in front of the TV, headphones on, reading through a science textbook. Nora's sort of in an iffy mood today—in fact she's been a little standoffish since Miss Pam mentioned college—but she still insists on whatever Olivia has to spill.

"Coach Kyle put on another movie today in English class—Kenneth Branagh's *Hamlet*, which he played, I swear, in like February, not even two months ago—and he kept looking up at the clock. At exactly eleven fifteen, and this has become a weirdly consistent thing, he left the room, and right away, I got this text from Bethany Lucas—"

Nora interrupts, miming puking, and says, "You're not friends with Bethany Lucas, are you?"

"No, not really."

"Too cool for school, just like her mom. Nothing I hate worse." She takes another big swig from the giant Styrofoam cup that holds her daquiri.

"You're right, she's totally stuck up."

Nora squints at Olivia, but then moves her hand in a slow circle, gesturing to go on.

"But anyway, Bethany's in Miss Lavender's class, and Miss Lavender also coincidentally leaves class at exactly eleven fifteen a bunch of mornings. Bethany texted with a question mark, and I texted back, *Yep*, and we both snuck out of our classrooms and ducked under windows all the way to that handicapped bathroom at the back of the gym. And yeah, when we got there—"

"Okay, stop," Nora says. Olivia tenses up because she really can't read Nora's mood and therefore isn't sure how to act. "What did you end up doing about Jaden Nickel?"

Nora upends her cup and finishes her drink. Olivia hasn't had any of hers since she's driving home later and since she doesn't really like to drink. She offers it to Nora, but Nora will only take it after she watches Olivia swallow a tiny sip. On her beanbag, Kasey bobs her head to whatever slow, depressing music she listens to.

"Jaden Nickel?" Olivia says.

"Yeah, Jaden Nickel. Mustard! Mustard!"

"Do about him? Nothing. I mean, Amelia Bordelon came to school today with one eyebrow shaved off, and in homeroom she handed Jenna Mullin a tape she'd recorded of her piano music, I guess as thanks for helping. Everyone's pretty much forgotten about it already. He's a dumbass."

Nora sits up from where she's curled on the other end of the couch, gets on her knees and straddles Olivia's body, crawls up past her legs and to her chest. Immediately Olivia's breathing goes shallow and her throat dries up. Nora bends down and puts her forehead to Olivia's, letting her soft, curly hair dangle from her ponytail and just barely brush Olivia's temple. Her breath smells sweet and alcoholic, and Olivia feels a strong urge to taste. Instead she clasps Nora's waist with both hands and squeezes, and Nora laughs and they both laugh together. Olivia turns her head and glances at Kasey, who shuts her eyes when they make contact.

"You can't let the Jaden Nickels of the world get away with stuff like that," Nora says. "Otherwise, they'll grow up and start raping everyone right and left."

"Wow. Right *and* left? I'd have assumed just left."

Nora pokes Olivia in the ribs. Olivia squeals and squirms and fights back, pinching Nora above her knees where Olivia knows she can't stand it. Nora pulls her head back and then headbutts Olivia in the boob, and Olivia throws her arm around Nora's neck in a sleeper hold, and Nora lays her body out over Olivia's and bounces, trying to crush her, though she's slim and smaller than Olivia, and the weight and the pressure actually feel fantastic. They are cracking up, as they can't help but do when they are together, best friends and somehow more, even though they are ten years apart in age, until they hear a loud "*Ugh!*"

and look up to see Kasey stomp from the room. Nora looks at Olivia and widens her eyes—not quite an eye roll, but suggestive of one—and then motions for Olivia to scooch to the edge of the couch so she can nestle in.

"Also, I'm tired of hearing about Coach Kyle," Nora says. She tells Olivia that he was both her volleyball coach and English teacher back in ninth grade when she got pregnant. Some of the moms tried to set up a daycare at the school because it's not like Nora was the only one.

"Yeah, it's still such a huge problem," Olivia says, and immediately regrets it because she can feel Nora tense. Fortunately, after a moment of silence she snuggles in even closer to Olivia and continues on about the moms' vision for a community-funded daycare. How they'd outlined a whole plan in a PTA meeting. But Coach Kyle, self-righteous prick, shot it down: *We cannot reward bad behavior!* And then he invited Pastor Goins to talk about abstinence, who went off the rails and preached that offering birth control to our daughters meant we hated them. Same with community-funded daycare. Giving of daycare, aka rewarding and/or encouraging bad behavior, would betray a deep-seated loathing of our very daughters whom we were professing to love and help.

"As you can tell, I was there," Nora says. "Walked in, sat in the back, and no one noticed me. I really think that if it hadn't been for that man, I would have finished high school. Instead I'm at a wood products plant that smells like rotten eggs doing an entry-level job that a seventeen-year-old kid—no offense—could do blindfolded on shrooms. So that's why I don't want to hear about Coach Kyle fucking some teacher in the handicapped bathroom. Plus it's depressing hearing about him getting some when I'm not getting any myself."

Olivia lies there soaking up Nora's body heat and radiating her own, even though they are both sweating. Olivia generally knows when to be quiet. Though Nora's comment about not getting any is laughable. One of Olivia's "babysitting" jobs is entertaining Kasey out of the house so Nora can get some. Or hanging with Kasey at the house so Nora can go out and get some elsewhere. Olivia doesn't judge. Nora told her once that men reach their sexual peaks at eighteen, whereas— at age twenty-seven—Nora is just now entering hers, which might last years, she'd said, hopefully! Nora is smart, funny, exciting, not very pretty, but with her that's somehow a plus. It's not fair she's stuck at home with a middle schooler. It's Friday night, and Olivia assumes at some point Nora will go out and try to get some.

"Anyway, you'd better call Don't You Love Jesus and tell her you have another babysitting job, another overnight. Then drink that daiquiri already. I've got wine coolers in the fridge, and we'll order pizza. You get it since I got the drinks?" Nora props herself up on Olivia's shoulder and calls past her toward the hallway: "Kasey. We're calling for pizza. Sausage and onion in your honor, Your Highness." Then she leans down and whispers in Olivia's ear, "Sausage and onion. What a freak show," and they crack up again.

※

By the time the pizza comes, Nora's pretty drunk. After she finishes Olivia's daquiri, she gets a text from the guy she was going to meet up with calling it off, and she starts right in on the wine coolers.

"Well, ladies, I'm all yours. What are we going to do?" She points a finger at Olivia: "Don't You Love Jesus said you can stay. Kasey's a stick-in-the-mud and never has any ideas. It's up to me, I guess."

They're all standing at the kitchen counter eating pizza. This is where they always eat at Nora's house, since the table and chairs are stacked with magazines and bills and schoolbooks, some folded laundry that hasn't been moved in the weeks since Olivia's been coming over, and a sizable collection of jigsaw puzzles. Olivia's excited that Nora's not going out but wishes she would stop drinking so that they can snuggle up in bed again and talk all night. She also wishes she'd stop calling her mother that, even if it's moderately funny.

Olivia's mother has recently become hugely into Jesus. This wasn't true while Olivia was growing up, but it is true now. Olivia's father hasn't lived with them in almost two years, but her parents are still married because Jesus doesn't believe in divorce. Her father lives on the nearby army base and volunteers for deployments any chance he gets, so he doesn't care. Olivia and her mother are not on great terms right now. Any time something comes up that they disagree on, she gets all weepy and asks Olivia, "Don't you love Jesus?"

It's funny because before her mother started asking her that question, Olivia hadn't *not* loved Jesus. She hadn't even questioned it. She lives in a part of the world where nearly everyone loves Jesus. But since she was put on the spot and had to think about it? No, not really. Some of the worst people around are those who most love Jesus: the sanctimonious, the hypocrites, that German family a few years back who lived in the woods and kept their teenage daughter locked up in a shed. Until one day a hunter with his dog came across the German grandfather's body covered in turkey vultures and picked clean enough that the death was ruled inconclusive. Hip crushed and skull fractured, but that could have been from when he fell. Common denominator? Jesus.

Olivia talked to Nora about all this a month ago, after her first night staying over with Kasey while Nora met up with some guy. Nora had crawled into bed with her just before dawn and they'd talked all morning. That is one of Olivia's best memories in all her seventeen years of life, but now Nora won't stop referring to her mom as Don't

You Love Jesus. To Olivia, it feels like they shared something private that should have stayed in that room, and it disappoints her that Nora doesn't get that.

Nora and Olivia pull their onions from their slices and deposit them on Kasey's plate. Kasey eats every single one of them.

"Do you know where Jaden Nickel lives?" Nora asks.

"No. Why would I?"

"Well, start texting around. We can find out. Kasey, get on the internet and do that thing you do."

"I don't look up people's addresses on the internet, Mom."

"*I don't look up people's addresses on the internet, Mom,*" Nora mimics with her jaw hanging open, a dopey look on her face. Kasey goes red. If only she had a friend, she could go away, and Olivia and Nora could spend the night together alone.

Nora walks to the fridge, on which is taped Kasey's kindergarten graduation certificate, adorned with the maximum ten out of ten gold stars. Olivia pointed it out once, and Nora said it's there to commemorate the pinnacle of Kasey's accomplishments, which Olivia thought was mean even for Nora, though she had clearly been joking. But admittedly, Kasey was average at best. Nora comes back from the fridge with a squeeze bottle of French's yellow mustard. She squirts some onto all three of their pizza slices.

"Gross!" Kasey uses her paper towel to immediately remove as much as she can.

Nora takes a bite of her mustard pizza and chews casually, totally unfazed. Olivia tries to do the same and immediately regrets it. Her stomach twists, and she has to run over to the trash and spit it out.

"It's not only mustard," Nora says. "Us women have all kinds of vagina condiments. Ketchup being the obvious one, about five days per month."

Even though Nora's being obnoxious, Olivia manages a half-hearted laugh. Kasey says, "Shut up, Mom. You're drunk."

"Once Kasey starts her ketchup, which will be any day now, we'll need to have a conversation about irth-bay ontrol-cay."

"No, but that evil pastor wouldn't approve, that would mean you hate her," Olivia says. She tries her best to keep it friendly because there's a charge in the room that feels dangerous.

Kasey grimaces at them with pizza sauce on her face.

"And you should have seen what came out when you were born, little girl. Thousand Island. Worcestershire sauce." Nora hops backward, laughing, when Kasey starts hitting at her and telling her to shut up. "One time, this guy, this firefighter—damn, he was fine. He passed me something, and you should have seen it. So much relish and mayonnaise until I finally got on antibiotics."

"I said shut the fuck up!"

"Come on, Kasey, you can't talk to your mom like that," Olivia says, but immediately knows it's a mistake.

Kasey is bent over, breathing hard, her hands on her knees. She glares at Olivia but addresses her mother. "Did she tell you, Mama, that they had a school-wide pep rally in her honor today? We all got out of second period so we could admire Olivia."

"What?" Olivia says. "The pep rally was for basketball playoffs. I didn't even know the middle schoolers were there."

"All *I* know is that they told us that the pep rally was for Olivia. She gave an inspiring speech about the big college scholarship she got."

"Oh, please. The principal made me do that. It was like two minutes."

"It was thirteen minutes. I timed it."

Olivia might be sick now. The mix of tomato and meat and onion-soaked cheese and the bitter-tart vinegar of the mustard linger in her mouth.

"Well, that's fancy," Nora says. She pushes some unopened mail from one of the kitchen chairs to the floor and sits. "Isn't that fancy?"

Kasey's calmer. She clears a chair next to her mother, placing a pile of books neatly on the edge of the counter. "Don't worry, I remember it all. She encouraged us to get perfect scores on the state assessment tests in eighth grade, like she did. She suggested we study at least two years for the SATs, like she did. Oh, did you know she published an article in the newspaper celebrating how poor we all are?"

This is perhaps the most Olivia has ever heard Kasey speak. It's an ugly voice.

"Actually," Olivia says, "your memory sucks. I started a campaign to send letters to our senators about the disparity in the Louisiana school system and how small-town schools are not equipped to prepare students for college. *The Washington Post* picked it up and then some more national media, which got the Louisiana state congress to allocate funds specifically to our school."

Kasey beams at her with her overlapping front teeth. "She's practically a saint. I should go get my notes. There's a lot more."

"No, I get it. There is a superior being in our presence and I'm duly honored." Nora slaps her palm on her thigh. "Go get your jackets. We're going out. I just remembered: I actually do know where Jaden Nickel lives."

After Kasey leaves the room, Olivia dashes to Nora, trying for a graceful slide in her socks on the tile floor that will bring her to another dramatic collapse at Nora's feet. But it goes wrong when she hits a patch of unopened mail and careens into the table, knocking a jigsaw box to the floor. Pieces scatter.

"Girl, calm down," Nora says.

Still Olivia tries for the grand gesture, holds on tight to Nora's shoulders, unable to help the anxiety that creeps into her voice. "Listen, I was going to tell you about all of it tomorrow before I go home. It's just that I've been looking at apartments in Baton Rouge close to campus. We could do it together. We could find like a two-bedroom."

Nora pauses and they lock eyes. "What are you talking about, 'we'?"

"I was just thinking, maybe, we could all go, when I go."

"Move to Baton Rouge?"

Olivia nods.

"And get an apartment together, a two-bedroom?"

Nora's voice has gone cold, but Olivia nods again anyway.

"And you and I are sharing a bed in this two-bedroom scenario?"

Olivia is flustered. She's definitely not opposed to the idea, but that wasn't what she was trying to suggest. "Or you and Kasey could. Or, I mean, I could get a bunk with Kasey and you'd have your own room. Or maybe we could even swing a three-bedroom."

"We'd be one big happy family." Nora smiles at Olivia, and Olivia feels that the older woman can see through her, through to the nights alone when her mind turns to fantasies that embarrass her. She's a virgin, not even certain she's interested in any of that stuff, but she's had a lot of trouble sleeping, thinking how she's worked half her life for this exact college outcome, and yet every part of her body feels like it might die if she's across the state from Nora.

Kasey comes back with her jacket and lingers in the doorway. Nora leans toward Olivia and whispers, "What do you think is going on here?"

❈

Nora, with her thermos of wine coolers, sits in the passenger seat and navigates while Olivia drives and Kasey slumps down in the back. First they go to Market Basket and march down a single fluorescent-lit aisle. The store is nearly empty at nine o'clock on a Friday night. The cashier chews a wad of gum and makes no sign if he thinks a basket full of mustard is anything all that special. After that, Nora directs Olivia down Main Street, a left at the stoplight onto Highway 171, another left a mile past First Baptist onto a dirt road marked with a series of newly painted mailboxes. The houses here are spread far apart, separated by fenced-off ranchland. A mile or so down, Nora tells Olivia to cut the headlights and pull over. Clouds obscure the moon and stars. Olivia sees the lit windows of a house at the end of a long driveway.

Nora dumps the squeeze bottles of mustard into her big purse and tells them to come on. Olivia wants to protest, but Kasey doesn't hesitate—she gets out of the car and clicks the door quietly shut. The three of them convene at the hood, all touching because their eyes haven't adjusted to the dark. Nora shoves her hands into Olivia's pockets until she finds her car key.

"So that you don't panic and drive off without us."

Olivia starts to protest, but Nora shushes her.

Nora peels the protective seals from the squeeze bottles and hands them each a couple. "What's the problem? Worried you'll get in trouble and be stuck in this pathetic town like the rest of us?"

Then they are going, bent over, hurrying toward the house. Kasey pauses at a playground set and squirts a stream of mustard on the slide. The bottle squeals when it replaces the spent mustard with air. Sound amplifies in the quiet night. They approach the side of the house, and they all splatter mustard on a window that's covered by an inside curtain.

Nora grabs both of their wrists and pulls them close. "Okay, if we hit all the doors, that's good enough for me. I want it to be the first thing that motherfucker sees and smells when he leaves in the morning." Olivia agrees to hit the back door while Kasey hits the garage and Nora hits the front. She just wants it to be done, that's all she wants, and she tiptoes toward her assignment. She squeezes out the mustard with all her heart as if Nora's going to come grade her on her performance. She's on the second bottle when she hears it, the blast of a car horn pounding the silence. A pair of headlights makes long shadows that try to reach her at the back of the house. The horn continues to blare. She runs toward the noise and sees her car at the end of the driveway, pulling in, backing up, and taking off toward town. She's running, sprinting across the gigantic front yard in the direction of the fleeing car, when someone shouts—a deep, familiar voice she's heard countless times. For a moment she considers rushing blind into the night, but a floodlight comes on behind her and stops her dead. She knows she's caught.

※

Monday at work, Olivia enters the office trailer with a large poster board she prepared the day before and asks Miss Pam if she can make a short presentation. Nora raises her eyebrows but doesn't look at Olivia when she passes by. Today it's a ribbed white tank under a solid burgundy flannel. Olivia's breath hitches when she sees her, but she already cried it out over what turned out to be the worst weekend of her life, and now she is steel.

Miss Pam comes and stands near Nora's desk, tells Olivia to go ahead with the presentation. Olivia pulls her note cards from her backpack and begins.

"Back in early 2002, Boise Cascade divested its pulp and paper assets, selling them to an investment firm. Since then, the company has been pushing to digitalize its records. That's over three years ago, and yet even though we have a scanner, it's never been used. This office is still one hundred percent paper-based."

She flips to her next card and can't help but notice the ironic little smile pasted on Nora's face. "Miss Pam, you said I should come up with a project, and so I'm proposing this office become fully digitalized by the time I leave for college in four months. It's ambitious, but I'll manage the work and Nora will execute. I'm confident we can rise to the challenge."

Here Nora breaths a series of short little laughs through her nose, and Olivia holds her poster board up to the wall directly in front of Nora's desk where she plans to hang it.

"This gives us until August seventeenth, since the LSU Dean's Scholars have to show up a full two weeks earlier than all the ordinary students." Olivia points out the rows and columns on the poster board and continues. "I took a community college class last summer on operations management and learned that one way to increase employee productivity is to break complex jobs into discrete tasks that are simple enough for anyone to follow. So, I made this poster for Nora. As you can see, the tasks are broken down in columns: 'Read Epson Stylus scanner manual.' 'Plug in scanner.' 'Scan three sheets of test paper.' Et cetera. Then the rows have blank spaces for Nora to log in her beginning time and her ending time for each task, a space for her to initial, indicating completion, and a place for a potential gold star sticker if I deem that the task was done thoroughly and efficiently. That's another thing I learned in operations management, that if an employee knows there's a potential reward waiting, they'll—"

"That's fine," Miss Pam says, cutting off Olivia. "Though I'm not sure the gold stars are really necessary."

"Oh, no, please," Nora says. "That's the part I'm most excited about."

Both women turn back to their work without another word. Olivia gets the masking tape out of her desk drawer and hangs the poster board. On Friday night, her mother had to come pick her up from Coach Kyle's house, because Nora had lied. It had not been Jaden Nickel's house they had driven to and slathered mustard all over.

Once home, she started texting Nora, at first trying to pass it off as a huge joke—*LOL!!!*—even if Nora had just tried to sabotage Olivia's future. But Nora wouldn't respond, and so Olivia stayed up all night sending messages that turned from increasingly desperate to nasty: *Wow, everyone was right about you. You really are just a dumb hick.* Finally, Nora texted her Saturday morning: *I put your car key in the glove compartment and the door's unlocked. Leave us alone. We're not home.* Her mom drove her to get her car and, when they returned home, tried to find out what was wrong. But Olivia screamed at her, told her she'd made herself into a person whom Olivia couldn't talk to about things, so instead her mom just lay quietly next to her and stroked her hair.

The three women accomplish more in their shared office than they have since Olivia started working there in January. The only talking occurs when Nora or Miss Pam answers a phone call, and before the day is over, Nora marks off four of the tasks with her time stamps and initials. When Miss Pam goes out to meet with someone in accounting, Olivia feels the heaviness that hangs in the air between them. But she stands up through it, straight and tall, and goes over to inspect the poster board. She sticks on two gold stars.

Then, suddenly, Nora comes up behind her, close, talking so that Olivia can feel her hot breath on the back of her neck. "I'm sorry for the way things went down Friday night. If I could go back, I'd do a lot of it differently."

It's completely humiliating, but Olivia can't help it—she squeezes her eyes shut and tears seep from the corners. After a moment, she turns and drops to Nora's feet, trembling, her body discharging all its heartbreak and anger. Nora helps her to stand back up, brushes a tear away, softly, with the knuckle of her thumb. Nora is everything, no matter how much Olivia tried to convince herself otherwise over the weekend.

Nora takes one of the gold star stickers from the sheet in Olivia's hand, sticks it on her own forehead, laughs. "These are priceless, you little brat." Nora locates the stack of stickers on Olivia's desk and picks them up, fans them out.

"I know. I think I have like five thousand. They only sell them in huge packs."

Nora takes about half the pile and puts it in her purse. "Kasey and I are going to have fun with these."

She motions for Olivia to sit and gets her to tell how Friday night ended.

"Well, first off, that definitely was not Jaden Nickel's house," Olivia says, and Nora starts cracking up. It's unbelievable, because Olivia laughs, too, and they laugh together even though she was positive only minutes before that she would now live out her entire life stoic, devoid of joy. She tells Nora about sitting in Coach Kyle's living room, his wife and five kids present so he could deliver his teaching moment. And how the teaching moment quickly swerved to the fact that everyone deserves a second chance after Olivia lobbed a non sequitur at him about how much she appreciates the handicapped bathroom at the back of the gym. How large and private it is. How for some reason she always needs to go at precisely eleven fifteen.

Nora shakes her head. "What a guy." She pulls her flask from her purse, and this time when she offers it, Olivia takes a real sip, endures the burn in Nora's honor.

Nora leaves about half an hour early, but Olivia doesn't mind. She'll see Nora in only twenty-one hours. She still has four months to convince her to move with her. In the big city, Nora will surely drink less. Pinecreek is so small that you need either Jesus or booze, Nora herself was always saying. But in Baton Rouge there will be so much more to do. Olivia will make an effort to be nicer to Kasey. Less bossy. More like a big sister, a role model. And Nora's smart, that's clear enough. She could finally finish school and actually *be* something in life. Olivia worries about a lot, but one thing she is certain of is her own resourcefulness. She'll always be able to take care of herself, and she could take care of a whole family if she needed to. Their family, hers and Nora's.

By the time Miss Pam comes in, Olivia is beaming, fidgeting in her seat, she can barely contain her happiness.

"What's up with you?" Miss Pam says.

"Nothing," Olivia says. "I just didn't notice how nice it is outside today. I didn't sleep last night. You know, putting this project together."

"Oh, honey, they don't pay you enough for that."

At five on the dot, Olivia walks to Lot C. The humidity keeps the creosote plumes from dispersing, and her eyes and nose and throat sting from the chemicals. She doesn't really mind; this isn't her life. Before she gets to her car, she sees it shining. An abnormal shine from something on the front window that reflects the sun. Dozens, maybe hundreds of gold star stickers decorate the windshield, screaming their upbeat messages:

Great job!
Nice going!
Superstar!

Part II
Beyond

One Trick
Tess

ON WEDNESDAY EVENINGS at the Fort Meade library where Tess had been working for almost two years, she took a theater class. It was led by a Johns Hopkins graduate student named Joel, an aspiring playwright, and it was kind of a silly thing to do, but Tess needed something for herself. Paul was completely wrapped up in studying for the exams he had to pass before they moved yet again to his next post at the end of the year. And their daughter, Summer, nearly four years old and the greatest of kids, could survive without her mom one night a week.

Tess's life wasn't exactly exciting, but it was stable, and most days she could convince herself that was preferable. She woke up at six. Got to bed most nights by ten. Flipped through *The Baltimore Sun* over coffee every morning. Worked five days a week. Handled the family budget. Ate three square meals a day and all that. Her younger self would have been appalled.

In the first half of her theater class, they set up for, rehearsed, and then performed a student's original one-act play, and in the second half they prepared for the next week's piece. At the break, Joel would say,

"I'm going outside for a smoke break if anyone wants to come." Tess knew that by "anyone," Joel meant her. She always joined him.

Now they leaned back on the hood of Joel's Volkswagen and watched the sunset, in the mostly empty parking lot next to the squat brown military library that looked like every other squat brown building on the base. Tess had a lot of bad habits, but smoking had never been one of them. She found, though, that it suited her. Helped limit some of her other bad habits—absent-mindedly biting her knuckles, fingernails, cuticles; pulling at her hair; picking at her scalp; fidgeting.

"Sorry about *The Turn of the Screw*," Joel said. "I know it's due back tomorrow, but I accidentally left it in my room. I wanted to read all the other stories anyway."

"No worries, I've got the inside hookup," Tess said. "A lot of people say 'The Jolly Corner' is the best in the collection, but I'm team *Turn of the Screw*."

It wasn't surprising that Tess was into the first guy whose favorite way of interacting with her was to exchange and talk books, who treated her like an intelligent human with worthwhile opinions. People usually didn't. It was something about the way she presented—small and country and a hell of a lot girlier than she felt. Men in her hometown had always been like, *Hey, you're cute, wanna get wasted? Wanna hook up?* She'd hoped when she got married that Paul would be the guy who recognized her intellect. He was brilliant, currently mastering his fifth language. But he was also constantly stressed and preoccupied. It's not that he thought Tess was dumb; he just didn't care that she wasn't.

Tess pinpointed the moment she fell for Joel at their first book exchange seven weeks back. She'd given Joel *The Shining* because he hadn't yet read it, and how anyone would even want to continue through life having not read *The Shining* was beyond Tess. And he'd given her *Topdog/Underdog*, a play by Suzan-Lori Parks that she'd never even heard of, even though it had won the Pulitzer Prize. It was so good, the way it used humor to reveal the mostly bleak lives of these brothers, the way it made you care about an eventual perpetrator of violence, the way it took you completely outside of time and your own life. But the bigger point was that it showed Tess that Joel didn't off the bat assume she was an idiot. Last week he gave her *Who's Afraid of Virginia Woolf?* Maybe it wasn't supposed to be a comedy, but Tess thought it was hilarious, in a sharp, shocking way, following that train wreck of a couple. She'd laughed so hard reading it in bed one night that Paul had glared at her and finished studying out on the couch, so of course Tess punished him for it by reading and laughing out loud wherever he happened to be working at home the rest of the week. Ah, marriage.

She took a deep drag on her cigarette and had a coughing fit until they both sat up and Joel hit her hard several times on the back. It was all very sexy. The fall days were getting shorter. The class was originally supposed to last ten weeks, but right away three people dropped and those remaining agreed to extend it into mid-December, when Tess and her family were moving to a base in Monterey, where Paul would complete his military linguistics training. Finally. The entire three years they'd been married his attention had been fully taken with his work and study. Summer was just under a year old when Tess met Paul at a bar close to Fort Polk where he was stationed. Things moved quickly, and a couple months later they stopped in at city hall and then left Louisiana for good, moving to Fort Hood for a year before relocating to Maryland.

"You're quiet tonight," Joel said.

"I'm just thinking about people talking about my submission after break." It's not what Tess had been thinking about, but as soon as she said it, she started to feel a little nervous. She'd never shared her work before. "Maybe we can just skip mine?"

"It'll be fine. You know we don't really critique; we're just brainstorming the best ways to bring it all to life. People's stories are people's stories, you know?"

Not really. In her experience people's stories were a jumble of inarticulable shit swirling in their brains nonstop until they struggled to get them down at a tiny fraction of their complexity. But she wasn't the one with all the schooling.

Joel turned toward her, and his knee pressed into her thigh. Her whole body suddenly felt very warm. "I have a hard time imagining what you're doing here," he said.

She wasn't sure what he meant—he had a hard time imagining what she was doing in his class because her writing was a joke? A hard time imagining what she was doing on the hood of his car since she was married? Whatever it was sounded condescending. But she was being sensitive; she knew him better than that. "What am I doing here? I'm smoking a cigarette. I'm talking to you. I'm learning how to write the next great American play."

He gestured out at the expanse of the concrete parking lot, the blinding fluorescent lights that had just blinked on, the nearly windowless library, squat and brown. "I just think you're really special. You're really smart."

Oh, dear god. Okay, so it was one thing to treat someone like they were smart and another to say it aloud as if it were some big revelation, which made her feel sort of pathetic. Tess eyed the kid from head to toe. He was not tall, about Tess's height. He wore small, round professorial glasses and had hair clipped short that he tucked back behind his ears incessantly as if he were used to it hanging in his face. He wore a button-down shirt under a gray sweater that looked so soft Tess had been distracted all night wanting to stroke it. Dark designer jeans. Distressed leather boots.

"I'm real special. I'm real smart," Tess said, leaning into, for a moment, her country accent, which she'd mostly managed to drop. She wasn't exactly sure why she was being so pissy. She often felt like a crazy person. "Am I real pretty, too? The full trifecta of original dude compliments? What am I doing here? What are you doing here? Remind me where you're from?"

"Chicago."

"And let me guess, you have parents putting you through graduate school."

He turned up one corner of his mouth and shrugged.

"Well, I'm from a small town called Pinecreek, in west Louisiana—that's not the interesting half of the state—and now I've managed to get out. I'm about to move to my fourth state, and after that we'll probably be stationed overseas. I have a college degree and I'm working my way toward a master's so I can become a head librarian instead of an assistant. I have a family and a life, and I basically have my shit together. That's a lot if you're me and you come from where I came from."

Joel shifted away and took another drag.

"And anyways, what? You can't be special or smart and be here?" Tess said. "Where should I be? At Johns Hopkins working on my art?"

"Sure, why not?" he said. "I don't think you're really all that interested in theater, but you'd be great in the Writing Seminars. You'd hold your own."

Tess was proud of herself for staying calm. The conversation had raised a huge well of aggression in her that made her jumpy. But instead of punching him in the face or tearing off his clothes—the two conflicting urges that took so much effort to ignore—she got up off the car. "God, you're incredibly young."

He fumbled his cigarette and slipped off the hood of his car to retrieve it. "I'm not that young. I'll be twenty-six in November. I'm not that much younger than you."

"Believe me, if you're telling someone when you'll be turning a higher number, you're incredibly young. You know my daughter—she's not three, she's *thwee and thwee-quarters*." Tess did this very thing herself, *Next year I'm turning thirty*, but Joel didn't need to know that.

He managed to get his cigarette, which had rolled under his front tire, and then opened his car door so they could both drop the butts in the armrest ashtray.

She took a last drag. Paul didn't know she'd started smoking, but that might have to change soon, because she was a fan. She also used to have a severe drinking problem, but thankfully she'd outgrown it. Now she could share a six-pack of beer like she had last week after class with Joel without ending the night a total shit show.

On the way back to class, he said, "I do that, by the way."

"Do what?"

"Say ridiculous shit. I can tell you're annoyed, and I'm just letting you know that it's a thing I do. I'm just surprised I held out this long."

Tess opened the heavy door to the library and gestured for him to go in first. "Don't worry about it," she said.

"It's just, I'm actually devastated that you're moving away in a couple months. And I'm freaked out that I feel that way."

Oh. Even though she knew, she hadn't expected him to admit something like that. She stopped and looked him in the eye. "I feel the exact same, okay?"

※

They returned for the second half of class, where the group sat in folding metal chairs around the plastic table, ready to discuss Tess's one-act. There was Sheldon, a Vietnam War vet who must have been in his eighties; Kurt, an army spouse like Tess; and Cassandra, who was frankly an asshole but had lost her left hand in Afghanistan so no one could call her out on it. Tess made coffee and put out the snacks Joel always brought, this time a veggie plate and a dozen doughnuts from a bakery near his campus.

She thought it would be better if she could keep herself busy while everyone judged her for her work—it's not as if she couldn't hear everything—but Joel said they'd wait for her to join them, so okay, fine, she sat down. The blood rushed to her head and a buzzing filled her ears when the group looked at the play she'd handed out at the end of class last week, *I Want More*. The way her body was responding as if this were at all important, which it was not, made her feel defensive before anyone had even spoken.

Joel read it aloud when Tess deferred. It was tough to make sense of the words she was hearing. Cassandra leaned over the page on the table, scowling, while she used her one hand to eat a glazed doughnut. Sheldon seemed a little bemused. Kurt, who was muscled up like a jock, nodded along. To everyone's surprise his first play had been about a man who plants a rose garden after the death of his wife.

When Joel was done reading, the silence spread thick. Finally, Cassandra spoke up. "So, Thea . . ." and then stalled.

"The main character," Joel offered. "Thea."

"But she only says three words in the whole play?"

"That's not totally accurate," Kurt said. "Don't lose sight of the *ha!* sound she makes. The *haha!* and the bird call, it's just buried in the stage directions."

Tess shut her eyes tight and pinched the bridge of her nose, regretting the play and the class.

"Lots of plays use little dialogue and rely more on stagecraft," Joel said. "For this one, we'll focus in on the shapeshifting choreography. We'll need sound effects."

"Back up really quick," Sheldon said. "Look, I admit I'm a literal-minded guy, and so maybe I just don't get it. But is this play about a cannibal snake? Thea starts out as a snake, and then when she turns into a woman, she eats raw snake meat. Am I reading that right?"

"That's a metaphor," Kurt said, looking at Tess for validation. "For the rage, for the extreme loathing Thea feels toward her former selves for the lives she had to ruin to get what she wants."

Tess got up and poured herself another cup of coffee. It was coming up on eight o'clock—her daughter was probably already sleeping; Wednesday class was the one night she didn't get to tuck Summer into bed and she missed it. The coffee would keep her up all night, but right now she just thought fuck it. That's not even what the story was about. Not that she could exactly articulate it.

"But to Sheldon's point," Cassandra said. "Yeah, I don't get the cannibal part, either. Why doesn't she just eat regular snake food when she's a snake and people food when she's a person and hawk food when she's a hawk? I also don't get where the bodies go when she kills. Do they just disintegrate, vanish into thin air? Or are there just, I don't know, rotting carcasses in these woods? Why is no one finding them? And why is this national forest in Louisiana? Couldn't this happen anywhere or, for that matter, nowhere at all?"

"Interesting question—" Joel began.

"Because that's where I'm fucking from, Cassandra. No other reason," Tess said, and she could feel herself shaking, could feel her temper flare up. And it was strange, because she was thinking, Just sit down and be quiet, it's not that hard. "You know what, I don't want to do this. Let's do someone else's next week and I'll think of something different. Or maybe I just don't need to be here. I'll still let you all use the break room and keep the branch open late and close up when you're all done. I-I—"

Tess stopped talking when she saw the looks of something like pity around the room. Not a single thing in this world worse than pity. She shut up for the rest of the class while everyone shifted to praising her work in fake, careful voices. At the end, Joel assigned Cassandra the part of Thea and Kurt the part of Frederick. Tess and Sheldon took joint roles of trees and puppeteers.

And unbeknownst to Tess, on three separate occasions the following week, Cassandra drove forty-five minutes to Johns Hopkins to work with Joel and a dance choreographer after her shift working the desk at the military police station. And in those moments of shapeshifting, from snake to woman, from woman to hawk, Cassandra moved in time to an eerie soundtrack that Joel put together, and she was spectacular, moving from the floor to standing upright, then sprouting wings so convincingly that the library break room turned into a vast expanse of sky. And Cassandra's missing hand became both beautiful and painful, the residual limb making Tess, even as the author of the play, keenly feel what could be lost by never being satisfied with what you already have.

※

The Monday after the class ran *I Want More*, Tess strapped her daughter into her car seat and they took off to meet Joel at the Patuxent Research Refuge visitor center. She had the day off, and they were going to collect sounds for Kurt's upcoming play, about two boys processing the death of their mother while skipping rocks.

It was probably iffy, spending all this time with Joel, but she'd be moving in less than two months, so any harm that could come from it was at least contained. In the years before she'd gotten married—her drunk years—she'd slept with everyone she could get her hands on, and it had gotten old. So even if, yeah, she was attracted to Joel and she thought about him alarmingly often, she wasn't going to do anything about it. In any case, Paul was glad for her and Summer to get out of their apartment while he studied at home. She hadn't lied about where they were going. He did not care. Paul was anxious by nature, singularly focused, and he'd warned her before they'd married that the next few years would be intense for him. Things would get better, Tess just had to wait it out. That was her plan.

The trees were at peak fall colors, the forest a vivid mix of reds and golds that amazed Tess even though this was her second season experiencing them. "*Ooh, pretty,*" Summer kept saying, pointing out all the colorful trees. As she pulled into the visitor center, she spotted Joel, waiting outside.

Without preamble, they started off down a path. It was about a mile to the Patuxent River, and Summer could make that, though she may need to be carried back. Joel had two heavy backpacks full of recording equipment that he'd checked out from his school. Tess took one. Summer wanted to help, too, so Joel handed her a small foam piece.

"This is called a windscreen," Joel said.

"*Wind-screen,*" Summer said, holding it right up to her eyes.

"And it's a very important piece of recording equipment, especially outside. It protects the microphone diaphragm from gusts of air. And it will be a big help if you carry it for us all the way to the river."

"Can you do that, Sum?" Tess said.

"Yeah." And not three seconds later, Summer saw a frog jump, squealed, and rushed after it, dropping the much less exciting windscreen in a mud puddle. Joel had seemed excited when Tess had mentioned bringing Summer, but she was curious how he'd do with a little kid.

"I have a whole pack of them," he said, and when Summer rejoined them on the path, he handed back the muddy piece of foam so she could continue to "help."

"You see all these pretty trees, Summer?" Tess said.

"Yeah."

"They're called deciduous trees. That one's called a poplar. I grew up with mostly evergreen trees that stay green all year long. Deciduous trees lose their leaves in the winter, but before they do, they turn lots of pretty colors."

"Purple!" Summer said.

"Yes, purple and also red, yellow—"

"And orange! Do you see the orange?" Joel said, and Summer spun around until she spied some orange and then did a little victory dance.

The two of them narrated the whole way about the types of birds and bugs they saw, the chilly air and how wet it was outside, the path that was treacherous with rocks and roots.

"Let's do more talking," Summer said any time they stopped.

Joel explained lots of theory around stagecraft, and then they both told her about their great friends Cassandra and Sheldon and Kurt and about how, when they got to the river, they were all going to skip rocks so that Joel could capture the sound and that they'd try to get some birdsong, too.

When they finally got to a clearing at the river it was so peaceful, no other people, nothing man-made in sight. The few paths they could see leading to it were narrow and overgrown, and the three of them were completely cut off from the rest of the world. It turned out Joel was terrible at skipping rocks. Tess was good at it, but it didn't matter because Joel couldn't capture the sound with the ambient noise of the rushing water and the chaos of nature teeming all around. So, he took recordings of buzzing and chirping, of Tess dropping large stones into the river, of Summer splashing around and giggling. And then he and Tess rested on a fallen log while Summer played on the shore a few feet away, gathering river stones and mounding them into a grand manor.

"She's pretty great," Joel said.

"She's the best," Tess said. Tess had been worried about becoming a mom, but Summer was so easy. Her best little buddy. Joel lit a cigarette and offered her one, but she wasn't yet committed enough to smoking to take it up in front of her daughter.

"Why do you think Kurt keeps writing about his dead wife when I've met his wife at least a dozen times around the base?" Tess said. "It's either because her death is his greatest fear or because he wants to kill her."

"I'm going to go with fear," Joel said. "Writing about fear is always a solid choice."

"I'm going with the other option."

Joel smiled at her. "So, about *The Crucible*. The real reason I gave it to you, the Baltimore Theatre Project is putting it on in the spring, and they hired me for lighting design, which is actually my first professional gig."

"That's so great," Tess said, reaching over and squeezing his hand. He looked down at their hands and she let go.

"I was thinking maybe you could fly back to see it."

"Okay, well, when I get on a plane in a couple months, that will be the third time I've flown. Ever. I'm not living the type of life where you fly across the country to see a show."

"But you wouldn't have to worry about that. My parents have like a million frequent flyer miles. You wouldn't have to do anything."

Tess pressed her lips together. His parents. Jesus, this guy was so young he didn't even understand how much better it would be to not remind her of it by invoking his parents. At the same time, though, she'd love to be a person who could flit away for a quick trip.

Just then, Tess heard a branch snap somewhere nearby. And then another. Before she could react, a man, tall and imposing, dressed in a black trench coat hanging open over flannel pants and a threadbare T-shirt that said "Berlin" with a bear in a coat of arms, emerged from the path close to where Summer was playing. Strapped to the man's back—the strangest thing Tess had ever seen—was an adult woman wearing dingy white pajamas stained brown down the front. She was facing outward, her arms and legs dangling from a leather harness. The woman had long black hair. She was pale, slumped. She appeared sluggish, maybe even drugged. The man stepped to where Summer was playing, positioning himself between her and Tess, and stopped.

Tess jumped up; a shot of adrenaline coursed through her veins so violently she almost blacked out. She gripped Joel's arm as he stood up beside her. "Sweetie," she said, although she could hardly hear her own voice.

Her body felt oddly paralyzed. Just as she'd gathered herself and was about to sprint over, two more people emerged from the woods. Two women: One in cutoff jean shorts and a halter top, a vine-looking tattoo winding its way up the side of her neck. The other wore a ground-length dress, sheer with no bra or underwear, nipples and a dark bush poking into the fabric. When that one saw Tess, she started wringing her hands.

"Sweetie," Tess said again, louder. "Come on over here. We need to get going."

"Yeah, it's getting late," Joel said. "Time to head on home."

Tess could see that Summer was standing in front of the man, her head tilted all the way back so she could see his face. "Hi," she said.

The woman strapped to the man became agitated, butting her head into his back, flailing. "Let me see it. Let me see it," she said, her voice hoarse.

He turned and crouched to his heels, looked at Tess and grinned. He had no front teeth. It all happened in a matter of seconds, but still, Tess should have already been over there, rescuing the only person in her life who really mattered. She could see the woman, the scary woman strapped to the scary man's back, stretch out her legs and open her arms wide. And then, unbelievably, Summer stepped in and gave her a hug, and the woman wrapped both arms and legs around her daughter, clutching her little body tight. And then the man stood, and both Tess and Joel rushed them.

She went straight to her daughter and wrapped an arm around her waist. She pulled, but the woman wouldn't relent. Joel was in front of the man, jumping up in his face and yelling. Summer started crying, "Mommy? Mommy!"

The woman wouldn't let go. She looked directly into Tess's eyes and spit at her, tried to headbutt her, tried to bite her. Her wet lips grazed Tess's cheek.

"Let go of her!" Tess yelled. "She doesn't belong to you!"

Finally, the woman with the vine tattoo came over and peeled the harnessed woman's hands away from Summer's body. "Stacy, come help me," she said to the hand-wringing woman, but that one never budged. The tall man just stood there and looked over his shoulder, grinning. Joel came around and wrenched the harnessed woman's legs from Summer. The woman wailed, then so did Summer. Finally, Tess managed to pull her daughter free.

Then they ran. Joel scooped up the recording equipment, and they barreled their way through the underbrush, not slowing until they were back on a main trail, in sight of a backpacking couple using trekking poles to hike.

Tess's arms burned carrying Summer tight to her chest, but it didn't matter. She smoothed her daughter's hair. "It's okay, baby. That woman wasn't trying to hurt you. I think she just needs some help."

Summer burrowed her head into Tess's neck. "Then why don't we help her, Mommy? We have to help her."

Summer had a fair point. But what was Tess supposed to do? She could barely even will her body to help her own daughter until it was almost too late. She was a very inadequate person. Tess flicked a tick from her daughter's shoulder—they'd need to do a full check and clean up as soon as they got home.

She exchanged bewildered looks with Joel. Then he started to narrate the walk for Summer in an upbeat voice, talking about the lizard that ran up the trunk of a tree beside them and the fat mushrooms near the path up ahead, then about how when he was little, he had a pet terrier named—

"Please don't mention owning a *d-o-g*. Summer wants nothing more than to have a *d-o-g*, and right now I just cannot."

—about how when he was little, he used to love taking trips to his family's place on Lake Geneva and going out on their boat. And then he told her all about the intricacies of waterskiing until she nodded off.

Just before she fell asleep, she whispered, "We have to help her, Mommy."

Once Summer was out, Tess let the tears stream down her face.

"What the hell was that?" Tess said. "Do you think it was some kind of weird religious thing, like a cult? Do you think they live in the woods?"

"It seemed more like a *Deliverance*-style clan of inbreeders to me. But I doubt anyone lives out here."

"So, tourists?"

"Yep, tourists."

"I think all kinds of crazy shit is going on in the woods at all times, I swear to god."

"Do we tell someone?" Joel asked. "Call the police?"

"Jesus, I don't know."

They stayed behind the backpacking couple, hesitant to let other, safe-looking people out of their sight, until they got to the gravel pathway that led to the parking lot. When they made it to the car, Joel helped her get Summer, still fast asleep, into her car seat. Before Tess got into the driver's side, Joel reached out and brushed her cheek. And that was it; she was worn down. She leaned in and kissed him, hard, hungry, pressing her body into his for a lingering moment, and then ran her hand down between his legs, rubbing him over his jeans, and his hands went up her shirt and under her bra, before she, panting, opened the car door and got in, shutting him out. Before she drove away, she looked at herself in the rearview mirror and saw blood on her cheek where the woman's lips had brushed, which it seemed Joel had been simply trying to wipe off.

※

In the end, they never told anyone about the incident in the woods. Tess had moved around the house for a while in a daze, clearly something wrong, but Paul either pretended not to notice or genuinely didn't notice. She kept expecting Summer to bring it up, but Summer seemed oddly fine, and then it just felt better to leave it between her and Joel.

The whole scenario had, however, gotten her thinking back to that Pentecostal girl, Gail Liebrecht. She reread the notebook she'd been using during the time they'd met, the one Lainey had given her with the cutesy horse stickers, now in various states of unpeeling. And the single decapitated horse on the back—it still made her grin. Most of it consisted of notes on the books that Tess had been reading at the time. One interesting find was a story snippet she'd written of a woman taken from her family and put away in an institute. She'd abandoned the story after only a page and a half, but there was something to it and she thought she might take it back up.

What she'd really been looking for, though, was the message Gail had written to her in German. Tess had looked at it many times and even made a few notes in the margins for words she felt had an obvious translation, before attempting to forget about it completely by folding it in on itself, accordion-like, to make it as small as possible inside the notebook. When she'd found the message, she brought it out to where Paul was working after dinner at the kitchen table. He could have read it to her in seconds, but as she approached him, he put out a hand as if to block her from his peripheral vision and leaned his head closer to his study materials.

So instead, Tess asked Joel to meet her at the library during story hour when she had a break. He showed up precisely on time, just as Tess was arranging the kids in a circle on the floor cushions, handing out snacks, and yielding the session to the volunteer readers. She led him to a table in the opposite corner, where they wouldn't disturb anyone as long as they were quiet. She'd already pulled the materials they'd need to translate: German dictionaries, verb conjugation guides, thesauri, a Barron's book on idioms.

Tess told Joel the entire story about the time Gail had visited, about how Tess hadn't helped even though she knew the girl needed it, about the rumor that Gail had killed her grandfather, who'd been found dead a couple years after Tess had met her. About how the girl went away and no one ever heard from her again. Tess had tried to look her up but had found no trace of her. Joel leaned in and listened, absorbing the details.

"Anyway, I know I could just use the internet to translate this note, but I thought this would be more satisfying."

"I completely agree," Joel said. "I'm really anti-efficiency. It's so much better to spend real time with something."

They got to work, smoothing out the notebook page, both of them flipping through books and Tess writing down their findings. Neither of them had studied German in the past, and they got to learn some quirks of the language. Such as: Nouns were capitalized. And the suffix *-ig* seemed to turn a noun to an adjective, which was lowercase. *Fish* was *Fische*, but *fishy* was *fischig*. *Filth, Schmutz; filthy, schmutzig. Egg, Ei; eggy, eiig.* Et cetera. It was all very interesting.

The process was choppy; they had to deal with Gail's looping handwriting and what they could only guess were spelling errors. Yet a message still emerged, one that Tess could polish later.

> *It is almost impossible to find me. Whenever I try to leave a trace, my parents find it and cover it up. But you can try.*
>
> *Start by finding a natural spring. It is the source of the stream from which we can drink. Try it out to see if it is right. If it is not fishy or eggy or filthy, you have probably found it. When you find the stream, follow it north to the spring. Then on the side almost to the east you will*

see four fallen pine trees. One, two, three, four, look like dominoes. If you find the trees, that is the first step. Actually it is not possible, not safe, to explain, so do not worry. Thank you for a good night and the pizza, and sorry for what I will do.

They both sat silent with the words for a while. Tess hated that she was only figuring this note out now, far beyond the point that anything could be done. Over on the other side of the room, children giggled in unison, and then there was an enthusiastic round of applause. Story hour was wrapping up.

"Sorry I tried to make out with you a few days ago," Tess said.

"Oh, that's okay. I mean, I'm not. But—"

She cut him off gently: "Joel, it's not that I didn't want to or even that I'm personally scandalized by it. It's just—it's hard to describe what a complete mess I was for several years and how badly I just want to live a drama-free life."

Joel pushed his chair back, put some distance between them. But his face was kind, open. "I hear you."

And that was that. From that moment on the energy between them shifted to friend mode, no questions asked.

※

It was the first Wednesday in December, and Tess was moving on Sunday. Getting ready had been hectic, especially since Paul wasn't much help. But his exams were finishing up tomorrow, and he'd done something amazing: suggest they hire a babysitter Friday and have an adult date night for the first time in forever. When she'd been surprised by his suggestion, he'd pretended not to understand why, but she could get over that.

It had begun to snow, which was exciting because Louisiana and Texas didn't have snow and California wouldn't have snow. Tess wasn't sure when she'd see it again. She was feeling strangely optimistic. As she entered their final class, she was eager for her next adventure even though she would genuinely miss the people in this group.

The energy in the room was festive. Since Tess had been at work all day and she'd bought a bunch of candles to light later, her potluck contribution consisted of disposable plates, silverware, and cups. Everyone told Joel to take a rest since he'd brought drinks and snacks all semester, but he still came with a case of assorted fancy beer. Cassandra brought stale fruit Danishes from the commissary and a box of wine. Kurt made classic lasagna—vegetarian to avoid the wrath of Cassandra—roasted brussels sprouts and butternut squash, and by far the best potato salad Tess had ever tasted. Sheldon brought his wife's homemade fudge.

They feasted and talked and had one too many drinks and laughed like old friends. Tess arranged their chairs in a semicircle around a pad of presentation paper on an easel she'd borrowed from the reading room. She lit a few dozen candles, shined Joel's portable spotlight on the easel, and turned off the overhead lights. Unlike the rest of the class, Tess hadn't finished her final one-act, so everyone had agreed to use this last section to help her work out a story idea. Joel took his smoke break alone since Tess had decided that smoking wasn't a habit she wanted to acquire after all.

When he got back, she began: "Okay, I'm calling this project *In the Wilderness*. It's set somewhere beyond Louisiana and Maryland, I don't know where yet. For tonight it's a generic, thick woods behind a generic town. There's a shed or cabin, hidden deep in the woods. It's like we're leading a hero on a mission. Step one comes to us from the voice of a Pentecostal girl who lives there. She needs help."

Tess flipped open the pad on the easel. Before class she'd written:

STEP 1 (SISTER GAIL): It is almost impossible to find, but you can try. First locate the natural spring. If you see a stream, taste the water to make sure it's the right one. If it's not fishy, eggy, or filthy, you've found it. Follow the stream north to the spring. Then, to the side of it, almost due east, you'll see four fallen trees, down one, two, three, four, like dominoes, pointing you in the right direction. From this point on, nothing else is safe. I'm sorry.

The class leaned forward as Tess wrote out her contribution for step two, and then they went one by one around the semicircle after that, working out the journey to the mystery dwelling.

STEP 2 (TESS): Realizing you won't be able to do this alone, you must befriend and tame a savage woodland creature—a wolf, a fox, a mountain lion, whatever's native to the area—to help you with what lies ahead.

STEP 3 (JOEL): Then you and this savage woodland creature have no choice but to enter the most dangerous stretch of the deepest part of the forest, where a disturbing clan of inbred timber poachers do everything they can to make sure that no one who enters exits alive.

STEP 4 (CASSANDRA): You do make it through somehow. But not without sacrifice. You lose something, I don't know what—an arm, a leg, your hearing, your eyesight—and then you have to figure out how to go on without the thing that before now you took for granted.

STEP 5 (SHELDON): Once you've adjusted, you and the savage woodland creature come upon a one-lane dirt road that leads to the dwelling. And you discover the cabin in a clearing deep in the heart of the woods.

STEP 6 (KURT): The most important step is this: You save her. But however you do it, it will involve carnage. Massacre. Extreme bloodshed. Things are gonna get fucked up.

Tess nodded as she wrote it out. Kurt's assessment felt true, even though she could tell that he had some unresolved issues. Tess didn't know what she'd do with all this, but she'd gotten what she wanted out of the exercise.

Joel handed out the last of the beers, and soon enough the night was over. They all hugged one another, Joel lingering with Tess only the briefest moment. He seemed to be the most broken up about the goodbyes.

"We're all like family now," Joel said. "Don't you think?"

Yes, they all agreed, they were like family.

"So, we'll all stay in touch forever, okay? We'll remain friends."

At that they all laughed. "Okay, son," Sheldon said, clapping a good-natured hand on Joel's shoulder. "If you say so."

Even Tess, who'd lived the transient military life for only three years, the shortest of them all, knew that none of them would ever see or hear from the others again.

※

Tess worked her last shift on Friday and left a little early to get ready for her date. The movers had already taken their personal items from their furnished apartment, and they were living out of suitcases for the final few days. But she'd made sure to keep on hand a sexy black dress for the occasion. The good thing about military life was that each new post offered the chance of a fresh start. And now that Paul had passed his exams and cleared this major career hurdle, California could be really great for them. Who knew, they might even turn into a family of beach bums!

Tess expected Paul to be working from home, but he'd left her a note on the kitchen counter saying he was finishing up some things at the office. Summer's daycare assistant, a bubbly camp-counselor type named Jeanne, was tonight's babysitter. Jeanne brought Summer home when daycare closed at five. The three of them hung out while Tess put on makeup and dressed for her big date. "*Ooh, pretty, Mommy*" was Summer's assessment. She and Paul would need to leave by six forty-five to be on time for their dinner reservation. At six, she first tried his cell phone, and when that went straight to voicemail, his office. His sarcastic coworker who'd never liked Tess and vice versa said he'd been called into a meeting with their boss, but he'd be sure to give him the message that he was expected home soon.

She made pasta for Summer and Jeanne and tried Paul again at six fifteen. Around six thirty Paul called back to tell her that he just found out he had to give a presentation on Monday in Monterey and had a ton of prep. And that their boss had offered to stay and work through some materials so he could make a good first impression. And that he couldn't pass up the offer. Tess replied that it was bullshit and she'd see him at the restaurant at seven o'clock, though of course she knew she wouldn't. Then she hung up, fuming, shaking.

She kept it together while she helped Summer pick out the books that she'd ask Miss Jeanne to read her at bedtime, which was "coming right up, Sum!" But Summer was so sensitive; she could always pick up on Tess's moods. "What's wrong, Mama?"

Tess left and considered going to Paul's office and embarrassing him, but really, did she even want to be out on a date with someone who so clearly didn't want to be on one with her? She went ahead to the Mediterranean restaurant, where the service wasn't fancy but the food was delicious, one she'd heard about from all kinds of people over the past couple years but hadn't had the chance to try. It didn't disappoint. She ordered something exotic called moussaka and a glass of the house red. It was unbelievably comforting to be at a point in her life where she could just enjoy a beer or a glass of wine, after a few years of thinking she couldn't drink at all without it turning into a problem.

She wondered how the hell she'd gotten there. To a Greek restaurant in a Baltimore suburb packed with happy couples and families. In a black dress with arguably too much cleavage, feeling sorry enough for herself to have to continually blot tears with her napkin throughout her solo meal. It was strange, because she'd wanted so badly for so many years to get out of her hometown. She'd been stuck. It wasn't that she wanted to go back by any means, but this wasn't better, and California wouldn't be either at the rate things were going.

Paul could be such a piece of shit sometimes. He'd swept her away from her home after mere weeks of knowing her, and then he lugged her around his life like the military-issue gear he was obligated to carry: necessary but burdensome.

But you know what, fuck that. Tess was fun! She'd always been popular and well loved, and just because she'd married someone who didn't notice her didn't mean there wasn't someone else out there who did.

She pulled out her cell phone and sent a note to Joel: *last minute and nbd if not but let me know if you feel like hanging out right now. grab a drink?*

She watched her phone while she finished her meal and paid the bill, but Joel never responded.

Still! She wasn't going home, that was for sure. She deserved a night out. The babysitter said she could stay as long as they needed, and Paul would presumably be done with work and get home at some point. When she got in her car, she wasn't sure where she was going, but she was still thinking about Joel, so she drove in the direction of Johns Hopkins. Grab a beer at a good old-fashioned college hangout, the kind she'd never had the opportunity to see. Why not? She was curious, she was restless, she was very pissed off. Maybe Joel would get her note and meet her.

She drove down Charles Street, past the idyllic campus built for people who were not her, and then pulled off onto a side street. Coming out of a McDonald's was a couple holding hands who looked freakishly young. "Hey," Tess called to them from her rolled-down car window. It was freezing outside. They walked toward her but kept a safe distance. She asked them to recommend a good bar, something divey, the type of place students could walk to after class for a five-dollar pitcher. She was considering coming here next year for fiction writing, she told them, and she wanted to check out the scene first.

Ginger's Ale House was everything she'd hoped for. Ridiculous, distracting, a place where she could sit in a dark corner with a beer and watch shenanigans. Not all that different from the seedy bars she'd frequented back home, except that it catered to fancier kids than she'd been.

Ginger's was attached to a Johns Hopkins–owned apartment building. She felt somewhat ancient. No way even half these people were old enough to drink. Still, who cared? She'd had her first drink at age eleven and her life was fine. She ordered a shot of well vodka and a Rolling Rock and sat in her coat in a drafty spot by the window. She texted Joel a line from Gail's note, already their inside joke: *it is almost impossible to find me ... but you can try.* After a minute with no response, she followed up: *at ginger's ale house if you want to meet up.*

And then she turned off her phone and forgot about him. Forgot about Paul. Even her beloved Summer for a few hours. Just had a good time. Which everyone deserved every once in a while, what was the big deal? Just let loose from time to time. It was true she'd had a drinking problem in the past, but that was behind her—had been for years!

She ordered another shot and another beer. She shed her winter gear down to her sexy dress and removed her shoes for maximum dance freedom. The night got later. The room filled up. She befriended a group who lived upstairs and had the hilarious tradition of meeting down in the bar in their pajama pants every Friday night. The bar was out of open tables, so they'd asked to join hers, and yeah, of course! Three girls, two guys, all senior engineering majors, finishing up their second-to-last semester. Tess bought a round of shots to celebrate them and then one of the girls bought another. They were so excited about her acceptance to the Writing Seminars. She should *definitely* take the offer, it was *so fun* here. They commandeered the jukebox, and Tess grew tired of their teenybopper shit and changed up the mood with some Metallica. And they got more shots, and why not stand up on the tables and headbang?! She had somehow before tonight lost track of her true self and how fun she was as a human person! Another shot. One of the guys, she could not remember any names, helped her up off the floor, and do you want to come up to my apartment, take a break from this place? No, of course not, Tess wasn't going to this guy's apartment. But. She did have to pee. Wink, wink. She slammed another shot and waited with that guy in line to pee and then got into one of the bathrooms and peed. And opened the door and pulled him in and locked it again behind them. Why not, it had been so long, it felt so good, who cared. This for her was autopilot territory, no different from riding a bike. His hands all over her and hers on him, and she unbuckled his pants and tried to get complicated by kneeling down in front of him but lost her balance. But why when all she actually had to do was turn and brace her palms on the wall? He was there from behind and so strong she flashed back to Louisiana days, but instead of the tons of drunk sex she had there, too, she flashed to a great big field, sun on her face while she rambled through. Not one care in all the world. So close to recovering a truth she'd known in her youth but since forgotten. Harmony, disquiet, impermanence. Something. So close, but he was done fast, and no big deal, she wiped off and arranged her dress and left the bathroom, and he left right after her, and there was Joel.

By two a.m., after hanging on Joel, trying to make out with Joel, trying to, haha, cajole Joel into taking a shot, saying actually, Joel, yes, I will fly back just to see a play in the spring, why not. Then after getting sick, chugging water after water Joel put in front of her, she was already in a cab, one Joel had called to take her home.

Palsgrave House
Thea

THEA, TAKEN FROM her children (or so the doctor kept saying) and forced to rest for her own good, resided at Palsgrave House until such time as Doctor Palsgrave deemed her cured. From her bed she heard the doctor's heavy footsteps echo his approach down the long hall, drowning out the voice that puffed through cracks in the stone walls of her bedchamber whenever she was alone. Barely a whisper, the voice murmured regrets, bemoaned a chronic lack of self-control, lamented drifting through life, one place to the next with no real aim. Thea found the voice to be a tiresome whine but had no power to escape it. She used what little strength she had to roll from her side onto her back, set to receive her morning treatments. She'd spent the length of the night staring out her barred window, through the single break in the trees that allowed her to glimpse a lone bright star. She wanted to be one with the star, a queen of the heavens, blazing. Down on the ground, everything about her was so much smaller than how she felt inside.

Footsteps halted outside her door. The key turned, a crisp click. Hinges shrieked. Doctor Palsgrave entered and got straight to work.

He retrieved the wool blankets from the wardrobe and lowered the safety rails on her bed. Thea kept herself limp as he cocooned her within. The blankets smelled of soured milk, and the doctor tucked them so tightly that Thea couldn't move her limbs. He placed hot water bottles at her feet, wound scarves around her head and neck. Stoked the fire. He rubbed his hands vigorously over the blankets, over the full length of her body, until his cheeks glowed red from the effort.

"How are you on this fine day, my dear?" he asked.

Thea opened her mouth, began to pant.

"Excellent, excellent." The doctor sat in the armchair, scribbled in his pocket notebook. "We need to get you well so that you can be a fine mother to your children."

"I have no children," Thea said, her voice a rasp.

The doctor tsk-tsked, reached out, squeezed her wrapped foot. "Nonsense. You have many children. Your life's purpose! We shall get you well."

But Thea felt unconcerned with wellness, with life's purpose. She desired one thing: ascent. Sweat pooled in the corners of her eyes. She squeezed them shut and lay still while her skin prickled and her muscles twitched in want of release.

In time she heard the hiss of smothered flames when the doctor threw water on the fire, signaling the end of the sweating. He flung open the window to let in the chilly outside air. Then he unwrapped Thea, dabbed the sweat from her face, smoothed back her matted hair, peeled and billowed her white cotton gown that had plastered to her skin.

Doctor Palsgrave picked up the rotary telephone on Thea's bedside table and dialed. "Yes, nurse? Stand by." He hung up the receiver and went to unlock the door. "Okay, you've been here long enough. I'd like to try an experiment. I'll make it clear for you. If you can stay calm and remain where you are, prove to me that you're able to control yourself, you'll be many steps closer to being discharged from this facility. Understand?"

The doctor flung open the door, and Thea didn't hesitate. On instinct she gathered her strength and burst from her bed, zipped from the room, bare feet slapping down the long stone hall to the stairwell. Energy already flagging; she hadn't been upright in so long. She collapsed on the stairs but found that if she stayed on all fours and leaned into the wall, her shoulder fit perfectly in a groove worn into the stone, in a long smooch that began from the first stair and wound all the way up to the nursery. The doctor followed behind. With each palm smack on cold stone she counted the steps to reassure herself of her progress. She kept going up, up, up. Seventy-two steps in total. At the top, the two nurses of Palsgrave House stood with their backs against the wall, observing.

Thea rose to her feet, wobbly without the help of the long smooch. Out of breath she reeled across the floor, past the nurses, to the small rope that hung from the hatch door in the roof. She jumped for it, her body sluggish, gravity fixing her firmly to the ground. Yet she kept on. The nurse with the snake tattooed on her neck took a couple of steps forward while the deathly pale one cowered and wrung her hands. Stay back, remain calm, the doctor ordered. Finally, Thea seized the rope in one hand, dangled in place, and then heaved herself to grab it with her other. The hatch creaked barely ajar. Thea crunched her legs up to her chest and caught the rope with her toes. The hatch continued to open slowly, slowly, and then swiftly all at once. Thea crashed to the ground but crawled up the ladder through the roof, and then there she was, out in fresh air. Wind gusting. Vegetal scent of decaying leaves. A thick branch of a towering tree hung several feet from the far edge of the roof. She'd have to run and jump. And she did; she filled her lungs and bolted. But just as she jumped and caught a little air, she felt the doctor's meaty hands clasp her ankle. She reached out, her fingers skimming the closest leaf, before he yanked her back to the roof. She landed hard on the clay tiles and scraped her chin. Over the side of the roof, through the leaves of the unfamiliar amber-gold-scarlet trees, she saw a river far below. Disorienting, not knowing where she was. She turned and looked up at the silhouettes of the doctor and the two nurses against the backdrop of the sun that had just broken above the treetops.

"You see what she does when offered a tiny bit of freedom? You see her tendency toward self-sabotage?" Doctor Palsgrave said. "Textbook hysteria."

The handwringer nodded. "Indeed, Doctor. As you diagnosed."

"But we'll make her well," said the one with the snake tattoo. "And then you'll release us from our work here, Doctor. As you promised."

※

Some amount of time passed, days or weeks or months, enough so that her chin healed and only a ghost of a bruise circled Thea's ankle where the doctor had caught her in the air. Each morning and evening, Doctor Palsgrave sweated Thea and then carried her up to the nursery, submerging her in an ice bath followed by a hot bath, holding her under each time until her breath gave out, alternating between the two until the temperatures converged to match that of the room. The nurses then fed her a breakfast or a supper of sixteen egg whites beat to a lather and poured over beef broth with a side of warm milk clotted with cream.

One morning, as Doctor Palsgrave observed to ensure she finished every bite, he said, "We want you to know how it feels to be weak and then to be nourished, so that you will go forth and provide your children with the nourishment they deserve."

Thea let the final sip of fatty broth run from her mouth and stain the front of her nightgown. "I have no children," she rasped.

"Let's try something new." The doctor slammed his fist down on the table, and the nurses jumped up. "Winter is close at hand; we could all use some autumn air."

The handwringer retrieved a leather harness from a peg on the wall and secured it to the doctor's back. The tattooed nurse lifted Thea to the harness and strapped her in. Thea's bare feet dangled and knocked the backs of the doctor's legs. They all left through the front door of Palsgrave House for the first time since Thea arrived, whenever that had been. The doctor entered a path in the trees that narrowed quickly as they approached the sound of rushing water. Several paces behind, the nurses followed.

"Here we are, my dear. Deep in the woods of Maryland, heading to the river," the doctor said, and continued to narrate their surroundings as they went.

Ah, and so Thea was in a land called Maryland. The tall, colorful species of tree she hadn't recognized, poplar. Though she'd moved beyond her home, it seemed she'd simply replaced one forest for another.

She wanted ascent.

But for now, she was exhausted, tethered to Doctor Palsgrave's back with no means of escape. The path tapered further until the brush took over completely. Thorns and brambles tore at Thea's skin. A tick latched onto her arm; she watched it scuttle up to her shoulder.

Soon they stepped into a clearing. The doctor stopped at a point where Thea could see the soles of his boots submerged in a shallow river rushing at his feet. Then suddenly she felt the presence of another being. Pure energy. Heard a splash, the vivacious giggle of a small child. The nurses emerged from the trees and stopped. The one with the snake tattoo frowned, while the handwringer looked down and wrung.

"Let me see it, let me see it," Thea growled. She thrashed her limbs. In her frantic state she bit down on the inside of her cheek and drew blood.

To her surprise the doctor turned and knelt next to a being of pure light. A pulsing magnet, brighter than the midday sun that shone feebly from above. Thea stretched out her arms, her legs, and the being came to her, allowing itself to be embraced. Thea held tight and felt an energy, a blissful well-being, fill her entire body. She felt her mouth stretch into a grin so wide that her lips cracked. For the very first time, she knew love. Perhaps they could ascend together. Or if not, perhaps Thea had finally found a reason to remain rooted to this earth. But the being of light began to squirm and cry out. Like Thea herself, it did not wish to be contained.

SHE DOES NOT BELONG TO YOU!!! A voice rained down from the heavens, the same weakling voice that whispered in her room, but now thunderous and filled with wrath. Trees shook. Branches splintered, fell. The nurses cowered. The doctor stumbled forward into the rushing water. Thea felt her grip loosen, only for a second, but long enough for the pure, radiant light to dash off and disappear into the dense woods.

※

Predawn the next morning, after hours of staring at the single star and thinking of the light she'd held ever so briefly, Thea again heard the voice that she now understood to be that of her creator, fizzing out through the cracks all around her:

My daughter has asked that I help you. And since you let her go, I shall. But first you must complete a task. You must call and allow your children to hear your voice. One final goodbye. Then climb to the roof and to the top of the tall poplar and jump with all your might! The key to success is gaining the right momentum.

"I have no children!" Thea roared.

Fine. The voice sighed. *But look, I really do need you to call these kids.*

"I only want one thing."

Yes, I know, I know. Ascent.

"I want ascent. Why do you torture me?"

After a long pause that made Thea twitch with impatience, the voice came back, barely audible:

I can't answer that. I really don't know. You're a compulsion I can't control. Now just be quiet already, please. I am bone-tired, Thea. Weary.

"You are weak."

Maybe. And yet where you're concerned, I'm almighty. You can't get out of here unless I choose to let you out.

Although Thea felt a desire to argue, she found that she could not speak. She'd been shut up.

※

"As I suspected," the doctor said after the evening sweating, bath submerging, and feeding, that same night as darkness saturated the sky outside. "It was a happy accident running into that little girl by the river. Exposing Thea to her has clearly ignited motherly instincts. Her spirit is revived."

"Yes, Doctor," said the handwringer.

Doctor Palsgrave opened the hatch to the roof and gestured to Thea to join him and climb up. Every muscle in her body longed to go, but she couldn't move. All she could do was sit there and appear docile while she listened to the crickets chirp outside. Her body and her will did not solely belong to her, and she resented her creator for it.

Yet the doctor was pleased. "Interesting. Very promising indeed."

The nurse with the snake tattoo didn't look up from her sewing when she said, "So this means that our work here is complete? That you'll let us go?"

"Sadly, our work is never complete. There is no lack of hysterical women in need of my services. As soon as one recovers, another appears."

"But you promised," said the handwringer, but very meekly, and if the doctor heard her, he didn't show it.

The doctor normally helped Thea change into her bedclothes, but tonight he allowed her to do it on her own. He watched her undress herself. "Yes, you'll keep a husband satisfied. Raise blameless children. If not, you'll come back here and more drastic measures will be taken."

Rather than carry her, the doctor let Thea walk while he accompanied her to her bedroom. At the top of the long, winding stone staircase, Thea hesitated for a moment to tie the bow on her nightdress that she'd kept loose for that very purpose. The doctor continued down a stair, his bootstep echoing throughout the house, and when she didn't follow, he turned to face her. Thea kicked out with all her strength, connecting with the doctor's soft midsection. The force of the kick carried Thea forward just enough for Doctor Palsgrave to catch hold of her nightdress. She nearly toppled, but she leaned down and gripped the pads of her fingers into the groove of the long smooch and managed to stay upright just long enough for the nurses to rush over and grasp her firmly by the shoulders. The doctor bellowed, still holding on to Thea's bedclothes, trying to regain his footing. But before he could, the tattooed nurse took a pair of sewing shears from her smock and cut through the material.

They all listened to the doctor's fall, prolonged and violent, his body striking each step until he hit bottom and there was silence. Almost immediately, Thea turned and looked to the open hatch.

"I must climb the tall poplar and jump. I must ascend."

The handwringer wrung her hands, but the tattooed nurse put an arm around her shoulders and said, "Come on, Stacy. We may as well help her. Then we can finally get the hell out of this place."

First, Thea must do as she was bid, make a phone call, say goodbye to two who had been called her children. Let them hear one final time her rasp of a voice. The tattooed nurse led her to the nursery's phone. Thea picked up the receiver, heard a tone, squeezed her eyes shut tight, let her creator guide her as she turned the rotary dial. And then:

"Hello, Thompson residence," a little boy said, and Thea responded with a hum that welled up from deep in her chest.

"Mom!" said the boy.

"Mama?" said a little girl in the background. "Give me the phone, Miles!"

"Mom, I dislocated my shoulder, and we popped it back into place. Twice!" the boy said. "Tess isn't sure if she needs to take me to the hospital or not."

"And a girl stole my doll!" the little girl cried.

"Okay, shush you two," said a third voice, *the* voice, but much younger and with more of a drawl. A young woman, who then spoke directly into the phone. "We all agreed I'd put us on mute, so there's no pressure. Just maybe read to us awhile so they can hear you, okay? I've got us on speakerphone now, Mrs. Thompson."

Thea did not recognize the name, but still, she looked to the nurses and said, "I must read something into the phone, and then I can ascend."

The handwringer went to the small desk in the corner and retrieved a book. Well worn, the cover said *Anne of Green Gables* by L. M. Montgomery. The nurse flipped through and then handed it to Thea, pointing to an underlined passage. Thea read: "Why must people kneel down to pray? If I really wanted to pray I'll tell you what I'd do. I'd go out into a great big field all alone or in the deep, deep woods, and I'd look up into the sky—up—up—up—into that lovely blue sky that looks as if there was no end to its blueness. And then I'd just *feel* a prayer."

※

Thea closed the book and stayed on the line, silent, until she heard a click. Then she and the nurses climbed together into the cold night air. The full moon lit the way to the tree. If she jumped with all her might, perhaps she would make it. But no need. The nurses led her to the edge of the roof, made an arm cradle by clasping one hand to their own wrist and one to the other's. Thea stepped up, crouched low, and the nurses counted one, two, three, and tossed her as she pushed off with her legs. She landed squarely on a branch near the trunk of the tree.

Thea didn't hesitate. She clawed her way up the smooth, cold bark of the poplar, looking up at the star and thinking about the being of light she'd held so briefly. Her creator didn't deserve something so divine. Weakling sadist. What right did it have to interfere in her life? To believe it had control of her just because it made her. If Thea wasn't on the cusp of achieving everything she'd ever wanted—ascent—ascent—ascent—she'd go and find her creator. Destroy it.

Suddenly the wind gusted. A cloud appeared from nowhere, blew across the sky and obscured her star. Thea had made it nearly to the top of the poplar, as high as she could go without risking the weight of her body snapping one of the slender top branches. She perched while she caught her breath and waited for the cloud to pass. From her vantage point, she could see Palsgrave House tucked into the woods, the nurses holding hands and staring up at her from the roof. And beyond, treetops, moonlight glinting on the river, and, farther in the distance, a town twinkling with little lights.

But Thea's sights were set on the stars, on one brightest star in particular that she now couldn't see because of the damned cloud. Ascent. The more she thought of her creator, the more she filled with rage. Thea was vengeance; her creator was stupid and weak. She inched higher and growled at the sky. If she wanted to, Thea could find the voice, crush it. It would be so easy.

Just then the cloud moved on and Thea forgot all else. She crouched down and then used all her strength to jump. But she'd positioned herself too high. The force of her powerful legs snapped the branch, killing her momentum, and instead of ascent, she dropped, hard, wood splintering as she hit one branch with her shin and then bashed her jawbone on another as the earth rushed up. And yet, just before she lost hope, the air caught her, held her tight as she floated up, up, up, finally on her way. She rose ever so slowly, able to look back and view the curvature of the earth. The higher she climbed, the icier the air. In her fist, she bunched together the material of her nightdress where the hole had been cut. The warmth she could sense but not yet feel from the brightest star became that much more desirable. But long, long before she made it to her destination, Thea became stuck. Stuck in the exosphere, where she could see so clearly where she wanted to be but couldn't arrive. So very cold this high up. Completely alone. The air so thin she couldn't breathe.

Mama Prayed
Olivia

THE WIND FIGHTS the two cyclists from the moment they enter South Dakota. A hurricane that tore up the Gulf Coast a week ago has made its way inland and is now reduced to simply battering Olivia's cheeks, relentlessly, with every pedal stroke, as she makes her way east through the Great Plains. The hurricane is also named Olivia. Hurricane Olivia made landfall less than a hundred miles from Pinecreek, forcing Olivia's mother to evacuate and forcing Olivia to call her mother to verify that she's okay. Life is weird if you think too hard, and Olivia has nothing but time to think.

No technology other than their smartphones, no work, no books. The wind makes the flat road feel like a constant uphill, and the monotony of the landscape isn't helping. It's all corn and soybeans with the occasional sunflower field to break up the view, which might be exciting, except that the sunflowers haven't bloomed. They're just green stalks this early in the season.

Olivia sees it before it strikes, an enormous flying beetle that the wind catapults directly at her face. Before she can react, it splats on her sunglasses. And still—since in order to ride across the United States in the short amount of time she and Valerie have before they begin their new jobs, one cannot afford to be fazed by this sort of gore—she might have simply taken off her prescription glasses and squinted through the last five miles to their motel, except that apparently the monster beetle was pregnant, and though it didn't survive the crash, its offspring did, the burst egg sac scattering dozens of microscopic horror-creatures to scurry across her glasses, across her cheeks, up her nose, in her eyes.

"Stopping! Stopping!" she screams, spitting baby beetles, but after she pulls off to the side of the empty farm road and wipes frantically at her face with her sweaty bike jersey, she realizes that Valerie's not even behind her.

This morning they'd agreed not to do this anymore. Or rather, Valerie had agreed not to. From their very first day setting off from the Oregon coast, Valerie would turn off the road without warning, to chat with locals or snap photos, and it *really* wasn't okay during these gusty plains days. Olivia's learned the hard way after a month of riding that going back to find Valerie isn't worth it. Best just to wait.

Sure enough, twenty-three minutes later, here comes Valerie with her inefficient approach to cycling through the wind: standing and stomping down on each pedal, making her bike pitch from side to side. Her light brown hair whips wildly out from under her helmet. How anyone could ride nineteen hundred miles in under thirty days and not develop better technique is beyond Olivia. She wants an apology—zero shade, infant beetle lodged in her tear duct, dangerously low water supply—but when Valerie comes along beside her, out of breath and grinning, she understands there's not one coming.

"We have to turn back, Liv. It's the most fucking gorgeous thing I've ever seen."

A couple things about Valerie: she's Irish, and so every time she says *fuck*—which is often—it comes out sounding like *feck*, and every time it's the cutest thing that Olivia's ever heard. The other thing is that the world seems to have deemed Olivia unsuitable for a nickname, but Valerie calls her Liv. Liv!

"There is zero chance we're going back." Olivia yells to be heard over the wind.

"But we have to. You thought the sunflowers aren't opened yet, but they are. They were just turned away, following the sun like us. A whole field of pure gold, Liv. All you had to do was take half a second to turn back and look."

"The last sunflowers were at least ten miles away."

"Only seven. I clocked it. Come on, the wind will be at our backs, and we'll be there in less than twenty minutes."

A car passes. It gives them a wide berth, but still Olivia flinches because the constant whooshing in her ears has drowned out any warning of its approach. This area is so middle-of-nowhere that she's maybe seen a dozen vehicles all day. Both women scoot their bikes over to hug the edge of the road. There's no shoulder, just a few inches of weeds before the corn starts.

"Sure, twenty minutes to get there and an hour to get back. We're so close to our motel, and I'm hungry. And you don't even know about the huge bug that suicide-bombed me. Plus, we still have the rest of South Dakota and then we're in Iowa. There's no way that's our last sunflower field."

"Oh, come on. Leave at sunrise, go, go, go. Check-in's not for three more hours. Why are we always in a hurry?" Valerie asks, but doesn't wait for a response; she just shoots Olivia a look of disgust and starts pedaling forward, in the correct direction. Although Olivia is the stronger rider—both because she has thicker legs and because she hadn't skimped on their year-long training plan—she stays behind Valerie for the last few miles.

Everyone's always in awe of Olivia for her productivity, her accolades, the fact that she's good at everything she tries. But then they're disappointed when they learn that she's not also laid-back, not also spontaneous. Well, guess what!? They're not unrelated. The way she moves forward in life is by making a plan and sticking with it. Every. Single. Time. Though honestly, as they pass a feed store and a post office and other signs that they're entering the unremarkable town they'll call home for the night, she wishes that she had turned back to see the damn flowers. The one thing that Olivia is not good at is relationships; she never has been. Too obsessive, too judgmental, though she'd like to be better. She and Valerie have known each other for nearly two years, ever since they were assigned to the same business school cohort. Valerie liked her right away, which, let's face it, isn't common for someone as driven as Olivia. Valerie started the MBA program married to a man she'd met in undergrad. She went through a bad divorce last summer—this trip was conceived as a distraction—and she and Olivia hooked up only a couple months before classes ended, on a school trip to Moscow and Saint Petersburg. Now, on this bike ride, they've gotten into a routine of using one of the motel twin beds to lay out all their stuff from their bike packs and the other to collapse in exhaustion and sleep pressed together. But last night Valerie cleared off the other bed and was still staring at her phone when Olivia finally fell asleep.

On their right they pass by a round metal building with a sign that reads: *Prairie Methodist Church of Getting Bread.* Valerie takes the next left. Too early—the road to the motel is one turn farther up—but Olivia follows because she's decided to yield the lead. And although they're off course, there's an immediate sense of physical relief because they're no longer fighting the wind. Olivia picks up her speed and rides alongside Valerie.

"I know this isn't our turn, okay?" Valerie says. "I just wanted to see the neighborhood a little. We can make a right where the street dead-ends and get to our motel the back way."

Olivia looks at the GPS mounted on her handlebars and is surprised to see that Valerie's correct, though it isn't the most direct route. "Yeah, sure. Sounds . . . fun," she says.

Olivia's not stupid, she knows that Valerie's finally sick of her. Which is tough, because even though they took jobs in different cities, Olivia has all kinds of plans for them. For instance, cohosting an annual retreat for only the most successful from their MBA class as determined by their two-person panel. Valerie would never actually make that list since she's dead set on a career in the nonprofit sector, but when you're a cohost you're automatically included. Another idea is that since their birthdays are nine days apart, and on this trip they both turn thirty—Olivia last week and Valerie in a few days—they'll plan an annual birthdays-spanning adventure, though maybe not a bike trip every year. Olivia has a spreadsheet of ideal locations compiled in her head. Or! A recurring fantasy from all of Olivia's Valerie-focused daydreams is the two of them living together in Ireland one day. Mobility is one of the main reasons Olivia chose to accept a consulting job instead of any of the investment bank offers. Or maybe she'll start her own firm and Valerie will marry her so she can have automatic citizenship if that's even a thing in Ireland. Olivia doesn't know. She just knows that she's not cut out for this much thinking time, because her brain is constantly toggling between playing out these fantasies and rehearsing a breakup speech that she's considering delivering to spare herself the pain of having to hear one first.

The street is lined with houses on one side and a cornfield on the other. The houses are nothing special, a little nicer than where Olivia grew up even before the hurricane uprooted trees and peeled off roofs, but not by much. Ranch houses with squat porches and small yards that are mostly kempt and fenced. Several people are outside tending their gardens, water from hoses misting away in the wind. Invariably, they pause to stare as the cyclists pass. Olivia imagines that these people are probably out here watering on Sunday afternoons no matter the weather. The routine of rural living. Total conformity.

But then they reach the very last house, the one at the corner before their turnoff, and Valerie brakes hard. Across the entire front of the house, spanning the windows and the door and the peeling beige siding, are the words *Mama Prayed* scrawled in black tarlike paint. Almost odder than that, though, since it's only late June, is the space around the house decorated in a Thanksgiving motif, with hay bales and overripe gourds of various shapes and sizes at the feet of one gnarled scarecrow.

Valerie unclips from her pedals and leans her bike on the fence. Her phone is already out snapping a picture when the screen door opens and a guy walks onto the porch. He's pale, young—twentyish—wears jeans cut off at the knees with strings that hang to mid-calf, a black T-shirt, and has black hair that's long enough to tuck behind his ears. He stops short when he sees them, stares. After a moment, he leans his head back through the door and calls into the house. Olivia, still on her bike, feels Valerie's hand on her arm, and she shifts closer to her.

When a second guy walks out, identical to the first from his facial features to the length of the strings hanging from his cutoffs, Valerie presses into Olivia and says, "Should we go?"

Yes, of course they should go! Just as Olivia had insisted with all the other disconcerting locals Valerie had been curious about along the way—the DIY-shooting-range guys in eastern Oregon who invited them to unload semiautomatic rifles into stacks of old rubber tires, the woman accompanied by seven *Les Mis*–looking children selling their kiddie art projects at a roadside stand midway through Wyoming. But because of last night and because of the sunflowers, Olivia responds, "It's up to you. We'll do whatever you want." The look on Valerie's face, a look of shock and uncertainty, a look of *Do I even know you?* is revealing. Has she ever ceded a decision to Valerie? Perhaps not.

They nearly jump out of their skin when a popping sound erupts like gunfire, and a rusted gray pickup comes into view down the road. A moment later it's parked in the driveway. The engine cuts. From the driver's side comes a third identical guy, carrying takeout in Styrofoam containers. Instead of just staring like the other two, he places the takeout on a hay bale, waves, and walks over.

"Hey," he says. "We never see strangers off the road, but just our luck. Do you mind helping us with something? It'll just take a minute or two."

The guy is friendly enough, but the obvious answer is no way. Obvious to anyone but Valerie, that is, because Valerie looks to Olivia, and when Olivia shrugs—*Up to you*—Valerie takes off her helmet. "What do you need?"

Without pausing to think, Olivia gets off her bike, too.

※

The yard is buffered from the wind, though it whistles in the distance. The guy who asked for help is named Cal. He and his two brothers are twenty-two-year-old triplets and founding members of an a cappella group, determined to get their first album out by Halloween. The house, which the brothers inherited from their grandmother who passed away three years ago, is the backdrop for their album cover. They've needed to repaint for a while, and they took the opportunity to first mess it up.

"So, 'Mama Prayed' . . . ?" Valerie says.

"Is the name of our group," Cal confirms, the other brothers lingering behind him, one scowling and the other staring at the ground. "I have the least talent, so I manage our group. And I'm the bass. I also do some vocal and body percussion." Cal motions the scowler forward. "Dean is our baritone. He extracts the stories and helps some with lyrics." Then both brothers turn and gesture with outstretched arms to the third brother. "Augustus is the real talent. Tenor, countertenor, lyrics, composition." Augustus moves forward and stands between them.

Unprompted, they place their hands in prayer position and tilt their chins slightly toward the sky. Olivia notices it as they look to heaven: Cal, standing on the right, has two dark brown eyes, while Dean, standing on the left, has two light blue eyes, and Augustus, in the middle, has one eye of each color. In their current formation it's three dark browns followed by three light blues. They start to sing the strangest song, so hauntingly beautiful that it borders on discomfort. Ache. Cal and Dean surround their brother and sing in what seems to Olivia like perfect pitch. They are competent, but Augustus is the one to watch. All intensity comes from him. Secure in his brothers' steady foundation of tone, the middle brother riffs. He's at times pitched high, at times falsetto. At times he'll hold a note in harmony, but it never feels static or even steady. At spots throughout the song, Augustus slurs his voice from harmony to off-key, creating a dissonance that makes Olivia's eyes tear up. When the brothers finish, Olivia feels a profound sense of release. She's breathing hard, but she recovers quickly.

Both women clap, and Valerie says, "I love a cappella, that's lovely. And what a messed-up story. Fucking brilliant."

Apparently, Valerie picked up on some actual lyrics, whereas Olivia was simply engulfed in sound.

Augustus looks at Valerie and mumbles something too low to hear.

"I'm sorry?" Valerie says, and Augustus shakes his head and backs away.

"He likes your accent," Cal says.

"Oh, thank you." Valerie nods at Augustus. "Thank you so much."

Cal tells them that all they want help with is snapping a few photos in front of the house for their album cover. "We would ask the neighbors, but they don't like us and they'd take crappy pictures anyway. It was good luck you showed up."

"Regular lucky charms, that's us," Olivia says. "If the neighbors don't like you, it's because you're talented and special. Believe me, I know what small towns are like."

"No," Dean says, speaking up for the first time. "It's because we've taken their stories from them and they hate us for it."

"You haven't taken them," Olivia says. "They still own their stories."

"Do they?" Dean says.

Olivia had been trying to be nice, but in the look Dean's giving her she sees the typical, unfortunate, chip-on-your-shoulder bullshit that infects every rural person she's ever met. She recognizes it because she's infected, too.

Valerie stands up and assesses the space. She moves some of the gourds to the porch railing and pushes the scarecrow an inch or two closer to the house. "Everything's too shaded now to get any good photos. The light's going to be so much better later on when the sun shifts. We'll go find a place to grab a bite and then come back when the sun's in our favor."

"No, you won't," Dean says. "You won't find anyone around here who will serve you on a Sunday. Especially not outsiders."

"Oh, we're easy," Valerie says. "A convenience store even. I'd eat the hell out of a Hot Pocket right about now."

"No," Dean says.

"We could go to our motel," Olivia says to Valerie. "I'm sure I can talk them into early check-in. We'll find something."

"You're staying here? Around the corner at the Kennebec? Sylvia won't let you check in early, she's a terrorist." Dean spits out every word he speaks.

Before Olivia can respond, letting Dean know he's an asshole, letting them know that they are riding EFI—Every Fucking Inch—across the United States and they'll figure it out, Augustus whispers something to his brothers. Dean nods and Cal says, "We've got a ton of food here, just picked up from this amazing Mexican place two towns over."

Valerie glances at Olivia and says, "Oh, that's brilliant."

Olivia shrugs, entirely committed to her control-freak moratorium, despite her growing unease.

※

Fajitas, chimichangas, chips and queso, cinnamon-dusted churros. A liter jug of Dr Pepper. The stuff of dreams, especially for two cyclists running constant calorie deficits. The brothers spread a blanket on the grass at the edge of the shade and make a picnic. They scarf down the food, and Olivia starts to relax. Valerie appears content.

The brothers tell them how they started out writing songs about famous instances of people hearing voices from God, like Abraham and Joan of Arc. Then they moved to horrifying Bible verses and wrote a bunch of lyrics that cover stonings and eternal damnation, fire-and-brimstone-type songs that aren't bad, but—

"Our passion lies in personal stories," Dean says. "The song you heard is dedicated to our dear mother. She's the inspiration for our band. She used to make the three of us kneel and pray with her, pray that we would all be better and stop provoking our father to violence."

"Jesus," Valerie says.

Olivia shakes her head. Thank god she no longer lives in the Bible Belt.

"It's all good," Cal says. "Neither of our parents is a problem anymore."

"Got it," Valerie says. She fans her hand out in front of her as if she's presenting a headline. "'South Dakotan Triplets Form Goth-Horror A Cappella Band Mama Prayed.'"

Olivia props herself up on her knees. "Oh, I like it. Niche, but I see a market for that."

"But personal stories," Dean says, ignoring them, "they're a lot harder to get."

"Really? Then I guess most people didn't have the type of childhood I had," Valerie says, and laughs.

But when she says it, Augustus, who'd been checked out for quite some time, leans in and stares her down, and his brothers follow suit. Their attention isn't even directed at Olivia, and yet she feels hemmed in by the weight of their collective focus. She also feels their curiosity like a contagion, deepening in intensity almost to pain.

"What was your childhood like?" Cal says. "Tell us."

Augustus murmurs.

What was Valerie's childhood like? Olivia realizes she's never talked about it.

"Tell us now," Dean says.

"No, nothing." Valerie takes the rubber band out of her sweaty, wind-matted hair and ties it back tighter. "Just, my dad had this aunt that came to live with us when I was about eight. My older sister, she—"

The brothers lean in farther, their fists pressed into the blanket, arms bearing their weight. Olivia looks down the street. None of the neighbors are in their yards anymore. A curtain falls across the window of the next-door house the moment she looks at it.

"Never mind," Valerie says. "I don't know why I said anything. It's really none of your business."

"You can't stop now," Dean says. "It's too late for you to stop now."

"Back off," Olivia says, hating how weak her voice sounds. The brothers ignore her. Valerie's eyes dart around like she's trying to find an escape route, and Olivia tries to think of something to shift their focus. She'll get the story from Valerie later. "I'll give you something. Just let me think..."

Olivia remembers: All the small-town zealots and the sanctimonious pricks. Nora, her first love (or maybe just a crush, she can never make up her mind), whose life was made harder by the hypocrisies of these people. Focusing on Nora has always been too humiliating, though—Olivia had been so immature back then, trying to make someone else feel small just because she didn't get her way. She thinks of her mother, who became born again after separating from Olivia's father, crying, *"Don't you love Jesus?!"* when she suspected Olivia of doing something wrong. But there's no real story there, Olivia understands now. Just a woman struggling to get by like anyone else.

Then something else pops into her head.

"I have one."

Olivia had only been in ninth grade when it all went down, but the whole rest of the time she was growing up, people talked about it or avoided talking about it, but it was always somehow there. Once she gets going with the story, Cal jumps up, runs into the house, and comes right back out with a portable cassette player that's already emitting scratchy piano music at low volume and a legal pad and pen he hands off to Dean. Dean flips to an empty page and starts taking notes. Olivia keeps talking, and she's happy to do it because she can tell Valerie is relieved, which makes her feel relieved. Heroic even? A creative intensity builds in the air around them.

Eventually, she finishes, and Dean looks at his notes and recaps: "Pinecreek, Louisiana. Fifteen-year-old Gail Liebrecht says she plans to move away to live with a distant relative and the parents seem to acquiesce, but what they really do is invite Grandfather Liebrecht, her father's father, over from Germany to quote 'take care of the situation.' Grandfather keeps her in a shed for two years, secured with a rope tied around her ankle—"

"Two years," Valerie says. "Fucking hell."

"—to try and perform an exorcism because God, who speaks to him, has told him that Gail Liebrecht is evil. But then one day Grandfather Liebrecht is found dead—or killed, nobody really knows, though his body has been mauled by animals. Parents put away. Gail leaves town not long after. That's the sequence of events. Town gossip continues, perhaps even to this day."

Dean looks at Olivia and she shrugs and then nods in confirmation. The piano music is barely audible, but she can make out a pounding of keys, followed by a frenzied interpretation of "Für Elise" that gnaws at her brain, the way she can't quite put her finger on why she believes she should recognize it.

"What really happened?" he continues. "Well, some conclude that Gail Liebrecht is, in fact, evil and brought this on herself. She's probably the one who killed Grandfather; there was always something very off about the girl. Others say Grandfather is the evil one. He had it coming. Or the fact that the family is German and therefore outsiders makes them all evil. Some suggest that the German language is the source of evil."

"Yeah," Olivia says. "I think it was just that some people heard them speak German once and interpreted it as devil-speak since they were too stupid to recognize a foreign language."

"Town consensus: evil exists somewhere," Dean says.

"Another thing," Olivia says, recognizing a parasitic thrill in the air that surrounds the growing wildness of her account. "The story goes that the shed around her kept trying to break apart, as if it couldn't contain the evil. Unexplained holes in the roof, in the floor, the walls. Trees falling down around it. Trees aiming for it. I mean, obviously that didn't happen, but that's what people—"

Augustus cuts her off and sings:

Gail Liebrecht

Gail Lieeeeeeeebrecht

His brothers match him, trying different keys, until he indicates with a nod that they found the one he wants, and then he sings:

*Gail LieeeeeeEEEEEEEE*EEEEEEEEEEEEEEE*brecht*

That sound, that dissonance of sound, the way the middle brother seems to have found a way to communicate feeling beyond simple words, and the tears come to Olivia's eyes. The response is so automatic that she feels manipulated.

Dean says, "What's the German word for evil?" and searches on his phone. "*Bose.*"

Valerie gives Olivia an odd look and then scoots toward Dean and points at his screen. "See the umlaut?" she says. "You pronounce it like *boo-sah*. Very nasal."

"You listening to this, Cal?" Dean says. "You're not so good at this stuff."

Cal mouths *boo-sah* to himself over and over while Valerie and Dean go through a list of words and pronunciations. Augustus sits still and listens, nods when he hears one he likes, and Dean writes it down. Then Dean points at Olivia. "Spell the last name."

She finds herself doing what he says despite herself. "*L-i-e-b-r-e-c-h-t.*" There's a pause in the piano music, and Olivia thinks the tape is finished only for a melancholic version of the same song to start back up. She feels drained all of a sudden, the exertion of the day catching up with her.

Dean scribbles out and rewrites. He points at Valerie. "Pronounce the evil words again."

"*Boo-sah. Ew-behl. Shleht,*" Valerie says, frowning, and the boys repeat the words in harmonic unison. Cal's pronunciation isn't quite right, and Dean punches him in the ribs, hard.

"I'll work on it," Cal says, and the brothers start right back in.

Gail Liebrecht. Böse, übel, schlecht. Gail LieeeeeEEEEEEEE—

Instinctively, Olivia slaps her hands over her ears, and Valerie does the same. Even Augustus's brothers cringe until he ratchets down the tone. The mood around them seems to have shifted, a thickness that wasn't there before. The wind gusts beyond the yard and, although all Olivia wanted all day was to be free of it, now she wishes she were in it again. The words in the brothers' mouths are an incantation, and she can't help but feel her carelessness, that she did real damage by giving away someone else's story to these people. She looks over at Valerie, who tilts her head toward their bikes when they make eye contact. They start to stand, and the brothers go silent.

"Sit!" Dean says.

And they do. For some reason they do.

"You know what? Don't use Gail's real name," Olivia says. "I'm sure she's still around out there somewhere. And no one knows exactly what happened. It's all gossip."

"Shush," Dean says.

"She's right," Valerie says. "The song should be about the grandfather, not the girl. He's the one with the visions. Maybe Herr Liebrecht. Or *großvater*."

"Shut up. Shut up," Dean says. But Augustus puts a finger on Dean's forearm and whispers, and Dean points at Valerie. "Pronounce that last one again. Is that 'grandfather'?"

Valerie stands. "Just fucking google it," she says. "It's not that difficult." She reaches out her hand to Olivia, and Olivia takes it and pulls herself to her feet.

They start off toward the bikes, and behind them the cassette player clicks off. Augustus claps loudly, and his two brothers run to cut off access to the gate.

"The sun's almost in front of us. You haven't taken the photos you promised," Cal says.

Olivia looks over to the front of the house. The bottom half of *Mama Prayed* is directly in sunlight and no longer looks like paint but like a hole, a void, the absence of light.

"Tough luck," Valerie says. "We're done here."

Augustus walks up behind them. Olivia feels him touch the small of her back and her skin crawls. She reels forward, out of his reach.

"You can't go," Dean says to Valerie. "Not without a story. She gave us a story, and we need to take one from you, too."

Olivia doesn't have the energy to protest, but Valerie steps right up to Dean and Cal. They're not much taller than Olivia, but they have several inches on Valerie. "Move!" she says, and to Olivia's extreme relief, they do. The women hurry out of the gate, put their helmets on, and throw their legs over their bikes.

Cal's voice is friendly when he says, "Tell Sylvia to give you room seven. It's the west-facing room at the far end of the property up on a little slope. You'll be shocked at the view that little bit of incline gives you in these flat parts. Tell her we sent you and she'll do it."

Olivia's heart booms in her chest. She has a hard time clipping back into the pedals. She gets one foot secured, but then almost loses her balance. Valerie grabs her handlebar and supports her, keeps her from falling over. Then she turns back, and before Olivia can stop her, she flips off the brothers.

They laugh. Even Augustus has a little laugh that's as cold and sharp as a bell.

*

Within half a mile they spot their shitty little motel. Olivia starts to turn in, but Valerie rides past and says, "Nope!" and Olivia follows her.

They turn west back onto the farm road they've been riding on the past two days, and Olivia doesn't complain, not even in her own head, that on a thirty-eight-hundred-mile cross-country bike ride retracing their steps makes no sense. Instead, she shifts her bike to its biggest gear and lets the wind and the power of her legs push her. She's up beside Valerie and Valerie matches her speed, and they're going ten, twenty, thirty miles an hour before Olivia stops tracking it, zooming back out of town, the rows of corn filing past on both sides.

Just over twenty minutes and there they are. They slow down when they get to it, the sunflower field. Still, all Olivia sees are green stalks.

"I told you they follow the sun. Come on."

And sure enough, because the sun is past its peak and beginning its long, slow descent, when they get to the western edge of the field and turn back to look, there they are. A vast field full of honest-to-god sunflowers. But there must be something wrong with Olivia, because she sees them and still can't grasp what's so special. These aren't particularly beautiful flowers, black pupils with a fringe of yellow lashes staring wide-eyed at the sun. The ones they sell in bouquets at the grocery store look better than these dusty crops. But Valerie seems to love them.

"Oh, wow," Olivia says. "So nice."

"Right? Aren't you glad you didn't miss this?"

"I'm so, so glad."

There's a narrow dirt path that separates the edge of the sunflowers from the neighboring cornfield. They pull their bikes off the road and sit in the shade of the corn. The flowers lean toward them, protecting them from the wind.

"Did we almost die back there?" Valerie asks.

The question brings Olivia some relief, poking a tiny hole in the veil that's covered her since the moment she first heard those brothers sing. "You mean did we almost get killed by really talented yet psychotic triplets in middle-of-nowhere South Dakota? Yeah, I think we just barely dodged that bullet."

"I'm not staying in that town, Liv. I was studying the GPS. I think if we walk our bikes to the end of this path, there's a parallel road that will take us a little farther north than we planned. We can still get to Sioux Falls the day after tomorrow and be back on track."

Olivia nods, grabs a handful of soil, lets it dirty her glove and fall through her fingers. Her eye is still bothering her, and she wonders if one of the bugs scratched her cornea or managed to burrow inside.

"It's so funny," Valerie says. "I kept expecting you to say we needed to leave. To get us the hell out of there. I realize I rely on you for that kind of thing."

"I just wanted to do whatever you wanted," Olivia says. "We've been spending a lot of time together, and I can tell that you're getting really sick of me."

"What? What are you talking about? Are you sick of me?"

"No, god no. Not at all. But I know I can get annoying. Wear on people's nerves. I just mean I can try harder. Or if you don't want to finish the ride, I'll understand."

"Stop talking shit about yourself, Liv. Seriously, you're my actual favorite person."

Why? Olivia wants to ask. *Why, why, why? What about me makes me your actual favorite person. Tell me in detail, because I can't see it.*

"And we've been training our asses off for this ride for a year," Valerie continues. "We've planned the whole thing down to water stops."

Olivia can't stop her brain from thinking that she was the one who did all the planning and Valerie skipped out on much of the training.

Valerie leans back into a stalk of corn that's way too young, and it immediately collapses under her weight. She laughs and rolls to her side on the dirt, props her head in her hand, and smiles up at Olivia. "I got fired, that's what's wrong. It's got nothing to do with you. Before I ever started. Jesus, that must be a record. My boss called me two days ago to give me the news."

"She can't do that."

"Why not? You know they laid off twelve percent of their workforce at the end of last year."

"But that doesn't apply to new hires."

"Well, it does to this new hire, who requested two and a half months off starting day one."

"But what about—"

"Liv, stop. I did all of the things. I contacted all of the people. Everyone. My boss said they'll keep me on the books until the end of summer, so I can finish this ride and I'm not immediately booted out of the country. It sucks, but you can't fix it."

But she could. If it were her, Olivia could fix it. She's always been able to.

Olivia suddenly feels hungry, empty, so light and insubstantial if she just stood up the wind would blow her away. The life she's built, now that she's away from it, feels trivial. And that feeling scares her, because the kind of life she's chosen, to be truly successful, requires total buy-in. She squeezes her eyes shut and says, "Move in with me. If for some reason you want to stay in this fecked-up country—"

"Did you just say 'fecked'?"

"—you'll figure it out. And I want you to. To move in with me, I mean."

Valerie doesn't respond, and Olivia keeps her eyes closed until Valerie pulls her backward to the ground. They lie on their sides and face each other. Valerie smiles, and Olivia feels herself smiling back. Valerie laughs, and she hears herself laughing, feels herself laughing with her entire body.

And Olivia wants, wants so much from this woman, so much *of* this woman, it hurts. Everything. "Tell me," she says. "Tell me what you wouldn't say back at that house. Please, I want to know."

Just as the panic enters Valerie's eyes, Olivia hears a rumbling in the distance over the whoosh of the wind. The *pop-pop-pop* like gunfire of a sputtering motor that makes them both scramble to their feet and grab their bikes and gear, run with them farther down the path and back into the cornfield. They huddle together, hiding, imploring any divine power that may exist to intervene as the threat grows louder, closer.

Slovenly Tess

Tess

WHEN THE RODGERS FAMILY landed in München, Tess stopped her German language lessons and took off her headphones. Paul sat next to her in the aisle seat, their thirteen-month-old son, PJ, straddled her in the middle seat, and Summer sat by the window. Paul was checking his phone, and she could tell something was off before he relayed the news, because his posture went from traveling-for-sixteen-hours disheveled to rigid, upright, *militärisch*. He adjusted his shirt collar, straightened the magazines and brochures in his seat-back pocket. Then, with a voice a notch deeper—his officer's voice—he relayed the facts: the duplex with the private yard they'd secured months ago got flooded by a burst pipe. The army housing officer realized it only that morning, and the damage was extensive. They were now assigned to a sixth-floor walk-up apartment on the northern border of the Garmisch-Partenkirchen base.

Sixth-floor walk-up. Tess closed her eyes and rolled her head in a slow circle, trying to force some mobility back into her fucked-up neck and shoulders. PJ was fast asleep. For the entire flight he'd stayed there, calm against her belly, unless they'd needed to eat or use the bathroom. Any parent's dream child. Except that PJ had never cried once since the day he was born, a fact that worried Tess daily, even if the doctors hadn't yet found anything wrong.

The captain made an announcement, in German and then in English, to expect a long wait on the tarmac, and Tess got to learn the words for *long wait*: *langes Warten*.

While the plane taxied, Summer read a picture book titled *Der Struwwelpeter* that she'd picked out from the children's section of the library on the California base where they'd been stationed. It hadn't been checked out in years, one of those disintegrating, dust-gathering hardbacks that librarians were always trying to weed out of circulation. Seven-year-old Summer had wanted it because it was Deutsche, and they were moving to Deutschland, and they were all learning Deutsche—except for Paul, who already knew German, and PJ, who had yet to even say *Mama*. Tess hadn't realized how creepy the thing was when she'd scanned it out of library rotation for her daughter. This version of the book, which was first published in the mid-1800s, featured parallel text, the original German next to an English translation. Summer had the book open to the titular story, illustrated with a dead-eyed troll boy, a shock of blond hair frizzing from his head and fingernails that curved out, long and sharp. A nineteenth-century Freddy Krueger. The charming text read:

Der Struwwelpeter	**Slovenly Peter**
Sieh einmal, hier steht er,	Just look at him! There he stands,
pfui, der Struwwelpeter!	With his nasty hair and hands.
An den Händen beiden	See! his nails are never cut;
ließ er sich nicht schneiden	They are grim'd as black as soot;
seine Nägel fast ein Jahr;	And the sloven, I declare,
kämmen ließ er nicht sein Haar.	Never once has comb'd his hair;

Pfui, ruft da ein jeder: Any thing to me is sweeter
Garstger Struwwelpeter!   Than to see Slovenly Peter.

Summer, who'd acquired a hopefully short-lived habit of pointing out her mother's many flaws, reached over and took Tess's hand, studiously comparing her mom's jagged nails with those of the boy in the illustration before turning back to her book. Her nails were pretty scruffy, Tess had to admit. She should have clipped and filed them before they'd left, but everything about the move had been hectic. She bit into a hangnail, pulled at the skin with her teeth, but instead of coming loose it ripped deeper into the meat, almost to her knuckle, and drew blood. She sucked at her finger and watched Summer flip through the book that featured kids with various slovenly habits who all got their comeuppances. Summer stopped on "The Story of Little Suck-a-Thumb" and began to knock the side of her head rhythmically against the Plexiglas window as she studied the scissor man *"Snip! Snap! Snip!"* off the thumbs—*"klipp und klapp"*—of a naughty little thumb-sucking *Daumenlutscher*. Tess thought maybe she should take the book away from her daughter, but she didn't. The only thing Tess could remember reading as a kid that young was *Anne of Green Gables*, over and over, and she had turned out neither good nor happy.

"What do you think?" Paul asked. "About the apartment?" He reached across Tess and PJ over to Summer and tugged on her sleeve to make her stop hitting the window.

"Well, first off I'm thinking about your knee. Six floors is a lot," Tess said. Paul's left knee was chronically bad. The army doctor in California warned him he'd probably need surgery in the near future.

"My knee's fine."

Paul's voice cracked an octave higher at the word *fine*. Really convincing. Tess pulled her daughter to her side. The captain made an announcement that their wait on the tarmac would be indefinite, infinite; that this would be their final resting place and that eventually the nose of the plane would angle straight down, break through the asphalt, and carry them all to the underworld. *Die Unterwelt.* Summer leaned into Tess and snatched her little brother's thumb out of his mouth. He blinked his eyes open and calmly reinserted it, and she snatched it again. Tess let this go on awhile, always hopeful that PJ would cry so she could know that nothing was truly wrong. But he didn't, of course, and so Tess took Summer's hand and gave her the *stop it* look.

Paul thrust his phone in Tess's face, showing her a map of the base. He pointed at a rectangle that was presumably their new apartment complex. "It's next to a playground and closer to the elementary school."

Paul's new assignment was to teach Russian at the Partner Language Training Center Europe, known as PLTCE. Paul was a military linguist and Mandarin was his specialty, but the current PLTCE Russian instructor was retiring, so Paul was to teach Russian, which was only one of his secondary languages. Since Paul was prone to panic attacks and he'd been inches from one ever since he got the transfer notice— and since Tess had, just a few days ago, concluded a months-long affair that had ended in a feeling of disgust despite it not being her first but simply the longest in duration—she threaded her fingers through his and said, "I think it's for the best. Good location, great exercise, you know? Really *wunderbar.*"

※

It was midnight by the time the Rodgers family left the airport. They took the autobahn an hour from Munich to Garmisch, showed their IDs at the gate, and drove through the base. This was Tess's first trip outside the United States. They were assigned here for the next two years. A potentially exciting adventure, though these empty streets could be any of the bases they'd lived on—Fort Hood, Fort Meade, Presidio of Monterey—or any on the planet. Same grid layout and squat brown buildings. Absolute uniformity. But then they parked in the lot in front of their apartment building, and behind it was a forest so dense and black that it swallowed all the light from the streetlamps, the moon, and the stars.

They got their bags into the lobby, and then Tess opened the door to the stairwell and looked up: steep concrete flights, harsh fluorescent lighting. Already, Paul was limping a little. She strapped PJ into the baby carrier at her chest. She handed a couple of small bags to Summer, took a medium bag and PJ's stroller, and started up. At the top of the first flight, she looked back to see Paul carrying the other medium bag and, of course, the heaviest suitcase that had all her notebooks, ascending the stairs by using his right leg to hoist himself up and resting his left leg at each step. She wanted to tell him to let her handle the heavy suitcase, but she knew he'd dismiss her. At the landing to the fourth floor, Tess heard him gasp. Summer, who'd been struggling already with little bags, dropped them next to Tess. "I'll help you, Daddy," she said, and ran back down to Paul, who was sitting on a step near the third-floor landing, bent over his hurt leg.

Paul said, "No, sweetheart, just leave it," but Summer already had both hands on the handle of the heavy suitcase and, pulling with all her might, she climbed the stairs backward, the wheels striking each step and echoing throughout the stairwell.

"Summer," Tess said. "Leave it."

"I'm already halfway," Summer said, her little face red with the effort. But then she tripped on a stair and lost her grasp. The suitcase crashed down and slammed into Paul's back, knocking him to the floor. Paul kicked at the suitcase with his good leg. Tess unstrapped PJ, who was perfectly calm despite the racket and his mother's pounding heart. She made Summer, wide-eyed, whispering, "*I'm sorry, I'm sorry,*" sit on the floor of the landing and hold her brother while she went down to Paul. A moment later, the stairwell door opened and a woman in pajamas peered down at them.

"Need help?" she said, and Tess confirmed that they did in fact need a shit ton of help. The woman left the stairwell, but soon came back with a gruff man, his eyes groggy with sleep, and a boy around Summer's age who seemed thrilled to be doing something so out of the ordinary and exciting in the middle of the night.

Later, after everything was inside and they'd thanked their fourth-floor neighbors, Patricia, Dom, and their son, Charlie, they were alone in their new apartment. As soon as the door closed, Paul dropped his friendly smile. "Next time someone asks if we need help, the answer is no."

Very recently Tess would have blown up at this comment, but not now. Now she was on her best behavior. Somewhere over the Atlantic she'd decided that this overseas move offered a fresh chance to be a better, less volatile person. So instead, she left him standing at the door holding his back. She left him to hobble on his own while she unzipped all their luggage in the middle of the living room to find what she needed to get herself and the kids ready for bed. Once she did, she placed PJ in his travel sleeper next to Summer's twin bed, then tucked her daughter in with a small stuffed giraffe that she'd pulled from a carry-on.

The master bedroom was a little box, clean and spare. Queen-sized bed. Chest of drawers. Two bedside tables and lamps. Paul was already propped up in bed with a plastic tray of ice on his knee, poring over his Russian language lesson plans that he was expected to present to his colleagues the next day, a Friday. Then he'd have the weekend off before he started teaching classes on Monday. Sleep would be way more useful than going over lesson plans for the thousandth time, but that wasn't Tess's business. He didn't acknowledge her, didn't comment on the newness of their surroundings, the curtainless window that framed a full moon or their new mattress that felt like a plank of wood. Or about how they were living in a whole other country! Tess made herself small on the far edge of the mattress, curled up, and stared out the window until Summer peeped her head in and said she couldn't sleep.

Tess was relieved. "I'm going to lie down with my daughter for a while."

She'd been doing that a lot lately, emphasizing *my* daughter, thinking of Summer as *mine* rather than *ours*, even though Paul had adopted her when she was only a year old. As if to highlight her unfair behavior, Paul called Summer over, and they gave each other a long hug good night. Tess knew he didn't want Summer to feel bad about the suitcase incident. He was good to the kids. She tried to catch his eye and offer a little smile—it had been a long, exhausting trip for them both—but he didn't look at her.

In the other bedroom, they clicked on the lamp and checked on PJ calmly sleeping in his travel crib. Summer reached and snatched her brother's thumb from his mouth.

"Sum, stop doing that," Tess whispered.

"I have to, or else 'the great, long, red-legged scissor-man' will come."

Tess pulled Summer toward the little bed. "Do I need to throw that book away?"

Summer picked a bunch of loose hairs off Tess's nightshirt and dropped them on the carpet. "It doesn't matter," she said. "I have the whole thing memorized."

Of course she did, her precious, weird, perfect little girl. Tess didn't know for sure who the real father was, and Tess liked to imagine that it was no one, that Summer was 100 percent her. She knew the candidates, of course. But the pregnancy had come during her out-of-control days when she drank like it was her job and screwed anything willing. Even Paul didn't know that Tess didn't know. She'd told him that Summer's father didn't want to be involved and left it at that. Even though she promised herself that she'd change once the baby was born, her old habits had ganged back up on her fast. But Paul came in at the exact right time, when Tess badly wanted to be better, and early enough the particular night she met him at a bar that she wasn't yet wasted. If it wasn't for him Tess would have been stuck in her hometown and her whole life would be a mess. She really did try to keep that in mind when things weren't great between them.

"But do you have the German version memorized?" Tess said.

Summer's eyes got wide. They opened the book and sounded out German words together until they fell asleep. Tess didn't go back to her own room.

※

For breakfast, Tess doled out stale granola from one of the airport layovers. Once Paul left to return their rental car and get to his work meeting, Tess would need to take the kids to the bus stop, get a shuttle to the PX, find a cup of coffee, and grocery shop at the commissary.

Tess held a tranquil PJ on her hip and took Summer out to the balcony so that Paul could look over his papers at the kitchen table in peace. From the balcony, they had a view of the forest she'd glimpsed last night. And beyond, the beautiful, snowcapped Alps. Their apartment was level with the tree line, and the massive pines extended all the way to the mountains. Soon, Paul would settle into his teaching position, Summer would be in school, and Tess would start her job at the base library that had a daycare for PJ. Then they could explore. Munich day trips. Alpspitze ski lessons. Kreuzeck Mountain hikes. Oktoberfest.

Summer recited *Der Struwwelpeter* in a weird singsong incantation while they looked out at the wilderness. This transient military life made affairs relatively uncomplicated. No one ever stayed anywhere for very long. Either Tess was about to leave or the guy was. Each move offered a clean slate. A chance to be a new and better person, a woman of her word. She'd been faithful her first three years married until breaking her streak with that random guy in the bar in Baltimore. After that she just kept it up. It was PJ's doctor whom Tess had been sleeping with before they left California—an affair that stemmed from her distress for her son and had been sufficiently distracting for a while even if Tess didn't feel much of anything for him. She suspected Paul had found out; he'd been particularly shitty toward her lately.

Tess realized she was chewing on her hair, an old habit she'd once broken by keeping her hair too short to reach her mouth for a number of years. Apparently, the habit was back, which meant time for a cut.

Something tickled the back of her neck. She brushed at it, and an iridescent blue beetle dropped onto PJ's cheek. Tess jerked backward and tripped over a patio chair, slamming into the sliding glass door. PJ didn't even react. The beetle stayed there under his eye for another second, then it flew off toward the trees. Summer rushed over to them and then Paul was there, too, picking up PJ, who then rested his head serenely against his father's shoulder.

"Fucking Christ," Tess said, shaking. "That fucking beetle."

"*Fucking Christ,*" Summer whispered.

They all went back into the kitchen, and Paul handed PJ back to Tess. "My first meeting is in two hours and I go all day."

"Do you want to talk to the housing department and see what our options are?" Tess said. "Or I can."

"This is our option, Tess. No other officer's family is assigned here, so if there was some other option, we would know about it."

"Fine."

Paul had taken on his military voice, but all at once he slumped into a chair, knocking his stack of neatly organized papers off the table. His face turned red, and he began that shallow breathing thing he did, often the last step before a full-on head-between-the-knees attack. This was the point that Tess usually stood by and rubbed his back in small, comforting circles, but now she just sat down in one of the kitchen chairs and ripped her thumbnail down past the quick with her teeth and then worked to try to bite it off without causing more damage. The way he was sitting, shoulders hunched forward and head tilted slightly, made his Adam's apple bulge grossly, and all she could do was watch it wriggling around like a little animal trying to escape, until finally he gathered together his papers with Summer's help and left.

※

Seventy-two was the number of stairs it took to reach their apartment. Tess knew because, after the shuttle dropped them at the curb with their dozen full shopping bags, she took PJ and his stroller upstairs and paid Summer a dollar a bag to make the trip back and forth while she unloaded the groceries and started to unpack their luggage. Summer reported the number—"Yep! Seventy-two"—each time she dropped off a bag.

"What's seventy-two in German?" Tess asked, putting the milk in the fridge.

"Zwei . . . zwei und . . ."

"Zweiundsiebzig," Tess said.

The next time Summer came in—"*Ja! Zweiundsiebzig*"—Patricia from the fourth floor was with her carrying one of the grocery bags.

"You know you owe Miss Patricia a dollar now," Tess said after greeting her neighbor.

Summer looked stricken but said, "Okay," and the two women laughed.

"Actually, Summer, that one's on me. My pleasure." Patricia had some sort of New England accent that Tess wondered about but didn't ask. It'd always pissed her off when people commented on her Louisiana accent before she'd managed to work it out of her speech.

When Summer left again, the two women set the groceries on the counter, and Patricia said, "Don't tell Charlie your pay rate. I only give him a quarter a bag."

"Well, he only has to climb four floors. It gets exponentially harder after that."

PJ stood in his baby walker and toddled a couple of steps in their direction.

"Look at that little angel," Patricia said. "He was so calm last night."

He looked up at them with his serene gaze and then toddled over to the wall until his walker hit, at which point he sat back, seemingly content with staring at paint.

"Yes. He never cries, never gets upset."

"Oh, wow. I'm jealous. Charlie cried nonstop for two straight years."

"I'm serious, though. Not one time. Ever. He's seen several specialists about it. Anyway, it's just on my mind a lot. What I need to do is text PJ's old doctor back in California, see if I can get a referral here so that

I don't have to start completely over. I'm just waiting until this afternoon because of the time difference."

"*Ja! Zweiundsiebzig*," Summer called as she came through the door. "Only *fünf* more."

She set the bag down by the women and gave her mom an odd look. Then she pulled herself up to sit on the kitchen counter next to where Tess stood. She reached over and brushed lightly at Tess's eyebrow, then moved her bangs back from her face and brushed harder. Patricia cocked her head, her long braid falling over her shoulder, and looked curiously at her, too.

"Jesus, what is it?" Tess said. She excused herself and ducked into the bathroom. Summer tried to follow her in, but Tess shooed her away and told her to go finish her job. She checked herself out in the mirror. There was a single hair, coarse and white, that curled upward from her eyebrow. It must have been at least three inches long. She felt her blood rush to her head, and quickly she pinched the hair between her fingernails, plucked it out, and dropped it into the toilet. Then she swiped at the dandruff that dusted her shoulders. She was so gross right now.

She went back out to Patricia, who she suddenly wished would leave. She tried to laugh it off. "Well, that was embarrassing. But I don't know, maybe a secret of womanhood is that every thirty-three-year-old starts to grow the eyebrows of a one-hundred-year-old man, but no one will talk about it."

"Then I'll have something to look forward to in a couple of years, and I'll be in the know. That's the hard thing about daughters. Charlie wouldn't even notice if I had a unibrow."

Tess smiled but felt irritated, as if Patricia were criticizing Summer. She blamed her sensitivity on the jet lag that was really starting to kick in.

"Look, I'm heading off to work," Patricia said. "But I wanted to tell you we're cooking out tomorrow night, at the barbecue pit past the soccer field over by the playground. I know you're just getting settled, but we won't keep you too late and everyone's got to eat. And don't bring anything or I'll throw you out."

"Sure you want us there? We're kind of chaotic right now."

"Yeah, I'm sure," Patricia said. "How's your husband's knee?"

Last night, since he couldn't hide his limping, Paul had told them that the suitcase had smashed directly into his knee. Tess didn't feel like lying for him. "Oh, it's messed up. It's been bad for a while, and he should tell the housing people that an apartment with *zweiundsiebzig* stairs doesn't work. *But*—here's a hint about Paul—just pretend like nothing's wrong when you see him hobbling around and everyone will be a lot happier."

Patricia grinned. "Don't worry, my husband's ridiculous, too. I'm sure you noticed how grumpy he was last night. He leads PRT, so he has to be up kicking ass at four thirty a.m., and he's always whining on and on about sleep."

Tess saw Patricia to the door. Patricia leaned down and squeezed PJ's little hand where he still stood facing the wall. "See you tomorrow," she said, and caught Tess off guard when she wrapped her in a tight hug.

※

Saturday after breakfast, Tess left Paul alone with his work and took the kids down to the playground. She brought her notebook, and while Summer showed her little brother how high she could swing, Tess studied the woods in front of her and made some notes. It was a fairy-tale forest, nothing like the pine forests she grew up with in Louisiana or the deciduous forests in Maryland. The trees were easily twice as large and twisty, the pine needles thick and sharp, the cones perfectly shaped like ornaments. There was a damp chill to the air that made her feel alert. Tess wrote several lines about a woman roaming the alpine forest for millennia in search of something: yes, it was Thea, in search of a little boy who never cries. And when she finds him, she *makes* him cry. But Tess quit before Thea could hurt the boy, and instead of writing, she challenged Summer to a race on the monkey bars and went down the slide with PJ in her lap.

Later that afternoon, when Tess got out of the shower, she discovered that they were, in fact, going to the cookout. Patricia and Charlie had come by to drop off a cake for their new neighbors. Although Paul had wanted *her* to say no to the invitation, he had been too much of a coward to say no himself. And so, at five thirty, already in a bad mood because of Paul's double standards, Tess followed behind as he held on to the handrail and hopped on one foot down all seventy-two stairs. She carried the stroller and their son, who got progressively heavier with every trip up and down. Summer had gone outside early to play with Charlie. Once they exited the building and got to the edge beyond which people could see them, Paul paused for a moment and took a couple of deep breaths. Tess unfolded the stroller and sat PJ down. She walked next to Paul while he pushed their son, using the stroller to help his limp, which had become so pronounced his shoulder dipped and every step became a lurch. She tried to ignore the aversion that the lurch inspired in her as they made it to the barbecue area, where their neighbors were unfolding a tablecloth over the picnic table by the grills.

Tess waved as they approached. "*Hallo!*"

Patricia gave Tess a quick hug. "You look good."

Dom glanced at Tess and quickly looked away. He was a big guy, all muscle. Not Tess's type, but there was something interesting in his permanent scowl. A challenge. He got his wallet from his back pocket and took out a business card that he handed to Paul. "This is a buddy of mine. A physical therapist, works over at the medical center."

"Thanks. Doubt I'll need it. I just need to let it rest for a few days and it'll be as good as new."

Tess caught Patricia's attention and rolled her eyes. The guys saw it, too.

"What?" Dom said. "What did I miss?"

"Nothing," Tess said.

"I don't think you were supposed to mention the *k-n-e-e*," Patricia said, and gave Paul a good-natured smile.

"What? Come on," Paul said. "No, I'm happy to have the referral. I'll wait a few days, see if it gets better, and if not, I'll give the guy a call."

"Okay, babe," Tess said, and patted her husband on the cheek. "That's going to be one *langes Warten*, I'm sure, but if you say so."

Paul pushed her hand away, and Tess had to hold her breath for a moment while a brief flash of hatred surged through her body, startling her.

Dom offered them a beer.

Tess released her breath and put up her hands in protest. "Not for me. I'm the type of drinker, one beer and, before you know it, I'm dancing on the table."

"I'd love to see that," Patricia said.

"No, you wouldn't," Paul said. "Believe me."

"*Kein Bier für mich!*" Tess said.

Dom tossed a beer to Paul. "You know we're all just here temporarily," he said to Tess. "You don't actually have to learn the language."

Tess knew he didn't like her, and for some reason this fact made her feel powerful, filled her body with adrenaline.

"*Ja?*" Tess said. "We don't really have to learn *die Sprache?*"

"Give it a rest, Tess," Paul said.

Before Tess could respond, Summer started shrieking, and all four adults looked at the kids, who were over by the swing set. Summer flailed her little body around while Charlie stood next to her with his arms raised.

"Kids!?" Patricia yelled, and started toward them.

"Summer," Paul called. "You two get over here."

Summer stopped her shrieking and got her book from where she'd left it on the swing, then she and Charlie ran over to the adults.

"We were just playing 'The Dreadful Story of Harriet and the Matches,'" Charlie said.

Summer opened *Der Struwwelpeter*. "See?" She showed them an illustration of a little girl in an old-fashioned green frock, flames shooting from the back of her hair and dress while she flung both arms and one leg into the air. A couple of cats watched her, hissing. In the illustration they looked menacing, though in the verse they were described as simply helpless.

Patricia took the book from Summer. "No, ma'am," she said. "In our house we don't read books like that."

Oh, dear god. Tess snatched the book from Patricia and placed it in the pouch of PJ's stroller. "No, you're right. We should just be reading *Anne of Green Gables*, over and over."

Patricia looked at her like she was nuts, and Dom went to the grill, lit the charcoal.

Tess was quiet for the rest of the cookout. She picked up their son, who was equally serene in the stroller as in his mother's arms, which for some reason made her feel unspeakably sad. She'd never been the type of person to have friends, especially when it came to women. Perhaps the only real friend of her life, the one she'd given her whole heart to, had been Lainey. Their breakup had hurt worse than the ending of any romantic relationship. For a long time, Tess had blamed Lainey for her inability to get close to anyone else, when all along it had been her own flaw.

Tess sat on the kids' end of the picnic table and watched Paul dispatch all his fake charm, his rare friendliness a rebuke to her. They all ate quickly and made their excuses.

While they were cleaning up, Tess said, "I never asked, how much longer are you here?"

"Not quite four months." Patricia's voice was colder now.

When she was sure no one would notice, Tess caught Dom's eye. At first, he quickly looked away, but then looked back and held contact for a moment.

※

On Sunday morning, Tess awoke disheveled. She'd stayed in the kids' room for the third night in a row. She didn't feel sick, but she'd tossed and turned all night and completely sweated through the sheets. Her hair was stiff with spit where she'd been chewing it in her sleep. After breakfast, she spent some time in the bathroom clipping all her nails, which seemed to have grown noticeably overnight. Her toenails were thick, even a little clouded. Her hair too tangled to brush. She tried to force it back into a ponytail, but the short layers kept falling into her eyes. She bunched it up, tucked it into a ball cap. Then she got the kids dressed and moved with them through the living room toward the front door. She avoided looking at Paul on the sofa huddled over his books, but she couldn't help but notice as she passed by the way he shrunk in on himself, mirroring the shrinking she felt in her own soul. They were two magnets, each repelling the other, neither willing to turn in line.

Tess almost had the apartment door closed behind them when Summer ran back and kissed her dad on the cheek. Then they left.

Past the playground and through the field, the three of them entered the German Alpine forest. They followed a path for a little while, but then made their own way through the underbrush, hopped over a brook that whispered over rocks, and stopped at a tree with a trunk so massive it seemed unreal. A thick blanket of pine needles covered the ground. Tess set PJ down. He couldn't walk yet, but he could wobble with support, and he grasped on to the thick bark with his little fists while Tess breathed in the pine air and Summer climbed onto a low branch. They weren't that far in, but already they were completely, blissfully, cut off from the base.

Some small animal rustled in the leaves nearby. On the trunk near PJ, an iridescent blue beetle landed. PJ slapped his open palm near the beetle, playfully, not trying to hurt it. Tess felt something loosen in her chest. The open palm, playfully slapping, was as much personality as PJ had really ever shown. And that was part of the problem, of course. Not just the lack of crying, but also the lack of personality. The lack of connection she felt because of it. So unlike her feisty Summer, her girl with attitude. PJ lost his balance and fell onto his butt, then scooched himself around to lean against the trunk. He began to suck his thumb.

Summer jumped off her branch, knelt in front of her little brother, and pulled his thumb from his mouth. "'*The great tall tailor always comes.*'"

PJ looked at his sister and then up at Tess. The look wasn't one of alarm, but it wasn't exactly serene, either. He put his thumb back in his mouth.

The wind blew, and though the trees shielded them, they could hear it rustling the branches above.

Tess knelt next to her daughter and loomed over her son. "Keep going, Sum."

"'*To little boys that suck their thumbs.*'"

Tess pulled PJ's thumb from his mouth, and he put it back in. "PJ, you seem upset. You seem like you wanna cry."

"'*And ere they dream what he's about, / He takes his great sharp scissors out.*'"

This time, PJ's mouth twitched into a frown before he popped his thumb back in.

"You can cry to Mama, PJ. You can cry to Mama."

"'*And cuts their thumbs clean off—and then, / You know, they never grow again.*'"

Tess held on to her son's hands, gently but firmly.

"Do you know the German now?" Tess asked her perfect daughter. She didn't know all of it, but she knew some, and some was enough.

Summer chanted, "*Lutsche nicht am Daumen mehr; / denn der Schneider mit der Scher,*" repeating it over and over, and PJ looked back and forth between his mother and his sister. Tess could feel him trying to pull his little arms from her grasp, and his strength surprised her, delighted her. Her big strong boy. She held on while Summer kept reciting, while the pine needles crackled underneath and fell around them like tiny arrows from above. His face changed. His first ever look of doubt, then his first ever anger. That's right, baby, you can do it. Mama's right here with you. So is Sissie. On a fallen log at the edge of the clearing perched a red fox, staring at them, front leg lifted at attention. Tess and Summer inched closer to PJ, crowding, chanting, holding. His face turned red. He squeezed his eyes shut, scrunched up his nose. The little chin was trembling. He was so close. Cry, just cry, baby. Come on, please. Just take everything that's bottled up inside you, gather it all, and then release it. Get out all that torment and aggression that can plague you your entire life so that you're never satisfied. Feel so much better.

Part III

Homecoming

Hintergarmisch
Thea

THEA AND THE RED FOX rested by the campfire while the lynx stalked them from the thick and wild understory. The red fox set his head on his front paws. Thea yawned, stretched her arms out above her, lay back, and looked up at the night sky's brightest star. She shifted her body to find a comfortable position for sleep, and just as she closed her eyes, the lynx pounced. Finally, they had it. Before the lynx could land, the red fox, less than half the cat's size, leapt straight for its throat. Together, the two animals struck the ground and rolled to a hard stop at the base of a massive pine. Thea thrust herself up onto her powerful legs and then crouched, ready. The lynx shook off the red fox, hissed and spit, rushed at Thea. She spun, landed a kick to the lynx's neck, hurling it into the fire. The lynx yowled a high-pitched shriek, burst from the flames, and tried to escape back into the safety of the Alpine forest. But the red fox was on it, batting ears and gouging eyes, while Thea pulled a knife from the holster attached to her leg. With one swift swipe she sliced the lynx's throat. It slumped. Dead. Immediately she hacked away a hind leg for the red fox and then got to work skinning the cat. Lynx hide would make a great addition to her overcoat of badger, deer, squirrel, and bat skins. When she was done, she tore her teeth into its flesh while gazing at her brightest star and eventually fell into a well-earned sleep.

※

The next morning, Thea worked her pelt. She removed scraps of flesh she'd missed last night and boiled roots she'd dug up to extract their salts for tanning. But then she heard the red fox, screaming his birdlike *wow-wow-wow* in the distance. She wasted no time. Smothered the fire and slung her pack on her back. She tucked the lynx through a strap on her overcoat to work later. Then she rushed through the forest, up the mountain, in the direction of her friend's cries.

When she neared, she saw that he simply stood at the edge of a gentle stream. She sensed no danger. He lowered his head and drank. She growled at him for interrupting her work. *Wow-wow-wow.* Again, he drank and then drew up his front leg at attention. Although she could not grasp what he wanted, she trusted her friend; he would not disturb her needlessly. She fought through the brambles and made her way over the roots and rocks that stood between her and the red fox. She was not thirsty, but she drank of the stream. In that instant, her entire world shifted.

The prophesy.

Thea sensed she'd possessed many lives but now could hardly recall a time she existed other than to roam this Bavarian forest, all alone until finally she befriended the red fox. Always in wait of the prophesy. Only by carrying out her life's mission would she be freed of this savage world. Her wish was to ascend and join the night's brightest star, a desire that had been with her so long it had rooted itself into her bones. She no longer questioned it. And here it began. Never once in this land had she tasted water that wasn't fishy or eggy or in some way filthy. But in this stream, the water was pure, refreshing, one sip and she wanted more, more, more. It could come from one source only: the natural spring of the prophesy.

She clicked her tongue, and she and the red fox rushed upstream, climbing higher as the water swelled from gentle to rushing, looking for the source. Neither could resist a quick sip every so often along the way. She did not know what her mission entailed, but she expected carnage. All she could do was follow the steps. Finally, after trailing the stream to the base of two Alpine mountain peaks, the water bubbled up from an underground spring. Thea and the red fox dropped to the ground and took their fill. They bathed in it. Never had they been cleaner or more refreshed. But then Thea remembered herself. Her mission. Life's purpose. The prophesy, a sacred though limited text from a young girl in need. She looked all around, and sure enough, directly to the east were fallen pines that had dropped one, two, three, four, like dominoes. The pines pointed in the precise direction they needed to follow, through a pass between the two peaks. Thea had long avoided moving in that direction because it brought them closer to town, where the most vicious predator—man—lived together in droves. But they could avoid it no longer. They must now go in search of the dwelling.

✵

The season moved toward winter as they journeyed on. At the narrow pass, three loathsome humans blocked their way. Thea and the red fox had no choice but to scale a treacherous cliff to avoid an encounter. From the ledge of the cliff, she observed them: adult man, adult woman, old man. Hacking away at the trunk of a noble spruce while they chanted prayers to a god that Thea did not hold in esteem. Normally Thea would have relished slaying these poachers and feasting on their flesh, but now she had been called to carry out her purpose. She must not be distracted. They waited two days and two nights for the humans to move on. The red fox hunted while Thea finished curing the lynx pelt before it reeked too strongly of rot, then she sewed it to the torso of her overcoat to stave off the coming cold. She sharpened stones and affixed them to the ends of sticks. Gathered the spears into a thick bundle at her back. At one lucky moment she stood at the top of the cliff and looked down on the man and woman rutting below, directly in the path of a boulder that she rolled off the edge. But it hit an outcropping and landed just to the side of its mark. After that, the humans grew agitated, packed up, left.

Thea and the red fox continued their journey through the pass with little trouble. Finally, they made it to the far side of the two tall peaks and looked down upon the land. In the distance was the town called Garmisch. Yet within the woods not too far beyond town, something she'd never seen in all her years of roaming the forest: a square cluster of fire-red trees surrounding a squat wooden structure that looked to be a shed of some sort. She was too far away to understand the exact nature of what she saw, but it could be nothing other than the dwelling of the prophesy.

"*Böse! BÖSE! BÖÖÖÖSE!!*" Thea heard a booming voice behind her and looked back to see the old man, bearded, toothless, skin thick and tanned like leather, shouting at her, pointing. The red fox zipped at the man, leapt, grasped his ear with his teeth, flailed, tore until the flesh ripped off. The man bellowed, chanted and crossed his arms in front of his body, backed up into the woods. Thea gave chase. She pulled a spear and aimed as she ran, but before she could release it, she felt a searing pain in her leg. She slammed forward to the earth.

Bear trap, torn into the meat of her calf. She roared, and the red fox screamed in turn and then darted around her in frantic circles. She pulled apart the metal teeth, only to have them clamp back tighter and snap bone. After that the trap locked shut. The old man came to her, looming, arms raised to the heavens, chanting to his god. At the same time the red fox leapt from the ground and sunk his teeth into a pulsing vein in the old man's neck, and Thea gathered her strength and released her spear into his heart. They could not be sure which of them killed him. The old man fell to his knees and then collapsed.

She heard bodies crash through the trees. Nausea welled within her. She pulled the knife from the holster on her trapped leg and began to hack away just below her knee. The man and woman burst through to the clearing where she lay, stopped, saw the dead old man, regarded her in horror. She ignored them. Though weak and loathsome, they were not the dangerous ones. Thea clicked her tongue, and the red fox helped her escape, tearing with his teeth the sinew on one side of her leg while she sawed at the other. The couple fled into the forest. Thea rested a moment, her breath fast and ragged. Then the red fox rolled a large rock to her with his nose. She propped her exposed bone onto the rock and slammed down her lower leg with all her might until it snapped. She roared, thrashed, eventually calmed, and took some hunting twine from her pack, tied off a tourniquet, and dragged herself with her arms into a cave at the base of the cliff, where she built a fire and cauterized the wound.

※

Though her leg would need much longer to heal, Thea took only a season until her stump stopped seeping fluids. Still, it smelled of decay. She ignored it. The red fox kept her fed, safe, stocked with firewood.

There was too much time with nothing to do but be still and think. Doubt about her desire to ascend invaded her soul. It was cold up there with the stars. Lonely. Perhaps ascent was not really what she wanted at all. But no, that couldn't be right. Ascent was why she existed. She must have been simply tired, run-down.

As spring arrived and the snow melted and gushed from the mountaintops, the red fox found two sturdy sticks that she fashioned with handholds for walking so they could resume their journey to the square cluster of fire-red trees surrounding the dwelling of the prophesy. The shed. Thea was in no shape to make the voyage, but what choice did she have? It, whatever it was, was her life's purpose. Her struggle. There was no other meaning. The trip down mountain took several days and she endured many tribulations. She fainted repeatedly. She developed a painful and itchy rash that blanketed her entire torso. She became half blind when a hawk swooped down and attempted to take the red fox and instead took her eye when she fought it off. A snake bit the hip of her good leg, and her skin turned a livid green around the wound. She became too feverish to wear her coat, too weak to carry it. For a while the red fox dragged it along, but there was only so much he could do. They left it splayed out over the stump of a black walnut tree for something else to find useful.

Finally they made it to the one-lane dirt road of the prophesy. There was nothing left to do but follow it, to try to fulfill destiny. Whatever it was. Help someone or something. Very likely carnage. One of her walking sticks snapped on the uneven terrain, and she fell hard. *Wow-wow-wow*, the fox wailed. Leg, eye, hip, rash. All the doubt that invaded her soul. She fought to hold on to consciousness. *Wow-wow-wow.* The red fox nudged his wet nose in her ear. The day late, sun nearly setting. She began to drag herself, clawing with her hands and thrusting with her leg, rocks tearing into her skin and dust making it so hard to breathe.

And they were there, a few feet away from the perimeter of the square cluster of strange trees: trunks and branches that appeared charred and dead but contained leaves that were fire red and vibrant with life. A windowless shed in the center. For a while there was nothing else. But then, the very moment that the sun dipped below the horizon and dusk overtook the land, the ground began to rumble and the roof of the shed caved in. Creatures poured from it in droves. A swarm of wraiths, of demons, the color of soot, droning as one giant horde, sucking the air and the light from all around. They were legion. The red fox moved his small body into Thea's and whined, quivered violently. Yet she felt an inner sense of peace that surpassed understanding, a calm she hadn't known she'd lacked. A figure emerged from the caved roof of the shed. Human girl, dazed, trailing behind her an impossibly long rope secured to her ankle. She stopped at the edge of the fire trees directly in front of Thea, looking down at her in expectation, as if she'd been waiting for this moment for so long. Thea could sense they'd known each other in a different forest, long ago in another life. The swarm undulated, waiting, beckoning. *Go,* Thea gestured to the girl, using the last of her strength to work the knot in the rope and release her, pointing away into the woods. *I am here for rescue, to take your place. I am here, willing. Go, be well,* she conveyed to her friend. The red fox looked her in her eye, pressed his cheek to hers, and licked her chin and nose. And as Thea clawed her way toward the demons of soot, the girl joined the fox and they walked off, never looking back.

As soon as she moved within the square of trees, they were upon her. Surrounding, enveloping, underneath, above, all sides. At once her body burned in an ecstatic pain and shifted from flesh to soot. Both her good eye and her missing eye were replaced with onyx like theirs. She rode the wave of the horde as they ascended the trees and perched in flocks, looking up to the sky in one pulsating mass of anticipation.

At dawn they would take her into the mouth of a silo, descend with her deep into the underworld, where it was warm and certain, where the deep roots of the fire trees fed and nourished them and were fed and nourished by them in turn. Nights in the trees, days underneath. Much, much later, the great reckoning would come to the overworld and the vast swarm of them would spill upon the earth, creatures of vengeance to reset all. But tonight, right now, dusk turned full dark and her onyx eyes took in the dazzle of the night's brightest star like never before, an eternity of worship and adoration without having to dwell lonely in sterile space. She didn't get what she'd wanted, but she'd found where she belonged. Just before she was forever freed from the relentlessness of conscious thought, she considered how strange it was to struggle, strive, fight, want her entire existence, only to find out that she could simply. Stop.

Banned

Lainey

LAINEY'S WEEKEND BAG sat by the garage door, and a pot of coffee was nearly finished brewing when a text materialized on her phone: *DON'T!!!*

Lainey was about to start the five-hour drive from Austin to west Louisiana for her dad's seventy-fifth. She hadn't been back home since she'd left for the job almost two decades ago. Amelia's ban, however, remained in effect, and for two decades it had been Lainey's main excuse for not returning home. But there were other reasons for not coming back.

Guess you told Amelia, she texted to her dad, and the dot-dot-dot danced around for a minute until: *Couldn't risk her having an episode when you drove up unannounced. Don't try to get out of coming!*

She turned off her ringer and put her phone face down on the kitchen counter. Then she poured herself a cup of coffee. Spilled drops hissed on the burner. Through the window above the sink, she watched the sunrise over Lake Austin. Leading up to the trip, she'd had a ton of nightmares, picked fights with Kevin, overlooked work meetings that she'd requested and marked on her calendar. She took a swig of coffee and gagged a little when she swallowed; she'd forgotten to add milk.

Mena, who hadn't yet gone to bed, entered the kitchen and hung back in the doorway. Three weeks ago, she'd dropped out of her second year of law school and had come to stay with them for an unspecified period of time, quickly adopting a nocturnal life. She held Lainey's miniature schnauzer in the crook of her arm. "Pepper says *auf Wiedersehen*." She moved the little dog's paw up and down in a gentle wave. The other dog, a mastiff mix, lumbered in at the sound of her voice. "Shadow says *auf, auf*."

Lainey tried to smile. She bent over and leaned her forehead on the countertop.

After a moment she felt Shadow nudge her hip with his nose and heard Mena say, "You're really disappointed in me, aren't you?"

Lainey turned her head and squinted across the room at her stepdaughter, experiencing the sort of disconnect that she sometimes felt as a stepmom. Disappointed? Mena was a twenty-eight-year-old grown woman. She'd already been fifteen when Lainey had started dating her dad, eighteen when they'd married. She'd gone away to college, graduated with a studio arts degree, and moved to Brooklyn, lived with a bunch of roommates, paid her rent bartending, and created incredibly intricate large-scale textile art mostly from found objects. A few years ago, several Brooklyn-based artists had broken into the padlocked old Domino Sugar Refinery in Williamsburg for an unsanctioned art exhibition. Lainey and Kevin had ducked under a fence and climbed through a broken window to attend. One of Mena's tapestries, a night sky packed full of lace stars, covered an entire two-story brick wall of the refinery. She'd spent eighteen months working on it, and it was by far the most dazzling piece in the show. At the end of the night, she had set it on fire. The entire room watched it blaze, and

Lainey had stood clutching tightly to Kevin's hand, silently crying in the dark room. The last time she had felt that moved by art had been listening to her sister play the piano when they were girls. Such a long time ago. All this to say that no, Lainey wasn't disappointed. Maybe a little judgy, because it was obvious to anyone that Mena should have never gone to law school—she was an artist—but judgy was different from disappointed. Lainey loved Mena very much, but from a polite distance because they were only thirteen years apart in age, and Mena already had a perfectly functioning mother.

After a while, Lainey sighed. "Of course I'm not disappointed." And then, without really thinking, she said, "What's happening for me, if you must know, is that I'm having my first real nervous breakdown."

Mena, suddenly interested, put the little dog on the countertop, and her nails clicked as she scampered over to Lainey. "Oh. You want to tell me about it?"

Lainey stood and picked up Pepper, putting a hand on Shadow's neck so he didn't feel left out. "Oh, it's just my dysfunctional family. My dad really wants me there for his birthday, but my sister doesn't want me to come. I don't want to get into it."

"Well," Mena said, "I've been wanting to say: I don't have a heck of a lot going on right now, if you think having company would help."

Lainey withheld another sigh. Mena had grown up with professional parents in a world of education and culture and vacations, and Lainey could picture her carefully neutral expression when they drove together onto the dirt road and passed the trailer park to get to the house where Lainey grew up. Lainey imagined Amelia peering at them, paranoid, from behind a curtain while they parked, and then hiding away for the whole visit. Lainey came close to saying, Don't worry about it, but instead said, "Yeah, I'd love company." She saw a light enter Mena's eyes that had been missing lately.

⁕

They got onto Highway 71 and had about eighty miles before they hit I-10 in Columbus, which would take them almost the rest of the way. Lainey drove it in silence, both hands on the steering wheel, breathing in through her nose, out through her mouth. She had kissed Kevin goodbye, and his enthusiasm for Mena joining Lainey on the road trip had energized her momentarily, but then quickly wore off on the road. She couldn't shake the feeling that something terrible would happen if she visited home, a feeling that had stopped her from going all the other times she'd tried over the years. Her sister's bans were powerful—Amelia hadn't been able to function without them while they were growing up, so the family had always treated them as reality. But this time her dad had insisted—so unlike him—said he had some news he'd share only in person. Which of course made her think he was dying, and then what would happen to her sister?

Her vision narrowed to a tunnel. She picked out a station wagon driving just under the speed limit and followed it closely all the way to Columbus, where she stopped at a gas station before they got on the interstate. She woke Mena to use the restroom. As she filled up the gas tank, she looked at all the texts that had come through from her sister: *Don't. Don't. DON'T!* Over the years, Amelia had extended her ban to include Pinecreek, their parish, the entire state. How could she do that to her own sister?

When Mena came out of the convenience store, she was loaded up with supplies—Snickers, Doritos, Nerds, two Smartwaters, Ziploc bags, a pad of paper, and a pen—and had the giddy manner of a little girl who was getting away with something. She put the waters in their cupholders, threw the junk food in the back seat, and put the Ziplocs, pen, and paper in her lap. She pulled something from the pocket of her dress.

"Look at this," she said. She uncrumpled a piece of cloth and smoothed it out on the dashboard. It was a patch, ragged and dingy gray, with "Gigi" stitched in red. "I saw this hanging off the cashier's shirt. By a single thread, if you can believe it. So I just asked her, 'Can I have that?' She looked at me like I was insane, but then she snapped it off and handed it over, just like that."

Mena flipped open the cover on her pad of paper and wrote: *8:43 a.m., April 17, Star Stop 71 gas station—*

"What city are we in?"

"Columbus."

Columbus, Tx. With Lainey on road trip to La. Saw this hanging off cashier's shirt <u>by one single thread</u>. She handed it over on request without speaking.

Mena held the "Gigi" patch to a rare, tattoo-free area of skin on her upper arm. "Might be good enough to make the collection," she said, then zipped the name tag and the paper into the baggie and beamed up at Lainey. "All good?"

Lainey showed the young artist some teeth, the best she could do, and pulled away from the gas station, feeling nauseated, feeling like she could barely manage a breath, her head hurting so badly she had to squint to get on the interstate. But once she pulled onto the entrance ramp and got moving on I-10, the strangest thing happened: her body relaxed, her senses sharpened, she felt great. Night and day. Maybe it was Mena's enthusiasm, this rare gift of one-on-one bonding, or the idea of seeing her family again after so many years or even believing once and for all that her sister banning her from visiting home wasn't some unbreakable spell. It wasn't real.

She put on some music and settled in for the long ride ahead.

※

Two and a half hours farther down I-10, Lainey found a local NPR station that was re-airing a segment with Yusuf Islam, the artist formerly known as Cat Stevens. They were interviewing him and playing music from his new album.

Mena stirred beside her and sat up, brushing her hair back out of her face. "I need to pee again soon."

Lainey turned the volume down a little bit. "I'll look for the next exit. We could get an early lunch, too, before we cross into Louisiana. This is Cat Stevens. Do you know his stuff?"

Mena didn't answer. She was staring out her window and then turned around in her seat to peer out the back.

"'Peace Train'? 'Moonshadow'? Literally anything on the *Harold and Maude* soundtrack?"

"Lainey?"

Something in Mena's voice made Lainey's heart pound. She tried to ignore it. "My sister used to sing Cat Stevens all the time," she said. "Our mom was such a mega-fan. Our whole family loved him."

"Lainey? That sign just said Kerrville. Did you not notice that we're in the Hill Country? That the sun's at our back? That we're going the wrong way down I-10?"

Lainey's fingers began to tingle. She leaned forward in her seat and turned the volume up to maximum, and Mena covered her ears, and the interviewer said, "*Do you think you may have benefited by taking a few years off from the industry?*" and Cat Stevens answered, "*Absolutely, I don't drink, I don't*"—and Mena switched off the radio, and Lainey took the exit and pulled to the shoulder of the access road and put the car in park.

"Damn, Lainey," Mena said. "You really are having a nervous breakdown, aren't you?"

※

Mid-afternoon, they pulled back into their neighborhood in Austin. They had driven a four-hundred-mile triangle. Lainey knew Kevin was working from home, since he had the house to himself, and she would have to walk in there right now and explain herself. She stopped the car a couple of houses before their own. She and Mena had both been quiet on the drive back, even during lunch, but now she said, "You know I love your dad very much, right?"

Mena turned to look at her. "You don't want to go home right now, do you?"

Lainey shook her head.

"I get it. My dad's the type of person who has never turned the wrong way on the highway."

Instead of going home, they decided to check into a rental cabin on Lake Austin, just a few miles from their house. The day had turned hot, and Lainey sat out on their screened-in porch with the door open so she could feel the breeze off the water. She texted Kevin a double pink heart emoji to his *Don't forget to have fun!* Then she texted her dad to say that she wouldn't be there today after all. Right away, he called, but she declined it, so he texted back, *Don't let Amelia get to you. I need you to come and you know I don't ask a lot.* Typical Dad.

Mena was gone for a while but came back with shopping bags. "I'm taking complete care of you. I'm stocked up, and I'm cooking you a gourmet dinner."

She riffled through one of the shopping bags and found a pair of cuticle scissors that she tore from the package. Then she inspected the porch screen until she found an excess piece hanging loose from where it was connected to the window frame. She cut off a little section and logged it and put it in a Ziploc. Lainey took a sprig of wildflowers from a vase on the side table and handed it to Mena. She logged that, too.

After dinner, Mena sat with Lainey on the swing, and they shared a six-pack of Lone Star. Mena opened a bottle and put the cap in one of the plastic baggies she had in her pocket. "I'll log that in later," she said. "You want to tell me what's going on?"

"I feel like I'm the one who should be asking you," Lainey said.

Mena groaned. "Please, don't. Really, the reason I'm staying with you guys and not my mom is that she starts crying every time she sees me and says, 'What's wrong? What's wrong with my baby?!' At least with my dad, I know he'll wait for me to talk. I just have to endure his looks."

Lainey sighed and leaned down to get another beer.

"If you don't want to tell me what's going on, that's fine," Mena said. "I have to say, though, you never talk about your family. I mean, I met your dad briefly at your wedding, I know your mom died when you were young and that you have a sister, but you don't talk about them."

Lainey thought back to last Thanksgiving when they all—she and Kevin, Mena, Mena's mom and her husband—had dinner together, as they did occasionally. She could picture her own perfect posture, hands folded neatly on the table, attentive and pleasant the whole time. Chitchatting but never offering anything real. Polite. If she was honest with herself, she acted this way any time Mena was around, receding so as not to detract from father-daughter time. From time with *real* family.

"Hold this. I need to show you something," Lainey said, and handed Mena her beer. She went in the cabin to her suitcase and unzipped the inside pocket, pulled out the letter from her sister that she'd kept all these years.

She climbed back onto the swing, handed the envelope to Mena, and shined her phone flashlight so Mena could see in the dimming room. Mena pulled the letter from the envelope, and a couple of paper cutouts of musical notes came out with it and fell to her lap.

Amelia's long, slanted print brought Lainey back to the last time she'd really insisted on going to visit. She and Kevin were engaged and had just returned from an entire month in Italy. By that point she hadn't seen her sister in almost ten years, and enough was enough. She'd go and make Amelia accept her back into her life, convince her to attend the wedding. But then this letter arrived by FedEx the day before the visit. Lainey had read it through once, immediately stored it away, and canceled her trip. She hadn't tried to go back since.

> Dear Lainey,
>
> **DON'T** forget you're the love of my life. **EVER** look deep within yourself and question your soul? **COME** to terms, as I have, that sacrifices must be made. **BACK** then it was just the two of us against everyone else. **TO** the future, though, is where we should look. **LOUISIANA**, you made clear, is not the place for you. **YOU** hath awakened from the dream of life, Lainey! **ARE** you remembering when we saw that etched into the cross? **BANNED** forever from this world so that you might thrive in the next.
>
> xoxo forever,
> Amelia

Mena read the words that stood out, capitalized and bolded with many layers of ink: "'Don't. Ever. Come. Back. To. Louisiana. You. Are. Banned.'" Then she turned over the letter and looked at the back, where Amelia had cut out little paper musical notes and pasted them onto a hand-drawn staff.

"It's part of Beethoven's 'Für Elise.' She's—"

"A really talented pianist. You have mentioned that." Mena folded up the letter and put it in the envelope. She gathered the loose musical notes and was about to drop them in the envelope, but Lainey said, "You can keep one if you want," and Mena picked out a delicate sixteenth note and placed it carefully in a baggie.

"Another beer while you tell me what's up?" Mena said, and Lainey stretched out her hand to receive the offering.

※

The next morning they were on their way to Louisiana again, Mena driving this time. Lainey leaned her seat back, stared out the sunroof, and tried to calm her racing heart. Mena had downloaded all the episodes of a podcast called *Hellseer*, about a psychic in New Orleans named Madame Trinae. Lainey had meant to listen to it—some friends at work were obsessed—but she hadn't gotten around to it. But three episodes in, passing Beaumont, she barely paid any attention.

"I don't think I can do this," she said, but she'd whispered it, and the volume on the podcast made it too loud for Mena to hear.

In no time, they were bypassing Orange, and Lainey began to drip with sweat. She closed the windows and maxed out the AC. She could now see the bridge that spanned the Sabine, the river that marked the border between Texas and Louisiana. On the podcast, Madame Trinae, who was hosting a French Quarter jazz trio, suddenly spoke in a voice that seemed directed at Lainey, cutting through her haze: "*I'm originally from a small town in west Louisiana. Very rural, very insular. And I found, once I left, it wasn't possible to go back. Now if you think about—*" Lainey clicked the radio off, and the sudden lack of sound packed the car, making the space feel claustrophobic.

They passed the Texas Travel Information Center on the left. Just up ahead, seconds away, was the final Texas exit. Lainey yelled, "Pull over!" and Mena said, "What? I can't," and Lainey said, "PULL OVER PULL OVER PULL OVER," and lunged for the steering wheel.

Mena pulled off at the last possible second, and the car fishtailed but straightened out. They took the U-turn to the left under the interstate. As soon as they were going west again, Lainey could breathe. And then they were parked at the visitor center.

※

That night they stayed at a motel in a rural Texas town about twenty miles from the Louisiana border and about forty miles from where Lainey's dad and sister lived. It was hard to believe she had come so close. And yet she could go no farther.

While Lainey had paced around the visitor center, Mena handled everything: motel reservation, calling Lainey's dad to break it to him that they wouldn't be there for his birthday after all, texting Kevin that all was well but that they were officially "off the grid" and they'd see him when they saw him.

As soon as they checked in, Lainey crawled into one of the two double beds, pulled the sheets and floral comforter over her head, and slept. She woke up at dinner time when Mena opened the door carrying a pizza box and a small bottle of tequila.

Mena had spent the day out collecting things, and she laid it all out on the other bed and logged it while they had a few slices of decent pepperoni. They passed the tequila bottle back and forth for little sips. They were quiet for a long time until Mena finished her work and packed it carefully away. Then Mena told Lainey how things had ended for her in law school. She'd plagiarized a paper, but since her dad was an "alum of the year" and a "very important person"—she said these sarcastically using air quotes—they asked if she'd like to quit before they expelled her. She'd been plagiarizing all semester, and they'd pretended not to notice until she made it so blatant that it was impossible for them to look the other way.

"Oh, Mena," Lainey said.

Mena suddenly seemed annoyed. "Are you disappointed now?"

"'Disappointed' assumes that I have some sort of greater wisdom. I don't."

Mena shot Lainey a dirty look.

"Do you want me to be disappointed?" Lainey said. "I mean, I'm definitely feeling a little like 'WTF, fellow human,' but that's different."

"Sure, Lainey. If WTF is what I can get from you, I'll take it."

Lainey didn't know what to say. She couldn't figure out why Mena seemed angry with her all of a sudden. Clearly there was a way to be there for your loved ones that a large part of humanity seemed to have figured out. But not Lainey. She hadn't known how to give Amelia what she needed then, and she didn't know how to give Mena what she needed now.

Mena turned on the TV and found a channel that was airing a Hitchcock movie marathon. Then she got into bed with Lainey and sat with her, shoulder to shoulder, while they finished the rest of the tequila and watched the second half of *The Birds*.

The next morning, head splitting from the cheap alcohol and mouth cottony from dehydration, Lainey looked forward to being done with this failure of a trip. But once they packed up after breakfast and got on the road, Mena bypassed the entrance to the highway.

"What are you doing?" Lainey said.

"I just thought we could spend a little time in nature today. Trust me, we're not leaving Texas, okay? So you can relax."

"I want to go home, Mena."

"We will, don't worry."

Lainey had no more energy to protest, so within half an hour they were parked in the nearly empty lot of a Baptist church that was situated next to some woods. When they got out of the car, Lainey could hear organ music through the walls, someone practicing inside. They didn't have cell service here, but Mena was able to pull up the GPS on her phone, and Lainey could see that their blinking blue dot wasn't far off from a red pin next to the Sabine River.

"There should be a trail over there," Mena said, pointing to a shed at the corner of the lot. She set out, and Lainey followed, going along, enduring whatever Mena had planned for one last day. She trudged through the brush and slipped on some moss when she tried to climb over a log that had fallen in their path. She picked herself up and kept going.

After a little while, she could hear the rush of the river ahead of them. And then she could see it, wide, the water clear and rushing over large, flat rocks. Shallow enough to walk across. And there it was—Louisiana—right in front of them, woods, dirt, shore, all exactly the same as on their side.

At the water, Mena looked around and rechecked the GPS. She seemed lost. But then she yelled out, "Hello?! Can you hear me?" and right away a voice in the distance called back to them.

"Is that . . . ?" Lainey said.

They went in the direction of the voice. They had to skirt the shore around a bend and push through a thick tangle of shrubs, but then they were at a clearing, and sure enough, he was there, across the shore. Lainey's dad. Too far away to see completely clearly, but still, she'd known the pitch of his voice, and she recognized the way he stood with his hips jutting slightly forward in his green plaid shirt and jeans. The trees were thicker on his side. No clearing like theirs. He was alone.

"He looks healthy," Mena said. "He looks better than when I saw him ten years ago."

He did. He looked bigger, stronger, not the same stooped, defeated man who had showed up briefly at her wedding, eroding a little of the joy she'd felt on that day. He certainly didn't seem like he was dying.

Her dad called out to them, but the river drowned out his voice. She and Mena cupped their hands to their ears. Instead, he threw something, underhand, and it sailed high over the river and dropped in the water close to their shore. Mena snatched it up before the river could carry it off. She handed it to Lainey. Wrapped in a trash bag and then a dish towel was an old walkie-talkie, just like the ones she'd shared with Amelia when they were little.

Lainey turned it on, and it crackled, and then, "Well, hey, kiddo. Over."

Lainey sat cross-legged on the sand, and Mena sat beside her.

"Hey, Dad. I'm sorry I missed your birthday. Over."

"It's okay. Over."

On the other shore, he was gesturing toward the trees, saying something, and then a woman walked out from behind a wide trunk. She was tall, overweight, dressed in a long black T-shirt and khaki shorts. Her thick white legs were so pasty that they almost had an inner glow against the brown-gray-green of the shore and tree trunks. How often did she get out of the house? Her blond hair was long, stringy, and she kept it in her face, completely obscuring her eyes as she shuffled over toward their father.

Lainey's chest felt so tight she thought she might suffocate. She heard a soft cry escape her and then Mena's hand was in hers, squeezing tight.

The woman across the river, her sister, Amelia, would be thirty-five now. When Lainey had left home, Amelia was only fifteen. Lainey had practically raised her and then never saw her again. Not even a picture because her sister, wary of cameras, wouldn't allow it.

"Hi, Mena," Lainey's dad said over the walkie-talkie. "Can you introduce yourself? I know we've met, and really good to see you again. But if you could just, you know, say who you are so Amelia can know you, too? Over."

Amelia stood on the other side of the shore, her back to them, near enough to the walkie-talkie so she could hear, but tensed up like she might bolt at any second.

"Of course. I'm Mena, Kevin's daughter. Lainey's my stepmom. So good to meet you. Over."

"Thanks for helping arrange this, Mena. So the plan is for you two sisters to be able to see each other, even though Lainey can't come to Louisiana and Amelia can't leave. And there's no reason why that can't happen here on these rocks where the water's fairly gentle."

The woman across the shore shook her head violently. Took a few steps away before their dad put out his arm to stop her. Static sounded through the walkie-talkie. Lainey wanted so badly not to be where she was, so badly to run away from this river. Mena's fingernails cut into the back of her hand.

"But, of course, for that to happen, there need to be some ground rules." Their dad kept pausing to listen to Amelia. "She's thinking that if I don't leave the shore . . . and, well, if you don't bring Mena, don't let Mena leave the shore . . . um, and the two of you don't meet right away, wait until the sun comes over these trees, and the two of you don't talk when you're out there on the water, then maybe it can work. Over."

The woman across the shore knelt down, her back still to the water, and cradled her head in her arms, the same way the little girl Lainey had grown up with used to do when she was stressed, overwhelmed. That little girl, who had always needed to give something up to allow for something else. No more toys so she could handle school. No more sleeping for a certain hour in the middle of the night and no more eating anything but the blandest foods so she could handle her piano lessons. Eventually, heartbreakingly, no more Lainey, or she wouldn't see a doctor and threatened to give up every single thing one by one until there was nothing left. They'd all pretended as long as they could that things were manageable, until pretending wasn't an option anymore.

"Lainey." Mena was speaking gently to her. "Maybe you can help her out?"

Lainey picked up the walkie-talkie. "Hi, Amelia," she said, and saw her sister raise her head at the sound of her voice. "That all sounds good to me. I'm also thinking that if I don't come out there until you have a chance to pick the best spot, and we don't wear shoes and don't let ourselves get too wet above the shoulders . . ."

Amelia stood, turned sideways, brushed the hair back out of her face.

"If we don't run away, don't shout, don't cry, don't react at all if the water's a little cold, and don't mind if we see some fish, then we can sit on the rocks together quietly, and I can put my arm around you while the water rushes over our laps. Over."

Lainey watched her sister and her dad talk for a moment, and then her dad hugged his younger daughter. "Sounds like we have a deal. When the sun's overhead, which should be in a little less than an hour. Over."

She regarded her father, looking so strong. "Dad, are you dying? Because you don't look like you are dying . . . Over."

A pause, and then his voice came from across the river: "No, Lainey, I'm getting married, and I thought that telling you in person would be a good excuse to get you two girls back together. And here you are, back together. But we'll talk on the phone in the next few days, and I'll tell you all about it. Over and out."

Lainey's dad was getting married to a woman she'd never met. He was healthy, happy, but he wouldn't be around forever, and then what would happen?

Lainey spotted a lizard close enough to touch. She reached out slowly and offered her hand. Improbably, it hopped right on and scurried to the front of her shirt. She also saw a piece of cloth, a scrunchie, that was packed into the dirt. She dug it up and held it out to Mena. Mena gave it a disgusted look and then said, "Awesome," and pulled some supplies from her pocket to log it.

"Sometimes the only way to get out of an unworkable situation is by force," Lainey said.

Mena wrote in her notepad and tore out the page. "Yeah, I know."

"At least you forced your own way out. I made someone else do it for me."

Lainey and Mena both looked across to the other shore where Amelia was dipping a toe, testing the water.

"I mean, anyone can see you're an artist and not a lawyer. And you know what? I think plagiarizing your way out of that situation was really brave."

Mena shook her head at Lainey. "Oh my god, woman. Just admit you're disappointed and we can move on."

"Never," Lainey said, and they both laughed. "Do you know what you're making yet?"

Mena zipped the scrunchie and the piece of paper into a Ziploc. "I have some ideas. But it's way too early in the process to discuss it."

"Okay," Lainey said. "Just promise me that I can be there when you burn it down."

Soon enough the sun was shining down over the treetops, and Amelia moved out onto the rocks. Lainey gave her sister a chance to pick the best spot. When Amelia looked up to indicate that it was time, Lainey removed her shoes and stepped into the river. The water was quite cold, but of course Lainey didn't react. She stepped carefully across the slippery rocks since they weren't to allow themselves to get too wet above the shoulders. Finally, she made it to her sister. They didn't shout. They didn't cry. They didn't run away. Instead, they faced upstream and lowered themselves to sit on the long, flat stone that Amelia had found, just big enough for the two of them. The water rushed over their laps, and Lainey put her arm around her little sister, who allowed herself to be held. Their breathing quickly fell in sync. And they were there, together, with the cold water and the sun-warmed air and the smell of pine trees and the great big blue sky. At one point they noticed a school of tiny fish dart at their feet, but it was okay. Neither of them minded, not at all.

Jesus & Booze

Olivia

FOR SEVEN YEARS, Valerie has told Olivia she wants to go to Louisiana with her. For seven years, Olivia has ignored the request. She doesn't like her hometown, and the only time she's been back before today was four years ago when her dad died, a trip she'd insisted on taking alone. Yesterday, Olivia booked a last-minute one-way ticket from Atlanta to Lake Charles, packing a bag so large that it alarmed Valerie, who once again was not invited. Olivia said she just needed some time, given everything, and as usual, Valerie completely understood.

Her mom, whom she called only this morning when she was boarding her six a.m. flight to ask for an airport pickup, wasn't so thrilled with the late notice. But of course she picked her up, with barely enough time to head straight to Pinecreek Family Worship Center for Sunday services. They scoot into their second-row pew while the congregation around them raises their hands to Jesus and sings, *Holy, holy, holy*. Olivia mouths the lyrics. This is the church she attended in high school after her mother became born again, and the church where her dad's funeral services took place even though he was a self-proclaimed atheist. She's always felt out of place here. She'd never bring Valerie—they'd be unwelcome even if no one said so directly. A large box of a room, very plain and packed with worshippers, with five double rows of pews, worn beige carpeting, an American flag next to a large wooden cross in the corner, amateur stained glass in the two windows framing the pulpit. Without a doubt, she'd rather be home with Valerie, in their sweet little 1920s bungalow in Decatur, but she's determined to make them both miserable for a while. Olivia is tired of herself, which in turn makes her tired of Valerie. Or at least tired of how being with Valerie makes her feel about herself. It's all confusing and it's all too much.

The congregation sits, and Pastor David starts in on a prayer that Olivia has enough experience to know will go on forever. Everyone's head is bowed, and as she has so often in the past, Olivia takes the opportunity to look around. She scans the backs of the heads in the pew in front of her until her eyes settle on someone she knows. Or knew. What the hell was her name? Minnie Thompson. She recognizes her dark, thin hair and the way her ears stick out—still. Minnie never grew into them. She's holding an infant, has two toddlers squirming for space on her lap, and has a row of children and teens sitting next to her, all with the same hair and the same protruding ears. Lainey counts. Nine. Minnie Thompson has nine freaking kids.

"Jesus Christ," Olivia says under her breath, and her mother nudges her with her elbow and squeezes her eyes shut tighter.

Pastor David continues apologizing for all manner of sins and imploring the holy father to grant copious personal favors while Olivia looks away from the unreasonably large family and around at the rest of the room. Her mother and her friends who share their pew all sway their bodies, so overcome by Jesus devotion they can't sit still. Past them are faces that are familiar, vaguely familiar, and unfamiliar.

Then she cranes her body all the way around until she locks eyes with a woman standing in the very back

Her breath catches, and she can feel herself flush. Not in a million years would she have expected to catch Nora inside a church. But there she stands, looking like she's barely aged at all. She has a surprising hairstyle, chemically straightened clavicle-length hair dyed a color Olivia can only pinpoint as magenta, but although on anyone else it would be tacky, somehow it works. Looks kind of hot. Olivia can't believe how her body's responding to the presence of this woman she hasn't seen in twenty years. She fidgets through Pastor David's surprisingly tolerant though bland sermon on unconditional love, puts twenty dollars in the tithing basket, stands for more hymns, sits through a closing prayer, and then tries to think how best to avoid Nora but also how best to orchestrate a run-in without being obvious.

Outside the church, a few people greet her, but no one seems happy to see her. It's a gray June day, overcast and humid, lovebugs not as bad as she's seen them in the past but still flitting all around. While her mom socializes, Olivia catches Nora's magenta hair on the far end of the lawn huddled together with a group of people who are all looking Olivia's way. Unfriendly. Angry even.

Then Nora detaches herself from the group and starts walking over. That's when she sees it. Can't believe she was so stupid. This isn't Nora.

"Olivia," Nora's daughter says.

"Kasey."

Olivia asks how she is and how her mother is. The response is rapid: Kasey teaches high school science, which surprises Olivia since that means Kasey went to college. She's married to a guy who drives a tow truck, and they have one kid. As for her mom—Nora waited until Kasey finished school and then trained to become an EMT. She works the night shift at an ambulance service and likes it just fine. There is a long pause, and Olivia expects to be asked how she's doing, but instead, Kasey asks her to walk with her to a new place called Dawn's for brunch, though the invitation isn't particularly friendly. "What is it you used to say? How there's only two things to do in this small town. Jesus or booze."

"I said that?" Olivia's mind cartwheels back, trying to remember. Wasn't it Nora who always said that? She looks over a little helplessly at her mom, who she can tell is assessing the situation even as she's listening to one of her friends.

Kasey lets out a short laugh. "But guess what? We can do both. Jesus and booze. Dawn's makes a solid Bloody Mary."

They cut behind the church, and Kasey opens a gate to take them through someone's back pasture. It's all so strange. Olivia's fairly certain that before today, Kasey has never spoken directly to her. She always either gave her the silent treatment when they were alone or addressed her mother like Olivia wasn't in the room. They wind their way past grazing cows and around a series of sheds holding cords of firewood. About ten minutes in, Olivia's beginning to wonder if Kasey has something in mind for them other than brunch. But then she sees a dirt road, and once they get to it, there's the restaurant in the distance.

Dawn's is a converted barn, modern, pretty nice actually, tables downstairs and an open loft area with pool tables. Robert Earl Keen's playing on the jukebox, and Olivia can hear and smell bacon sizzling on the griddle. Even though there's a line for a seat, Kasey talks to the host, and they're taken immediately to a booth in the back corner. The energy in the room seems to shift in their direction for a moment, and then it goes back to normal. Right away, a teenage waitress comes to take their order, and it's yet another thin-haired, stick-out-eared offspring of Minnie Thompson. Given the resemblance there is no question about that. Kasey recommends the chilaquiles, and that sounds fine to Olivia. Kasey orders them each a Bloody Mary, and Olivia doesn't complain, though she's not much of a day drinker. When the waitress walks off, a silence settles over their table that eventually becomes so awkward Olivia has to break it.

"Am I crazy, or does Minnie Thompson have like ten kids?"

"You mean the Landrys? She married Brandon Landry. Yeah, they have a big family."

"A big family?" Olivia shakes her head. "That's the understatement of the year. God, Minnie's been popping them out her whole adult life."

Kasey's face darkens. "Wow, you haven't changed at all."

"Oh, come on, Kasey. You have to admit that's a lot of babies to drop, even for Pinecreek."

"You're such a jerk the way you talk about other people. You always were superior. There are consequences for that shit."

Olivia's trying to think how to respond to something like that—remembering how much Nora loved to dish, consuming Olivia's high school gossip like shots at a bar—when an eight ball smashes into their booth from one of the pool tables above, denting the wood. Olivia flinches. Kasey picks it up and marches up to the loft, telling some guy off who just keeps saying *"sorry, sorry, sorry."*

After that, the Bloody Marys come. Kasey holds hers up, and they clink glasses. "Here's to Jesus and booze."

Olivia cocks her head questioningly. With that, Kasey sets the record straight. Tells her how when Olivia last visited four years ago, she stayed up with a group of people and just started shitting all over the place, making fun of the town, of the people, performing a mocking impression of the pastor, going on and on until everyone finally decided they hate her.

"But, Kasey, I didn't even see you last time I was here."

"Yes, that's my point. I heard about it. Consequences."

Olivia hesitates in responding. The way she remembers it is that she was grieving the loss of a father she never had much of a relationship with, and Pastor David delivered an aggressive sermon about heaven being a place for believers—in other words, not a place for her father. The church funeral was solely for her mother's benefit. She'd been very pissed off and remembers the people who stayed up with her laughing with her about it all. She tries to explain to Kasey, but Kasey cuts her off. "It really doesn't matter."

While they sip their Bloody Marys, rather than sit in more silence Olivia goes ahead and tells Kasey about her life, which is the story of her life with Valerie. How they met in business school, rode their bicycles across the entire United States, lived in Chicago for a while as Valerie's career took off and Olivia's faltered, moved to Costa Rica for Valerie's career, moved to Atlanta for Valerie's career. How Olivia most recently worked for a third-rate mortgage company but lost that job, too, after a few bad performance reviews. How something had flipped in her several years back, and she simply lost the ability to pretend that the work she'd been doing was important. How sometimes she thinks she'd like to just get a job at their local coffee shop for the employee discounts and do the things she loves the rest of the time. How leaving on this trip was a way to punish Valerie.

"Olivia." Kasey leans back in her seat and gives her an incredulous look. "Olivia."

"What?"

"You're telling me there's a person in this world who can not only stand you but who actually loves you? Who's at home most likely pining away for you as we speak? I don't know how that's even possible, but I got to ask, why are you here?"

"You invited me, I believe. Jesus and booze, remember?"

"No, I mean in Pinecreek. What are you doing here?"

Minnie Thompson's tenth child interrupts them with their order. While they eat their chilaquiles, the restaurant's loud buzz takes over for a time, and neither speaks. But then Kasey lays her fork down and tells Olivia how intensely she couldn't stand whatever was going on between her and her mom back in the day, how deeply uncomfortable they made her, and how she'd felt that Olivia—and sometimes both of them—would rather she had just disappeared.

Olivia remembers. "All right. I can admit I was really immature, and honestly, I'm still confused about all that went down with me and Nora. I mean, I was pretty much a kid back then. But were you like scared I was going to turn your mom into a lesbian or something?"

"Oh, fuck off, Olivia. No, if I was scared of anything, it was that someone was going to steal her away. And sure, in that short window of time you two were doing your thing, that someone was you. Do you know how hard it was to get her to even pay attention to me back then?"

Olivia opens her mouth to argue, but honestly, Kasey has a point. Olivia would absolutely have stolen Nora away if it had been an option. "Kasey, I—"

"Were you in love with her?"

"Hell, I don't know. Maybe. I was scheming for a way to get her to move with me when I left for college."

"Yes, I heard. We laughed hard about that one."

Olivia turns up one corner of her mouth but otherwise ignores the comment. "I mean, did you know exactly how you felt back when you were seventeen? Look, I get that Nora was the adult in the room, but like, she got knocked up at fourteen, and I felt I really wanted to take care of her. Wanted to be the support she never had growing up. It's crazy, but I really knew I could be if she would just let me."

Kasey scoffs, takes hold of the saltshaker and spins it in place.

"So, I guess, yeah. I think Nora was the first person I was ever in love with, as weird as it is to be sitting here telling you that."

Kasey narrows her eyes at Olivia. "And did she love you back, do you think?"

At this Olivia is speechless. The two of them, she and Nora, did share something, she's certain of it, but the way Kasey's looking at her keeps her from speaking.

"Because she didn't, Olivia. Believe me. She was bored, you were amusing for a little while, end of story."

"Okay," Olivia says. Her chest feels tight.

"She used to mock you when you weren't around, talking in this deep, manly voice." Kasey tucks her chin and demonstrates: "*I'm Olivia, I'm perfect, and I will do whatever you say.* I mean, we'd both do it. *I'm Olivia and—*"

"Hey," Olivia says, reaching over and stilling Kasey's trembling hand. She takes the saltshaker and places it back at the edge of the table. It's as if the touch has woken Kasey from a trance. Olivia sees her jaw muscles relax as her eyes tear up. She also sees the scared preteen, the one she never really considered at all, sitting across from her, still alive today inside this woman. They stay like that while the jukebox switches to some country song Olivia's never heard, with lyrics about guns, pickup trucks, God's country. The pool balls clack overhead.

Finally, Kasey uses her wrist to wipe at her eyes and says, "Give me your phone."

"What? No."

"Just give it to me. I want to get out of here, but I need to make a quick call and mine died a little while ago."

Olivia takes out her phone, unlocks it, and hands it over, too worn down to protest. Kasey tells her she's heading outside for reception, and then she's off. Olivia takes the last sip of her Bloody Mary, gets a mouthful of pepper and Tabasco, and chokes it down. She's alone for so long she wonders if Kasey stole her phone and left her there. She thinks about this place, Pinecreek, how the people make no sense to her and vice versa, and how there really is nothing left for her here. The knowledge that she'll probably never return leaves her with an ache in her chest that surprises her.

She goes ahead and pays their brunch bill, and as she's signing for the tip, Kasey returns, telling her that she checked and there are still flights available for later today. Before she walks off for good, she puts Olivia's phone face up on the table, the screen revealing a new text exchange:

Olivia:	Hey. I'm coming back today. Is that okay?
Valerie:	oh wow, u sure?
	i mean fuck yeah. i've been miserable but i know i'm so needy, Liv
Olivia:	I'm the needy one, believe me.
Valerie:	u ok? u seem off
Olivia:	I'm getting a bad feeling. Like hostility vibes. Like something might happen to me if I stay. I want to come home.
Valerie:	???
	oh my god
	can I call u
Olivia:	No, no.
	This place is so backwoods. Jesus & booze, you know?
Valerie:	... wut?
Olivia:	Sorry, I'm just upset. Sitting in a loud restaurant waiting for my mom to pick me up for the airport. I have an early evening flight. I'll call you when I get through security and tell you when I'm supposed to land.

Valerie: ok. love u

Olivia: Valerie, can you tell me why? What do you love about me?

Valerie: ha! sure. you're funny, witty, you're a shit talker

Olivia: What else?

Valerie: you make me feel safe. you make me feel strong

Olivia: Keep going. What else what else what else what else?

Valerie: you sit on the porch swing with old ms. whitehead and tolerate her thousands of hours of stories
you let shannon's 4 yr old decide your halloween costume and went as a fork
you're good at everything you try and don't waste your time trying things that don't interest you
you're awesome in bed
you handle all our finances
you're learning to play trumpet which is so so cute
you're the only reason we're ever on time
you made me face all my shit I never thought I could
you charm my coworkers and make them believe I'm the greatest
you keep our plants alive!!
you do all the cooking and like it
you let me pick out the music
you painted the trim of our house a delightful pale yellow and I catch a little smile on your face every time we get home and you notice it
babe? you still there?
i can keep going. i can write a multivolume encyclopedia on the topic
liv?

Sistercreature

Gail

GAIL LEFT HER Tribeca condo in the early morning hours. She rode the elevator twelve floors down to the lobby and slipped past the doorman slumped in his chair, asleep. She envied him. Since Kate cut her off a few months ago, she hadn't been sleeping much. Two to three hours a night. Which was cluttering up her brain, giving it too much time in the day to think, think, think, but not enough recovery to stave off the debris of her past.

Later that same day, in the evening, she was running an event with an enormous budget for Google. It was one of her biggest professional opportunities to date, and roaming the city had to be better than lying in bed obsessing. She paced the gridded streets one by one all the way to the East River and back to the Hudson. Hours passed, until she found herself in front of Kate's West Village town house as the sky began to lighten to a hazy gray. She didn't want to bother Kate; she just wanted to be near the only person she cared about in the world. She stayed out of sight.

Eventually, when a woman out walking her dog waved her phone in Gail's face—"*I don't know what you're doing here, lady, but I ain't afraid to call the cops*"—Gail walked to the Hudson River Park and found a bench just south of Pier 40, where the Google event would take place that evening. The day was so foggy that she couldn't see across to New Jersey, couldn't see south to the Freedom Tower or north to Hudson Yards. A mural spanned the side of the Pier 40 warehouse: *I WANT TO THANK YOU* in big crimson block letters that cut through the mist. Less than six months ago, Gail had walked over with Kate to admire the mural. Meaning less than six months ago things were still good and life wasn't a hellscape of memory and regret. Kate had been fine that day. A little stressed since she'd been about to start finals to finish out her junior year at NYU, but there was nothing off between the two of them. Gail had entered motherhood young. It had always been just her and Kate. Kate was her mini-me. People mistook them for sisters all the time, from when Kate was a little girl and particularly now that they were both adults. Kate had always loved it. It made her feel so mature. The first time someone said to Gail, *Is this your little sister?* Kate's lanky body, goofy, expressive, flailed humorously. She laughed and threw her arms into the air: *Why, hello, sister!*

Hello, sister! Gail said back, and they said it back and forth, laughing, bowing, curtsying, until whoever asked the question looked at them like they were crazy and walked away. Sister Gail, Sister Kate. A single contained world. No two people had ever been closer.

Just then Gail felt something hit her head, hard, from behind. She cried out, jumped up, and whipped around to see a woman walking away from her toward the pier. The woman was dressed in a gray sweat suit, the pants tucked into bright red rubber boots. She had pale blond hair, frizzing out in the foggy morning.

Gail shouted after her, and the woman stopped, cocked her head sideways. Ever so slightly shifted her weight back. There was a pause when it seemed she might turn, a possibility that cut through Gail's shaky calm and made her feel that she would lose it, that everything would finally come crashing down if the woman actually turned to face her. Gail squeezed her hands into fists and held her breath. After a moment the woman resumed her walk, and Gail, standing stock-still, waited until she disappeared into the mist, before collapsing back on the bench.

But then she saw that it was somehow already a little after nine. Briskly, she walked the short distance to the Pier 40 garage entrance that faced the West Side Highway. Google had bought the entire property, in addition to the full city block across the highway. The old pier warehouse held a marine biology field station and a rooftop trapeze school, among other beloved community amenities that all wrapped around a center soccer field. Next week it would be demolished to build more office space. In order to alleviate neighborhood outrage, Google was throwing a huge party highlighting its charitable commitments. That's where Gail came in. She ran one of the most sought-after event planning businesses in the city. She'd apprenticed with her aunt, eventually taking over her business and growing it exponentially. Booked out two years in advance. *New York* magazine recently ran a profile on her—"Gail Carrington Makes Real the Unreal"—after the Met hired her for next year's gala. One of the photos it had used was of her and Kate in matching dresses at the New York Public Library's annual spring dinner. In the photo, sitting at their table in candlelight, they looked identical. Even Gail wasn't quite sure who was whom.

When she walked up to the loading bay, she saw her longtime vice president, Luca, chatting with a guy in a semi whose truck was blocking the garage entrance. Behind him vehicles were already honking, drivers yelling.

"It's all the setup for the stages and the VIP tent," Luca said when she approached. "They don't fit in the garage. I guess someone from our team told them they'd fit."

"You're going to have to park it along the curb here. You can't just logjam this entrance."

The driver started complaining about bad information, and the honking behind him increased.

"Ah. Okay, I'm on it." Gail picked up her phone and mimed making a call. "Yes, hello? I need a team right away to come with an enormous crane to stretch out the garage entrance on Pier 40 so we can fit a truck that doesn't currently fit. That requires special authorization? Yes, I'll hold for the governor."

Luca shook his head.

"Madam Governor?" Gail nodded with her phone pressed to her ear. "Yes, ma'am. It is an emergency, ma'am. And send a couple helicopters. A pair of Black Hawks is fine, yes. A SEAL team while you're at. They can rappel in. We absolutely must stretch the garage entrance for these gentlemen, because they're blocking all of my vendors."

Finally the driver relented with a glare in Gail's direction and shifted the semi into gear. Luca followed after the truck, which would now need to be unloaded at the curb, the equipment carried piece by piece through the walkway onto the pier and all the way to the center field. She'd send an assistant to get the crew coffee and doughnuts so there'd be no hard feelings. Gail located the rest of her staff and helped direct the vendors—tables and chairs, music equipment, flowers, alcohol, fireworks, party favors, and everything else in appropriate-sized vehicles—into the garage. She shook hands with Google's head of corporate social responsibility and assured him that the evening would be even more magical if the fog didn't lift, sending him off with her lead event planner to run through everything step by step.

The party started at eight. She knew the space inside and out; that was her job. For weeks she'd been stopping by almost daily and sometimes even at night. She'd paced the perimeter parking to scope out the best setup for fireworks, watched youth soccer games on the field, visualized the desired transformation. As she was about to head to the field, Luca called to her and walked over. He looked her up and down, frowning, as he approached.

Gail waved him off. "I'm going home to change after setup. I just need to be back here to meet catering at five thirty."

He didn't seem convinced. She noted the concern in his eyes, and it filled her with dread. Luca was the closest thing she had to a friend and Kate's only steady male presence growing up. She'd always had to fight her tendency to exclude everyone from their lives. It was a by-product of her isolated childhood—she could count on two hands the number of people she'd interacted with during her first sixteen years of life. One thing she loved about New York City was how people, millions of people, were omnipresent, but not a single one cared about her personal business.

"I need to talk to you about something."

"Is it a work something?" Gail asked. "Because we're at work, and I'm sensing it's not a work something."

"It's not a work something. But it's an important something. It's an it-can't-wait something. It's an honestly-I've-been-worried-about-you-for-a-while-now something."

"Luca," Gail said, "you've always asked me why you're a perpetual second-in-command while I'm someone who's run my own business since before I turned thirty—"

"I've never once asked you that."

"I'll tell you why. It's because you are incapable of drawing a line between work somethings and personal somethings."

"It's about Kate," Luca said. "We met for coffee yesterday."

Gail felt a sharp pain in her back teeth. She moved her jaw back and forth to calm the muscles. "Okay?"

"She said you've been—and these are her words, not mine—stalking her. That you've spent several nights outside her town house where you just stand and stare at her front door."

Gail let out a short laugh. Stalking. As if it were even possible for a mother to stalk a daughter. Gail ran her hands through her hair, thick with humidity, and felt the back of her head. There was a knot forming, tender to the touch, where that woman had hit her. Had she punched Gail? Or thrown a rock? She honestly had no idea.

"Are you sleeping? You look tired."

"Don't you love it when people say you look tired? Just tell me I look like shit already. I can take it."

"I think you're scaring her. I was going to wait until tomorrow to talk about this, but Kate called me at like five a.m. and left a voicemail saying you were creeping around outside."

"I'm pretty sure she doesn't have superhuman vision." There was a pin oak across the street, and Gail had been sure to keep her body a sliver behind it, shifting her head only slightly to peer at her daughter's door.

"So you were there?"

"Of course I wasn't."

"She's not doing well. Did you know she's taking the semester off, seeing a therapist three days a week?"

"Come on, Luca. You're not her dad."

"She told me things, certain things about how it was when she was growing up, things she said she's only recently realized."

"Yeah, what did she tell you? Did she tell you how she's always been the number one priority in my life. How it's an actual miracle, coming from where I came from, that I managed to give her all the opportunities she's had. World travel, the best education, this city. That town house I'm supposedly stalking."

Luca placed a hand on her shoulder, pulled her a little closer. "Those weren't really the things she focused on, no."

"Did you know I was never allowed to own a single thing when I was growing up? Not one. Every once in a while, I'd go out and bring something home. A necklace I found in the dirt, a ceramic mushroom I took from someone's garden, an ugly doll I stole once from a little girl. But every single thing they took and destroyed."

"No. You've never talked about any of that."

"I come from the Deep South, Luca. My parents were these Jesus fanatics. I mean, the best friend I can remember was this possum I hid for a while out in our shed and snuck food to whenever I could get away with it."

"Okay, wow, um . . . does Kate know any of this?"

"Of course not! I've always protected her from all of it. That's my point!"

Luca wrapped his arm around her and tried to guide her away. "Come on, I'm taking you home. You've planned this event to the last detail. We can take it from here."

A few workers around them were staring now. More than eight hundred people would be at this party—celebrities, tech moguls, influencers, community organizers, philanthropists, and regular folks who had their names drawn from a lottery. She had a $12 million budget. It was a huge deal. "Is everything good with the Google board? And the nonprofit grant recipients. We have their plaques in hand for when the CEO presents?"

"Gail—"

"The city inspector is coming at three. I'll meet with him and then go get ready."

"Kate's considering filing a restraining order against you. I'm one hundred percent certain she will if you don't lay off. And I promised her I'd deliver that message."

Something red caught Gail's eye. The rubber boots on that woman from the park, who was turning onto a walkway to enter the pier. Nobody was supposed to be accessing the space except for Gail, her team, and the vendors.

"Message delivered, message received. Now let's get to work."

Gail hurried over and got to the walkway just as the red boots disappeared onto the soccer field. She jogged to catch up but lost sight of the woman. The area was chaotic with preparations. The stage was already well under way for the lineup of nostalgia-inducing one-hit wonders who agreed to this paycheck. A team unspooled thick cables on the ground, which they would eventually install in suspension above the field to hold strands of twinkling lights and tightrope performers who would entertain throughout the evening.

She scanned the area one more time and glimpsed the red boots turning onto a second walkway that led to the river on the far side of the field. Gail ran across the Astroturf and almost the full length of the walkway until she came to a door, slightly ajar, a rusted padlock lying broken on the ground beside it. She pushed in the door and found a grimy custodial room. One bare bulb flickered from the ceiling when she flipped the light switch. Utility shelves clung to the walls, overloaded with bleach, solvents, paint cans. In the corners, piles of warped wood and corroded piping. In the center of the small room lay a filthy mattress littered with vending machine food wrappers. On the floor, countless cigarette butts. The room reeked of mildew and whatever had stained the mattress. The concrete floor near the side wall was cracked as if something heavy like a bowling ball had smashed down. She touched her toe to the crack, and the concrete crumbled further. She wondered if it was structurally sound.

Her last two years in Louisiana she'd spent in that shed in the woods, where she'd slept and prayed and fasted after Großvater had pronounced: *Meine Enkelin ist böse.* My granddaughter is evil. But she was never forced, that's what no one would understand. She'd stayed there because she believed. There was rot inside her. She could feel it then, she could feel it now. The shed became a place she preferred, one of comfort, where she'd sit isolated all day every day and hold dialogues with herself or sometimes with somebody else. Somebody whom she conjured and who shared the weight of the rot she felt deep in her soul.

Gail jumped when a huge rat scurried across the room, brushed her leg, and disappeared into the far corner. She stumbled backward out of the room and slammed the door behind her.

※

Instead of staying to meet the city inspector, Gail assigned her lead planner and left for home. Her calm had eroded, replaced by the strung-out manic intensity that plagued her during her worst bouts of insomnia. Never this bad, but yes, it had happened before. Often.

This time, though, she couldn't tell for sure what was real and what wasn't. For instance, just before things had blown up with Kate, when she'd been feeling the best she'd felt in years, like she'd truly left it all behind, she was on the subway coming home from a meeting in Queens with a glassblower who was making custom centerpieces for one of her events. Sardined in a train car at rush hour. Someone very close was playing music through their phone speaker—obnoxious, but she always minded her own business. Then, just as they'd descended onto the tracks underneath the East River and the lights in the train car flickered, she heard this singing. Voices, male voices, a cappella, eerie, singing her name from that phone speaker. Her name from more than two decades ago, before she legally changed it. Singing *Gail Liebrecht*, singing an inaccurate version of her childhood. Singing isolation, Jesus, grandfather, thick, thick woods. Singing about that devil language. They sang in German. *Böse, übel, schlecht, sagt Großvater.* Gail Liebrecht is bad, bad, bad. Evil, says Grandfather. But she was never forced like the lyrics suggested. She was never tied down. She'd listened in a daze, and when the music switched to something heavy metal, she pushed through the crowd to a twitchy guy, sallow, skinny, strung out. *What was that song?!* she'd asked, and squeezed into the sliver of space on the bench beside him as an old man cursed her but got out of her way. She couldn't get the guy to tell her anything. Either he didn't know or he was too messed up. Or he hadn't heard it. Had anyone else heard it?! No one would answer her. When the train doors opened at the first Manhattan stop, the guy shot up and slipped out just before they closed. She'd since tried to find the song online by searching the lyrics. She hadn't been able to, so what had that been? Had she really heard that song?

Gail took a slight detour instead of going straight home. Away from the pier, she got directly off the parkway onto Morton, followed by a right on Bedford to Kate's narrow little town house. She walked up the five steps to the front door and stood in front of it. She could sense Kate's presence.

"Sister! Hey, Sister Kate!" Gail called to the window. If she could just see Kate's face. Kate was part of her; Kate belonged to her. If she would just come out and talk to her for five minutes, Gail would be fine. That's all it would take. All would be well.

Gail could picture her daughter cowering behind the door. Weak. Kate had always had it so easy. Gail had protected her daughter, held her tight in her arms and never let go. Protected her from all kinds of people, but especially the true believers, the zealots, her own family. Even when Kate couldn't see it, Gail was protecting her. That's what had happened recently between them. Gail had felt it impossible to concentrate on her work and knew the only way to get back to the level of focus her successful life required was to go away and reset. Gail knew that Kate needed a rest as much as she did, so she rented a little cabin in the woods north of the city outside Beacon. It was during their little retreat that everything had unraveled. They'd gotten there, and Gail had started to move the furniture to the living room walls to make space on the floor for sleep, explaining that they'd be fasting through their three-night stay. This was something they'd always done periodically to cleanse body and soul, though it had been several years. Kate had gotten upset for no reason at all and wanted to leave. Gail had no choice but to guilt her into staying, threatening to harm herself until Kate relented. Had it really been that much to ask? They had electricity. They had running water. Two things Gail never had growing up, and still Kate had acted like she was afraid of her own mother, made it so that Gail felt even worse after the much-needed retreat. Then came the hellish insomnia.

She heard a siren and turned to see the flashing lights of an NYPD squad car. It was dark outside. In her disorientation, Gail thought the dark was a result of the fog, but then she pulled her phone out of her purse and saw that she had over a hundred missed calls and texts. It was after eight. Her event had already started.

That had been happening lately: With increasingly little sleep, chunks of time disappeared unaccounted for. With little sleep, personal somethings bled into work somethings. Past somethings into present somethings. The best thing Gail could do was keep her cool. Stay calm. She put on her winning smile and walked down the steps to meet the police car, which had stopped at the curb next to the town house.

The officer, a young woman, rolled down her window. "Gail Carrington?" When Gail reached the squad car, the officer stepped out to stand with Gail on the sidewalk. "You are standing outside the home of Kate Carrington and harassing her. I am making an official documentation of this harassment. Can you verify for me that you understand?"

Gail turned back to look at the town house, and a curtain dropped quickly across the window.

"Can you verify for me that you understand?"

"Yes, I understand." Gail's voice was raspy, and her throat hurt as if she'd been singing, or perhaps screaming, for an extended period of time.

"Okay, good. I need you to leave and not come back to loiter outside of this town house. Otherwise, I will make this official and serve you with an order of protection, ban you from coming within three hundred feet of Kate Carrington, make it part of public record. Can you verify for me that you understand?"

Gail looked down the street at a small crowd forming to watch the spectacle, a couple of people filming on their phones. In the center was the woman from the park with the red boots, her features indistinguishable, somehow out of range of the streetlight that illuminated every other face.

"Yes, I understand. Thank you, officer."

Gail thought she needed to rush home and change, but she looked down at herself and saw that she was already dressed and ready for the night: gray suede pants and a matching silk top, red strappy heels. She didn't remember owning these clothes, but they'd work. She'd head straight back to the party.

The soccer field was packed with partygoers in gowns and suits. It wasn't quite nine o'clock and already people were a little drunk and rowdy. A rock band was onstage, covering "Blitzkrieg Bop." She marched through the crowd. It was her job to emcee, to welcome the attendees and kick off the event. Better late than never. She pushed past one of her assistants blocking access, walked onto the stage, and picked up an unused microphone, turned it on and tapped. Feedback screeched through the amplifiers and the instruments went quiet behind her one by one. Someone from the band said, "All right, New York, let's take a short break."

Spotlights blinded Gail, but she could feel the hush of attention from the crowd. She started right in on her welcome speech, didn't even need her notes. "There's so much evil in this world. So much evil inside each one of us. Unspeakable evil. It's impossible to be told from an early age that there's evil inside of you and not believe it. There is a small part of you who will always believe—"

Before she could finish and sing a festive little song from her childhood about walking over burning hot coals for Christ to set the right tone for her segue into Google's philanthropy initiatives to combat the world's evils, the primary focus of the night's event, Luca was onstage rushing toward her. He took the microphone from her hand, apologized to the crowd, and told the musicians to please resume.

Gail allowed herself to be guided from the stage; she didn't want to make it worse. Luca had overstepped. He'd embarrassed her, and if she hadn't known in her heart that this was her last job—because she did know it, suddenly—she would have fired him on the spot.

Ever since that song on the subway and the failed attempt at sanctuary in the woods with Kate, she'd been plagued by flashes from her past. But for some reason, one particular memory bubbled repeatedly to the surface. She'd been fifteen or sixteen, staying for a year already in that shed, her entire family speaking only German because her grandfather was living with them now and her grandfather, the patriarch, mandated it. But one day she woke up with the thought that maybe she wasn't evil, maybe it was them, and she stumbled, weak, through dense woodland until she reached a road and the first business in town, a gas station convenience store. Her family had followed her at a distance, so as not to contaminate themselves, to keep the flood at bay. She'd spoken only German for the past year, and it didn't occur to her to switch. *Hilf mir. Hilf mir bitte.* Help. And her parents and her grandfather spoke behind her, angry, ordering her to return home. *What's that they're talking?* a guy with a thick beard buying a case of beer said to the gum-smacking girl behind the counter who was about Gail's age. The counter girl shrugged, and the beer guy guffawed. *Fucking psychos.* And Gail, and her family, left. That was the only time she'd seen anyone else, besides her parents and grandfather, for the entire two-year period she'd agreed to go live in the shed.

Backstage, Luca clasped his hands onto her shoulders. "What the hell was that, Gail? That'll go viral by morning. You're going to ruin this night we've worked so hard for. And you went to Kate's? She left me a couple messages, but I couldn't pick up. I thought you were going home to change." He was so frazzled.

"I did." She removed herself from his grasp and did a little turn to showcase her party outfit. Then she looked around. It was so foggy she could barely see the night sky. That wasn't supposed to matter, though. There were supposed to be cables installed overhead with tightrope walkers and twinkling lights made even more luminescent by the mist. But there was only emptiness. "What happened to the cables?"

"You didn't meet with the city inspector. You just left! He was pissed, so no cables. I had to bribe him to authorize the fireworks later. But look, that doesn't matter right now. I'm really, really worried about you. You need to go home and rest. I should take you to a hospital, but we're in the thick of it here. I'm taking you tomorrow, okay?"

Gail knew he wouldn't leave her alone unless she agreed. "Okay. I'm going."

He seemed skeptical, but he offered his arm, and she took it. They walked together behind the stage and behind the bar, trying to encounter as few people as possible as they moved toward the walkway that led back to the street. He went so far as to place her inside a taxi, give the driver her address, and wait until they were on their way.

※

But Gail wasn't going home. There was somewhere else she needed to be. Something inside of her could sense it. She told the driver she'd left something important at the party and she was back in no time. She avoided the crowd completely by walking along the outer perimeter of the pier warehouse and getting to the custodial room the back way. But when she entered, she was in a completely different space. Warm and welcoming, lined with shelves that were filled with lovely dolls and delicate figurines and all manner of beautiful trinkets she had not been permitted in childhood. They were arranged pleasingly among rows of leatherbound books. A king-sized bed covered in a purple velvet bedspread occupied the center of the room, a chandelier blazed with light above it. Incense burned over an elegant ceramic dish on a bedside table. It was all so warm, cozy, inviting.

Sitting on the edge of the bed was the blond woman from earlier, still wearing the same sweat suit and red rubber boots. For the first time, Gail could register the woman's face. It was her own face. She felt no surprise. If she felt anything, it was relief at the inevitability of it.

"Doppelgänger," Gail said, the corner of her mouth twitching up into a smile.

The woman on the bed laughed, a low rumble that saturated the air and made the ground below shudder. She wasn't beautiful, but she had an expressive face, large eyes, and a sharp chin that gave her an air of intelligence, a crooked yet dazzling smile that made it impossible not to smile back. Gail began to understand why she herself had been so successful in life, even after the childhood she'd endured. The woman was magnetic. Gail couldn't take her eyes off her. Gail felt uneasy, seeing that this woman might be too much to handle for a child such as Kate.

The woman grinned coyly from bed. "Not doppelgänger. Doppelgänger is a harbinger of evil. You are German—Liebrecht. Gail Liebrecht. You must know."

"No, I am not German," Gail said. "You of all people must know I am American. And like most Americans, my people came from somewhere else and I know little about it. How in God's name I ended up where I am is beyond me."

On the bed, the woman's shoulders shook with laughter and the room vibrated. "Using the Lord's name in vain. Evil." For a moment the walls blurred and rippled. Gail lost her balance and staggered backward, grasping at a bookshelf to stay upright.

"But you're right," Gail said, steadying herself. "A doppelgänger is not a good omen. Twins then?"

"We are not twins. We are one and the same."

Okay, yes. Gail could see how that was true. She tried again. "*Doppelschwester?*"

"Ah," the woman said. "But that sounds just as evil, no? Perhaps it is true that German is an evil language."

"Perhaps. You know I always used to dream about having a sister, someone I could really talk to."

"Yes, I dream about a sister as well."

"Sisterdouble?"

"No. Evil, evil. Double is evil."

A book, thick and heavy like the Holy Bible her grandfather carried everywhere, fell from the top shelf in the corner and cracked the marble floor. Gail began to sweat.

"Sister . . . person, thing." It was essential she get this right. Everything hinged on it. Nothing in all existence had ever been as important. Yet she felt that it was just beyond her grasp.

The woman pulled her legs up onto the bed and moved to the center. She beckoned Gail over.

Gail went to her and couldn't help herself. She reached out and touched the woman's brow, her nose, her cheekbones. Her skin felt smooth and warm. Though she felt shy, she had to ask. "You are also Gail?"

"Gail? Me?" The woman's eyes narrowed to slits, and the air droned around them, became something solid, drowning out the music and the partygoers outside. "Oh no, I am not. No, no, no."

"My apologies. Forget I said anything."

"But you know what I am called," the woman said. "My name begins with a *t-h*, with a *th, th, th, th*. With a *th, th, th, th, th, th, th, thhhhh, thhhhhhhhhhhhhhhhhh—*"

The room contracted, claustrophobic, and Gail started breathing fast. "Okay, stop, stop! Shhh. Please shush. Let us talk about something else."

The woman turned up one corner of her mouth. Winked.

Gail stared at her mirror image. Something wasn't right. "I turned forty-one last month, but you look young. I don't think I ever looked quite like that."

"Not young. Very, very old. Ancient. I have been around since the Prior World. I escaped the Maker, Modeler, the Bearer, Begetter. I survived the Great Flood. I'm God's Failed Experiment."

God's failed experiment. Gail's grandfather referred to humankind, to Gail in particular, as God's failed experiment. *Gottes gescheitertes Experiment.* For this reason, Gail had to be isolated or something terrible would befall them all. And her parents, fanatic, weak, had agreed. These were the things she'd spared Kate, and Kate had no idea. No idea.

Gail took the woman's hand. She felt a tear well in her own eye and watched it run down the woman's cheek. She'd only ever had herself, and she'd wanted someone else, a sister, so badly that she could sometimes feel her there. And now she had her, her sister self. "Finding you here is an extreme comfort to me. I want you to know that."

At that moment the racket of the party intensified—the door was flung open. A couple stumbled in, arms around each other, pawing. Gail felt the woman let go of her hand. The couple stopped when they were just inside. The man looked around, settled his eyes for an instant on Gail, and then looked down to the bed. "*Fuck, fuck, what are you doing? Why do you have that in your lap?!*" He threw an arm out across the woman he was with, pushing her back. For a single instant the walls faded, the bookshelves flickered and became utility racks, holding dried-up paint cans and soiled rags. A strong reek of mildew. She reached down and felt that there was something warm and substantial in her lap. It hissed. She hurled it away.

The room pulsed with the gravelly laugh. When Gail tried to look over at whatever she'd hurled away, the woman held her head in place, prevented her, as the couple fled and the door slammed shut behind them. Gail felt tense until the woman lay down and pressed Gail back into her. Then she felt peace. The room was back to normal. Warm, welcoming.

Seconds or hours passed. Luca came in and spoke words at her, but she didn't have to hear them because she was safe now.

"Are you a mother?" she asked when they were once again alone.

"Many times over," the woman said. She smoothed Gail's hair off her forehead, ran her fingernails down Gail's scalp, soothing in the way Gail herself had always tried to be.

"Then you understand," Gail said. "I was only nineteen when I got pregnant, my aunt's intern, and he moved back to Norway the second he found out. You understand that we do not have a child and then miraculously become a perfect being who never makes mistakes. That if we were prone to breakdowns before the child, we are not going to miraculously have it together all the time after the child. You understand that no matter how much we want nothing evil to befall the child, we cannot control everything. We never intended—"

"Yes." The woman pressed her palm firmly onto Gail's back and made little circles, massaging tight muscles. "Yes."

"Kate and I used to lie just like this. We would spend whole days like this, finding comfort in each other, any time I wasn't working. I always prided myself on being able to separate my personal somethings from my work somethings."

The woman sat up and took off her sweatshirt. Gail took off her top, too, and they lay back down in their bras.

Immediately Gail felt like nothing bad could ever happen again. "See how much better this is? Warmth. The way my skin feels against your skin."

"Yes."

"There is nothing indecent about this! I never intended anything other than comfort, other than getting as close to that feeling that we are one, as close as we were when I carried her as part of myself for nine months."

"Yes."

"And she fooled me. She made me think we shared our own little world. That we were one way when together and another with the outside world. But now she is spinning it, corrupting it. The worst part is that things were going so well until recently, and then all I needed was a tiny little reset. But she would not even grant me that."

"Yes," the woman said.

Gail nodded, resigned. Then she tried to sit up, but the woman held her tight in place. Gail tried to jerk loose, but the woman wrapped an arm and a leg around her and held her as tight as her grandfather had held her at times in that shed when he risked contamination for her own sake. Gail's heart began to race. Her memory flashed to a small Kate in the same position she was in now, Gail holding her like this for hours on end through Kate's cries and panic. It had been the only way to keep out the evil that was always trying to seep into their lives. There had been no other choice. She knew that just as her parents and her grandfather had known it before her.

The woman released Gail, and Gail flipped over so that they faced each other. They lay with their noses touching, breathing each other's air, looking into each other's eyes.

"I believe it was a kindness, proving Grandfather right all those years ago," Gail said.

"Showing ourselves to be what he'd known us to be all along," the woman said.

"I am never clear," Gail said. "Sometimes I feel the rock in my hand, heavy and smooth. Yet sometimes I see you swinging it with all of your might. The way he looked into our soul, truly seeing us before he stumbled off to die. Was it you, or was it I?"

"Yes, yes, sister. It was."

Once again, the door burst open, and she could hear thunder crashing down all around them. She clapped her hands over her ears and huddled low. There was nowhere to hide.

But then there she was. Kate.

"Oh my god, Mom. Oh my god. What are you doing? Put your shirt back on." She began to cry, to tremble. Luca was outside the room for a moment, but then the door closed, and it was just the three of them. Kate cursed, though she knew her mother didn't like it. She grabbed a bucket and flipped it quickly upside down, trapping something in the corner that began to screech and thrash in rage. Then she pulled Gail up to sitting and dressed her gently in the gray sweatshirt. The woman shook with laughter, vibrated the room and the air around them. The thunder continued to clap.

"Tell me what's wrong, Mama, please. Luca's calling an ambulance. You need to get off that filthy mattress."

"It's too late. The storm's coming. Can't you hear it?"

Kate was hovering over her, looking around the room at everything except the woman. Willfully blind. "I hear fireworks, Mom, that's all. I hear the party."

"No, baby. The evil is rising up."

"What evil?"

"Mine. From inside me."

"There's no evil, Mom—"

"We're all closed in together. I brought the flood."

Gail grasped Kate's wrist and tried to pull her daughter down beside her, but she was surprisingly strong for a weakling, stronger than Gail, and she almost managed to drag her off the bed. But then her sister self joined in, circled Kate's other wrist and dug in her nails. Gail dug her nails in, too, and together they grasped her shoulders with their other hand and pulled their daughter until her face was all the way down to the level of theirs. When they saw her look of wide-eyed panic, they laughed, and their laughter mingled with the thunder outside and with the water that was beginning to fill the room from the crack in the concrete. And then they let her go, because for the first time they sensed her separateness. They didn't need her anymore, they only needed each other. Kate could go face the end with all the others, and they would face it together alone. Just the two of them.

The Strays
Summer

SUMMER STOOD in the stacks and watched her mom for a good ten minutes unnoticed. The library was grand, there was no other word for it. Certainly the grandest Summer had ever seen. Marble floors and polished wood furniture, a skylit center atrium that swept up five tiers, bordered with wrought-iron railings, that held hundreds of thousands of books, all nestled within the towering Douglas fir trees of coastal Washington. The library served as the epicenter of the Garrard Institute, which granted artists and scholars the space and resources to set their own course of study, from animal rights to climate change to reproductive freedom to ancient languages to pure mathematics to obscure literary research, on and on ad infinitum. Summer had watched the promotional video on the website. Impressive. It was impossible to believe that Tess was in charge here.

Mid-afternoon in mid-May, and the library was calm, at least on the ground floor. A few people were spread out at sprawling tables. Tess sat alone at the circulation desk, dozens of open books fanned out around her. She was absorbed in a thick hardback, ran her finger over a few lines of text and then wheeled her chair over to a wide, floppy children's book. The cover illustration, at least from Summer's vantage point, appeared to be of a dark storm cloud brooding over a little girl. Tess riffled the pages and then thumbed through slowly until she found whatever she was looking for. After reading something, she gave a surprised little laugh and immediately wrote in her notebook, followed by a vigorous underlining of whatever delightful fact she'd happened upon. The last time Summer had seen her mom was after her college graduation three years ago, when Tess had been so hungover from her previous night's binge that Summer got to watch her puke in a trash can outside airport security. Good times. Now she looked healthy. Fifty-one next month and honestly never better. She also looked like she'd googled *How to appear intelligent* or *Interesting librarian looks*. Once, when she and Summer were still close, Tess had complained that she'd never be able to transcend her aging cheerleader looks. Maybe she finally had. Dirty-blond pixie cut, chic gray sack dress with a scarf tied loosely and fashionably around her neck. A pair of thick-framed reading glasses with a nerdy-hip beaded chain attached to them. A body that clearly ate well and got plenty of sleep and exercise. If Summer didn't know her, she'd think this woman fit in perfectly here, as the senior librarian of the grandest library she'd ever seen. Way to look the part, Mom. Way to chameleon.

Tess looked up. Her brow furrowed as if trying to work out a thought, pen still poised over her notebook. She brought her hand up to her hair, pinched some, and tried to pull it toward her mouth, absently. But it was too short, and so she settled for her large thumb knuckle, first just toothing it, and then really going to town. Lifelong oral fixation. Tess's eyes scanned the room and passed over Summer, then snapped back. Locked on. By reflex Summer hid. She shifted quickly out of sight, flattened herself against the shelves, tried to get her breathing under control. Fuck. She wanted to flee, but then it would seem as if she was overaffected by seeing Tess after so long, not since her drunk-ass mom had dumped all over her. It wasn't worth it back then, maintaining the relationship. Maybe it wasn't worth it now. She heard Tess rising in haste, papers falling to the floor, chair wheels rolling over wood, the squeak of hinges, footsteps. And since Summer couldn't stand for her mom to find her hiding, she peeled her back from the hard spines of the books and stepped out from the stacks. She held her hand up in a halt just in time to stop Tess from embracing her.

"I haven't showered in like a week."

"Okay," Tess said, smiling. But it was as if she couldn't help herself. She grabbed a handful of Summer's hip-length hair, picked it up, then let it fall. Reached to touch her face but managed to control herself. "I wasn't expecting you until tomorrow."

"Well," Summer said, "I can leave if you want. Come back then."

"Don't you dare."

Tess looked more like the mom Summer knew now that she was close up. Spilled coffee on the front of her dress, a light dusting of dandruff, a faint line of eczema in the corners of her nose. Fat, dark whisker peeking out from the otherwise cute mole on her left cheek. Tess had always presented as put together and even beautiful—unless you knew where to find the seams.

Tess shifted on her feet, and Summer could see a crumpled Post-it stuck to the seat of her dress. She reached around and pulled it loose. Five lines:

Double: doppelt, zweifach
Setting: "wilderness" or more specific?
Böse
Research Chaoskampf. Books??
Thea Thea Thea

Summer handed it over. The Thea stories. In a lot of ways her mom's life's work, but nothing to show for it. And what was up with her obsession with German? They'd lived in Germany off and on for six years, and Tess had never managed to pick up the language. It wasn't that hard.

As if she could read Summer's mind, Tess said, "I know, I know." She threw her hands up to the cathedral-like ceiling. "To all the gods up in the heavens and writers down on this earth, if you will take these stories and write them for me, I hereby bequeath them to you, willingly!"

Summer stared at her, and Tess's smile dissolved.

"Oh god, I'm so stupid," she said. "Here I am talking about me, and I haven't even congratulated you on all your stuff. Placing in all these races. A fellowship. Barcelona! You're killing it, Sum."

"It's no big deal." She hated when her mom called herself stupid. Plus, Summer wasn't killing it. She wouldn't be moving at all if she hadn't been dropped by Hoka, who'd been sponsoring her running since college. Now Summer had to learn to support herself and her dreams if she still planned on being the best of the best someday, which she did.

"But I want to know all about it. I want to know everything." Tess reached out and touched her shoulder lightly and then remembered herself and pulled away. "I just can't believe you're really here."

"I said I was coming, didn't I?" Summer heard the brattiness in her voice and hated how Tess could make her switch from full-grown adult to obnoxious kid in an instant.

Tess cocked her head at Summer, then excused herself for a moment and asked a woman shelving books across the room to take over at the desk. When she came back, she said, "Come on, let's go see your brother."

They climbed the inner staircase that zigzagged all the way up to the library's top tier completely encased by glass that looked out to equal parts trees and sky. PJ had dropped out of high school the day he'd turned seventeen but almost immediately passed his equivalency exam. Now, at nineteen, he was enrolled in an online bachelor's degree program in environmental sciences and also working part-time for the institute doing whatever menial tasks were needed. Tess explained that they were headed upstairs because one of the institute's permanent chemists, Andreas, had invited him to sit in on a meeting, a big opportunity for PJ.

They made their way across the top floor to a back corner, where a small group sat around a table strewn with papers and drawings. Among them was PJ, who'd changed a lot since she'd last seen him. He looked like their dad now: tall and athletic, handsome. But he also had a terrible, choppy haircut, and he wore a T-shirt with an illustration Summer wondered if he'd done himself. A diagram labeled with the layers of Earth's atmosphere: troposphere with trees and clouds, stratosphere with airplanes, mesosphere with what looked like meteors, thermosphere with satellites, and finally the exosphere. But in the exosphere was a suspended woman, floating on her back, her long black hair splayed out around her. Artistic, but possibly also creepy, Summer wasn't sure.

The group was discussing forest fires and natural flame retardants. PJ held up drawings of various snails, worms, and beetles, arguing quietly with an older man across the table from him. "Perfect timing. My sister's here," he said, though he'd given no indication that he'd noticed her come in. Now they locked eyes. "You drove up the coast to get here, right, Summer?"

Everyone in the room turned toward her. "Um, yeah. I took I-10 to Santa Monica and drove up the coast from there."

"And there were fires?"

There had been some smoke in the air, yes, especially in Northern California. She ran thirteen miles in it, which she'd known was a mistake, something her lungs had confirmed when they wouldn't stop burning afterward. "Aren't there always fires?"

PJ waved her off impatiently and continued his debate. Tess caught Summer's eye and pressed her lips together, trying not to smile. Summer did not recognize this talkative version of her brother. Last time she saw him was when the whole family was there for her graduation from USC; when Tess had just received this job offer and decided to leave their dad, though she hadn't told him yet; when Tess stayed an extra night and got shitfaced, and everything went downhill from there. Back then, PJ had been an antisocial, skittish boy who didn't work well with others and had just been held back a year in high school to give him a chance to mature cognitively and socially but wasn't old enough yet to quit. Clearly, there was a new confidence in him, an intensity, and the people at the table seemed to take him seriously.

After the meeting PJ hugged his sister and then immediately side-eyed her. "Yo, I thought you were getting here tomorrow."

"Oh my god. What is it with you two and my schedule?" She didn't know why she'd shown up a day early. She'd had a couple weeks' break before she needed to join her new training group, and her one-year fellowship in team sports medicine didn't start at the University of Barcelona until the fall. For some reason that didn't make sense to her anymore, she decided to spend part of the break with her mom and brother. She'd used every excuse possible to avoid seeing Tess for the past three years but felt that a quick visit before leaving the country might be okay. She'd dragged out the road trip, every day finding an area where she could get out and exhaust herself with long runs and plyometric drills before driving a few hours and parking for the night.

But this morning she'd started straight off and drove the final three hundred miles. It had been a mistake. She was feeling the lack of physical activity. Twitchy, grumpy, pent up.

"We're glad you're here early, Sum," their mom said.

Back down at the front desk they stopped to talk to the woman who had taken over for Tess. Her name was Claire. She looked fragile, with a delicate bruising under her eyes and skin so pale it was as if she'd never experienced the sun. "I thought you weren't coming until tomorrow," she said when they introduced Summer. Summer gritted her teeth, but Claire didn't seem to notice. "Before you go, Tess, I've been listening to these megachurch preachers and getting some ideas for my research project. I really want to go over what I'm thinking with you."

"Great," Tess said. "Pencil something in on my calendar and we'll make it official."

"I'm down for talking megachurch preachers with you," PJ said. "Any time."

Claire reached out and squeezed PJ's forearm. "That would be great." Was this woman flirting with her brother? She was older than him—at least five, six years older. "I keep following these rabbit holes, and I'm at the point where I need to stay focused." Then, turning back to Summer: "I have epilepsy. I'm here on a work-study researching the neurological relationship between epilepsy and religiosity. I'm not religious, but my seizures come with these weird hallucinations, so I can definitely understand some people go there. So that's what I'm doing here, in any case."

"Cool" was all Summer could think to say. She tuned out the rest of their conversation—she wasn't a part of this—but then grimaced when her brother said, "See you tonight at dinner."

Both Tess and Claire glanced at her, and Claire said, "Actually, I'll take a rain check. Let you guys catch up as a family."

"What? No. No one cares about catching up as a family," PJ said.

But it was decided that Claire wouldn't, in fact, be joining them for dinner. "Come on," Tess said. "Let's walk Summer home."

※

"My whole life now is just trees," PJ said with a bad British accent, raising his arms to the sky and twirling as they approached their home. A one-story main house with a guesthouse in the back. It was only a ten-minute walk from the library, but the woods were so thick there was nothing else man-made in sight.

"Trees and, um . . . and champagne," Tess said, also British, holding, Summer could only guess, an imaginary champagne flute with her pinkie out.

"Ever since I've been a little girl, I've adored trees." PJ walked over and hugged the trunk of a large pine.

And then they talked over each other:

"It's riveting!"

"I'll hear what's going on beneath the bark as they burst back into life in the spring!"

"Isn't that just beautiful?!"

"How they fight back against the invading hordes?!"

They both looked over at her, proud of themselves, clearly dying for her to ask so they could share their little inside joke. But she couldn't do it. This, their home with the fresh air and the breeze delivering a perfect chill, with birdsong and squirrel play, and yes, it did make one feel alive here. Still, she found she could not ask what bit they were doing. Couldn't grant them that tiny speck of satisfaction. It had been a long trip, and her body ached from sitting so long behind the wheel. What she really wanted more than anything was not to have come in the first place.

Her brother looked her dead in the eye. The playfulness was out of his voice, but he still kept the British accent. "Do you know, there are more trees on the planet than there are stars in our galaxy?"

※

Summer left all her stuff in the car other than her overnight backpack and a bag of dirty laundry. She'd decided that she'd clean up, spend the night, and head to Seattle tomorrow to stay with an old college friend until her flight in six days. Tess and PJ cooked dinner together, a really good steak and baked potatoes. With sparkling water. The way they navigated like a perfectly contained family unit was for some reason too annoying to bear. All she had to do was get through a meal.

"How's your dad doing?" Tess asked when they were all sitting down to eat. Paul lived in Bern with his new wife, and everyone knew Summer had visited them a few times since she'd last seen Tess and PJ. Altitude training in the Swiss Alps. Paul had remarried dramatically quickly after the divorce from Tess was finalized, less than three months. His wife, Masha, was odd. Deadly serious. She was a pharmaceutical rep and, as far as Summer could tell, had no other interests. But her seriousness and blandness seemed to keep her dad calm. Paul clearly loved her. They got along well, and he was much less anxious with her around. Tess had driven Paul crazy.

"He's great," Summer said. "I think you'd really like Masha."

PJ snorted.

"I'm sure I would," Tess said. "Maybe we can come visit you and that would give PJ a chance to see your dad in the same trip."

"It's ten hours by train from Barcelona to Bern. Flying's not much better." She dug into her dinner. It was delicious. She was always hungry since she trained so often, and she'd been living off crap food the entire road trip.

"I'm not going. I already FaceTime with Dad once a week, and I hate flying," PJ said.

"We just flew to Philadelphia with Claire," Tess said.

This got Summer's attention. "You did?" Although she'd made excuse after excuse to not have to see her mom, PJ had an open invitation to visit her in Flagstaff, which he never took her up on because he claimed a fear of flying.

"Yeah, but come on. It's Claire. That's different."

"She visited her grandma, and then we all drove a couple hours to a tent revival she wanted to check out for her research," Tess said to Summer.

"It was really intense," PJ said. "It definitely felt like we'd stepped into some cult."

"That sounds familiar," Summer said. "I'm kind of picking up that cult vibe here, too."

Tess smiled, but Summer could see underneath it that the comment had bothered her. She wouldn't engage, of course. Instead, she got up and grabbed a tray of peanut butter cookies from the kitchen and put them on the table.

For some reason, the fact that they went to Pennsylvania with this woman Summer didn't know existed until today killed her, even though she did stuff all the time without telling them. Summer really needed to get out of there.

"Look, I'll settle in and let you know if the coast is ever clear to come visit, okay?"

Tess reached across the table toward Summer. Opened her mouth. Closed it. Opened. Closed. Just say whatever it is you want to say, Mom. Christ!

"Oh, and by the way, I'm heading out in the morning. I have a lot I need to get done before my flight. That's why I showed up a day early."

"But you said you'd be here through the weekend." Tess leaned back in her chair. The wounded look on her face made Summer want to slap her.

"Hey, Summer," PJ said. "Why don't you let me show you the guesthouse? All my stuff's set up over there. You could even stay there if you want, on the pull-out couch. We can leave Mom alone to get some work done."

"No," Tess said. "Please don't go. Not yet."

"Come on, Mom," PJ said. He took a mound of peanut butter cookies and wrapped them in a paper towel. "You always write after dinner. And honestly, Summer and I could use some time."

PJ to the rescue. Without a word to Tess, Summer grabbed her overnight bag and followed her brother from the room.

※

The guesthouse was attached to the main house by a screened-in outdoor patio. Before PJ turned on the lights, Summer saw a skylight above that revealed the stars and a huge picture window that took up the entire back wall and looked out to the thick, dark forest. It was a mostly clear night with a half-moon. A few scattered clouds. When the light came on, the window became a mirror. The space was set up like a studio apartment, its barely ordered chaos giving Summer some insight into PJ's precarious brain. The walls were completely covered with all kinds of things. Papers and posters and photos tacked on to a series of corkboards. An enormous mounting board full of carefully displayed beetles. Countless diagrams of bugs, frogs, snails, and other small creatures. One section of the wall held swaths of fabric in various shades of gray that PJ explained were dyed hemp. He'd worked on them with a past resident, a master artisan from Japan who'd perfected the art of creating smoked soot dyes. Turpentine soot made by smoldering the roots of a pine tree and mixing them with water and natural latex. The dyes were deep and strong and absorbed the surrounding light.

On the other side of the room, a massive abstract embroidery hung on the wall, yellows and oranges and purples and greens swirling and darkening to a center almost as if they were being sucked into a black hole. Just looking at it made Summer dizzy.

"That's from a textile artist on residency, the stepdaughter of one of Mom's old friends. The three of us made this wall covering together. It took us almost a month and most of our free time. I think it turned out, though."

"You and Mom sure do a lot together."

"That was me and Claire, actually, working with the textile artist."

"What's up with you and epilepsy girl, anyway?"

"Epilepsy girl? God, what's your fucking problem?"

His calm demeanor evaporated. She'd pissed him off, which was not her goal. She apologized immediately, but couldn't help but add: "Are you two together or something? She must be like five or six years older than you."

"She's ten years older, Summer. Who cares? But to answer your question, no. She doesn't love me. Yet. But she will. I'm going to spend my life with her."

Well, that was concerning. The way he said it left no space for things not working out according to his desires, but there wasn't really anything Summer could do.

"Okay, sit. Let's get to it," PJ said, situating his lanky frame cross-legged on the opposite end of the couch from Summer. "It seems to me that your only point of being here is to make everyone as miserable as you are. But I'm going to give you a chance to tell me what's up."

"I'm not miserable, PJ. I'm just—"

"I honestly don't care. Tell me what's up with you and Mom."

Fine. She went ahead and told him the whole story. After graduation, after Paul and PJ had left, Tess stayed an extra night to help Summer pack up her room in a house she shared with three friends. Even though Summer's relationship with Tess had always been challenging in many of the typical mother-daughter ways, she'd needed the one-on-one time. She'd had a lot going on during her last semester—a bad breakup, her barely contained rage after an incident during a training session, stuff like that—and wanted to talk to her mom about it. She offered Tess a glass of wine. Sure, Tess didn't drink, they all knew that, but it's not as if Summer had forced it on her. Summer suggested it, and Tess had said, *Nah*, and then immediately changed her mind. She sipped one glass, then downed another. Eventually she'd guzzled all of everyone's alcohol in the entire house and passed out in and even *peed* her roommate's bed. But that part was after she dropped the bomb about divorcing Paul. After going into detail about affair after affair after affair their whole marriage, and why had they stayed together more than twenty years? About not having an actual clue who Summer's biological father even was, she'd been such a drunk slut, which had been *Tess's* words, not Summer's. Of course, they'd all known forever that Paul was her adopted dad and PJ was her half brother, but still. That was news to her.

Summer had never seen anything like it. Tess was so sloppy. *You're my best friend, Sum. Why don't you just have a kid and you can move in with me and we'll raise it together.* What a weird thing to say. She was slurry and kind of gross, and Summer responded that she'd never really wanted kids. *That is so smart! Kids will just keep you from having the life you want!* Which in theory Summer didn't disagree with, but it's not exactly something a girl wanted to hear from her mother.

It got worse from there. Sobbing, tears and snot pouring down her face, chugging more and more. *There are times I've tried to protect you, Sum, and I couldn't do it.* The whole thing had been an unbelievable shit show.

"And?" PJ said when she stopped talking.

"What do you mean 'and'? Did you not hear anything I said?"

PJ sighed and performed a slow clap. "Well, congrats, Summer. On experiencing that typical coming-of-age moment when you realize your parent is human."

"I know Mom is human. But come on, she's also my mom."

"Is the problem that you want an apology?"

No. Tess had tried to apologize a hundred times, and Summer had finally warned her, *If you ever say "I'm sorry" again, Mom...* "I just had a lot of stuff I needed to talk to her about—I mean, I still do, actually—and since then I can't talk to her at all."

PJ seemed to consider this. "Yeah, Mom is kind of a narcissist."

"She's not a narcissist, PJ. Come on!"

"I think what's really getting to you is seeing how happy she is. Seeing that Mom's capable of living a life after you've cut her out of yours."

"Oh, please," Summer said. Though it was true: Tess had never seemed better. Not at all what Summer had been expecting.

"Look, as interesting as this all is, it's a few minutes to ten and I need to go take my meds and then I'm heading out to a bonfire over at the main pavilion. Here's the deal. Mom's pretty basic. Her reality is she finally has a job she loves, and even though the divorce sucked, she's happier being single. And she's good most of the time, but she's also still kind of a hot mess. We've learned that we cannot, under any circumstances, keep alcohol in the house, which is obviously no shock. And I'm pretty sure she had a fling with Andreas—he was the guy across from me at that meeting today—even though it's never a great idea to hook up with someone from work. She's just a basically . . . basic person, Summer. She spends a ton of time in her own head, but she's pretty rooted to the ground. She doesn't have access to all the unseeable strangeness in the world. Some people do and some people don't."

"You do, I take it?"

He nodded.

"I bet Claire does, too."

He ignored that and continued: "Mom likes to think she does, but she doesn't. You definitely don't. It's just a fact."

Summer stared at her brother and shook her head. Who was this guy?

"Here's the deal. If you leave tomorrow instead of staying as long as you promised, I'm going to be really pissed at you, okay? Just suck it up. Fake it till you make it. It's five days. This place is actually really cool if you stop being such a loser. I'll give you the full tour. It'll be great."

Summer was exhausted, too exhausted to argue.

He got up and stood by the door. "Come on. You can come with me to the bonfire."

She just needed to sleep, to make sure that, no matter what, she got out in the fresh air tomorrow and got some exercise. She told her brother good night.

※

Once PJ left, she made up the pull-out couch and got into bed. It was pretty uncomfortable, not a lot better than sleeping in her car, a rail digging into her lower back. The air outside was still, and the sounds of the forest should have been soothing, but she was used to living in an apartment with feet trampling above her and TV shows coming through the walls and HVAC units whining. Too much peace, though one could probably get used to it. The room was pitch-dark until her eyes adjusted to the half-moon night, and then she began to make out something there, inside. Something long and dark and slender, stretched out in the rafters above her. A figure. A body. Summer's breath caught. She tried to distinguish details in the silhouette, black against the skylight that framed a single blazing star. But then cloud cover drifted into view, obscuring the star. At that moment, there was a *clonk* and something, the head, slipped off the beam that supported it, twisted around, and—hanging in the air—fixed its gleaming eyes on Summer. She was paralyzed, and time passed.

Finally, heart racing, she got up and very slowly moved across the room, pushing the side table as close as she could to the edge of her bed, climbing up, and reaching for it. She took hold of its arm and felt a rough material, scratchy and raw. She pulled gently, not wanting to damage it, until it shifted from its equilibrium in the rafters and fell all at once through Summer's arms onto the pull-out couch.

It was a hand-made doll, so long it took up the full length of the bed, and still its legs dangled off the edge. Hemp fabric like the swatches on the wall, dyed a dark soot gray. The eyes a glossy black onyx. It was sewn in sections, each section filled with sand, so that the weight was distributed evenly. Heavy, too heavy for Summer to put back in the rafters. Eventually Summer lay back down next to it, the doll on its side, watching her. There was a sort of comfort in it that she couldn't explain. She was drifting off when a low hum vibrated the bed. Summer opened her eyes, first looked at the doll and then up to see that the cloud had moved on and the star shone bright again through the skylight.

"Sorry about that," Summer whispered, and rolled the doll onto its back so it could gaze up at its star. She didn't worry about the hum that had vibrated the bed. She didn't worry about where it had come from. And soon Summer had fallen into a hard, dreamless sleep.

※

Summer woke close to noon; she hadn't slept that many hours maybe ever, but she did feel a lot better. When she walked into the main house, Tess and PJ were sitting in a pair of cozy recliners in the living room, Tess jotting down notes amid a pile of loose papers and PJ examining with a magnifying glass an iridescent blue beetle in the palm of his hand.

Tess looked up. "Can I make you something? Breakfast? A sandwich? Anything."

"No," Summer said, and Tess nodded, looked back down toward her notebook, but Summer could tell that her mom was just staring at her lap. "I mean, okay. I'm going to go for a trail run a little later, but can you make pancakes?"

"Sure, no problem," Tess said, her attempt at sounding casual clashing with the huge grin that spread across her face. "Plain, blueberry, or white chocolate chip?" She rushed off toward the kitchen.

PJ rolled his eyes, and Summer followed her mom. Tess pulled out the ingredients she mentioned, plus strawberries and peaches, even though Summer said she was fine with plain. Tess knew Summer liked all the stuff, no matter what she said.

"Also, I'm staying, until my flight. If that's still okay."

"Of course, babe."

While her mom cracked eggs into a glass bowl, Summer leaned her back against the counter. "Mom, will you still love me if I join a cult in Spain?"

Tess whisked the batter and nodded. "A cult? Cults are so super interesting. You'd be amazed at how many people are writing research papers on cults. I'm slinging cult books in that library on an hourly basis. Definitely yes, I will still love you. *Cult* is such a vague term, anyway."

"Okay, but what if I'm the cult leader? Will you still love me if I actually already started a cult and the reason I'm even going to Barcelona in the first place is because my Flagstaff training group are already converts and our collective goal is to send me over there so I can start another cult offshoot?"

"Sweetheart, you are brilliant, dynamic, and highly organized. If anyone could manage to run a successful cult, it's you."

From the other room, PJ called out, "Wait, can this cult not be another weird Jesus thing?" And then he was in there with them, putting on a pot of coffee.

"That's fine. Mainly we eat babies."

"Oh, thank god," Tess said. "Yum."

The white-chocolate-and-every-fruit-in-the-house pancakes sizzled on the griddle.

"There has to be a sci-fi element to this cult," PJ said.

"Inherited planets, shit like that," Tess said.

"Only for the most senior acolytes," Summer said.

Over pancakes and coffee they constructed their perfect cult, whose members planted a tree for every struggling soul and believed that after a trillion years of service they were freed to dissolve to nothingness. And all three of them were open to the possibility that maybe it wasn't a cult, maybe the followers were the only ones who knew the truth, who had a chance at glory and near-eternal life. PJ suggested that maybe Mom's favorite character, the one she had been writing about for decades, was the true leader of this cult, and Tess said, "No! I swear if Thea would just leave me the eff alone and let me try and write about something else it would be a major breakthrough."

"But, Mom," PJ said. "She's family!"

"Rude," Summer joked, though a stab of unease shot through her, leaving a strange taste in her mouth. Then noon breakfast was over, and PJ said he was returning to work. She called after him as he was leaving and, without really having thought about it, said, "You know Claire's welcome to join us for dinner tonight or any time."

"Okay," he said cautiously.

When he was out the door, Summer asked her mom if she ever worried about PJ, and the look Tess gave her told her, *Yes, always, so very, very much.* But all she said was "I can't think of a better place for him than here. Can you?"

Summer couldn't.

She sat with her mom on the couch. Tess reached out and stroked her hair. At first tentatively, but when Summer didn't resist, she ran her fingers through it, picking it up and play chewing on it. "Nom, nom, nom," she said. "I could never have beautiful hair like this. I'd eat it all up. Nom, nom, nom."

God her mom was such a dork. And Summer asked her, "Don't you think it's weird that I need to physically exhaust myself every single day in order to not feel like I'm crawling out of my skin?" And her mom considered and said, "No, it's not weird, it sounds like the human condition. You've got to keep the wilderness at bay somehow. If not exercise, it would just be something else. Jesus, drugs, extreme routine, meditation, career, video games, booze . . . some strategies healthier than others, but all with the same end goal."

Summer snuggled on the couch with her mom and said she wished she weren't such a nightmare sometimes. That she'd done things and treated people certain ways that made her hate herself, and maybe she'd tell Tess some of it later on in her stay. Tess said yes, please do that, and reminded her that she loved her anyway, and not less. And we all fucked up every so often and maybe it didn't actually have anything to do with who we really are. Or we're many different people in this one life. Or there's free will. Or there's predetermination. Or nothing matters. Or everything does. Tess sat there with her daughter and reminded her that she had no special knowledge. None at all. She was just trying to make it through like everyone else. With that, Summer excused herself, going back to the guesthouse. She had to at least try to figure out a way to lift Thea up and get her back into the rafters.

Acknowledgements

I'm incredibly grateful to my agent, Chad Luibl, and my editor, Chris Heiser, for seeing the value in my work and helping shape this book into its best version—none of this would have been possible without them. Also to Roma Panganiban and the rest of the Janklow & Nesbit team for shepherding it through to publication. At Unnamed Press, thanks to Allison Miriam Woodnutt and Cassidy Kuhle for their publicity efforts and book advocacy, and to Jaya Nicely for her fantastic art direction. To freelance copyeditor Nancy Tan for making it shine. To the exceeding-all-expectations Angela Melamud for the extra publicity help.

Thanks to my Columbia University MFA professors and mentors, particularly Heidi Julavits, Rivka Galchen, Elissa Schappell, Joanna Herson, Binnie Kirshenbaum, Joshua Furst, the late Paul LaFarge, Katrine Øgaard Jensen, Susan Bernofsky, and Clare Beams.

The friendship and support of my Columbia classmates is such a gift. Their acceptance of me as an artist is one of the main reasons I am one. We're the Covid class at Columbia (most of our degree was online), and although it wasn't ideal, I think we're somehow closer because of it: Abhigna Mooraka, Brooke Davis, Cameron Menchel, Ji Hyun Joo, Jinwoo Chong, Kage Dipale-Amani, Kate Sullivan, K-Yu Liu, Lin King, Robert Rubsam, and Rona Figueroa. A special shout out to Kat Tang, my most trusted reader who tolerates endless WWKD questions.

The following organizations and individuals were instrumental to my development as a writer. Thanks to the Louisiana School for Math, Science, and the Arts for opening up my world at the age of sixteen. To the Tin House Summer Workshop, particularly A.E. Osworth, Kelli Jo Ford, and my fellow Egrets. To the Kenyon Review Summer Workshop for four summers of community and inspiration, with extra thanks to Patricia Donahue and Mary Luvisi for nine years' worth of monthly writer check ins. To my Poets & Writers Get the Word Out cohort and our mentor Jennifer Huang. To my first teacher, Ann Napolitano. To Steve Adams for his coaching and encouragement.

Thank you to the literary magazines and editors whose early championing of my fiction gave me the confidence I needed to keep going: Michael Nye at *Story*, Evelyn Somers Rogers, Kristine Somerville, and Speer Morgan at *The Missouri Review*, Brenna McPeek, Abigail Wessel, and Shannon Elward at *Fatal Flaw*, and Kenneth A. Fleming at *Joyland*.

Endless gratitude to my parents, Rick and Anita Gilbreath, for giving me a happy and stable childhood with unconditional love. To my dad for modeling the joy of lifelong learning. To my mom for her friendship, her attitude, for teaching me not to be scared of people, and for reading and discussing many versions of these chapters throughout the years.

I married into a family of creatives—actors, weavers, film makers, ceramicists, art teachers, glass blowers—and I never would have become a writer without seeing what it's like to center a life around creative pursuit. Thanks to my adult stepkids Jessica, Zach, and Max, and their partners and families for inspiring me daily. Most of all, thanks to my husband Tom, for reading my work and believing it's important, for bike rides and bourb o'clock and laugher and true love for twenty years and counting.